Retribution

The Reckoning Series
Book One

Cheyenne Grey

For all who take their books like they take their coffee-
pitch black and hot.

Trigger Warnings

Please note that Retribution is a dark romance novel
that discusses situations and themes that are
uncomfortable, such as but not limited to:

- On-page violence
- Forced captivity
- Kidnapping
- Murder
- Explicit drug use
- Forced drug use
- Dub-con and non-con scenes
- Explicit sexual content

If any of these triggers you, Retribution might not be
a good fit. You've been warned.

Table of Contents

Georgia

The graveyard shift isn't for the faint of heart.
"Coming, Frank!" I shout. We're busy- it's to be
expected for this time of night, considering we're the
only spot within twenty miles that's open all night.

I've been in the weeds for hours and there
doesn't seem to be any end in sight, considering the
group of nine high schoolers that just walked in.
They're already making my head hurt as they drop
into a booth, loud and boisterous. Watching them
gives me an ache in my chest- I remember when I was
like that, too. *What I wouldn't give to be that again.*

The kitchen is shouting for me to pick up the
plates of food crowding the window, and I rush over
to collect them. I load each plate onto my tray, careful
to layer them just right.

As I arrive at my table to drop off their
orders, my mind is anywhere but The Lucky Plate.
I've picked up a job here to float the bills, and sure
the tips *are* nice, but having to flirt with middle-aged
men just to keep my lights on is really getting old. As
soon as the plates leave my hand, I hear another
shout from the kitchen.

"I said I'm coming, damn it!" I yell back, hoping to quell their demands long enough for me to walk back to the window. I'm the only server on the floor tonight since Kitty left to take care of her sick kid, and I'm ready to walk. *Only three more hours, Georgia. You can do this.* I can't help but look over my shoulder at the glass front doors as I walk back to the kitchen, nearly colliding with two women leaving the bathroom.

"Watch it." One of them bites out.

The other dissolves into a fit of giggles, no doubt noticing the red blush that creeps over my face.

"Sorry." I murmur, pushing past them.

I try to ignore their sneers as I stare out the glass, losing myself in thought. Ever since I ran, I can't help but feel paranoia every time I'm in public- they could be anywhere and probably have eyes on me everywhere. It's only a matter of time before he finds me. I was stupid to think Oakridge was far enough away, but I don't have the money to go anywhere else.

"Georgia! Get over here and take this shit out of my window." Frank screams from the kitchen, and it's enough to get me moving- quickly- back towards the kitchen to retrieve the next order.

"What is up with you tonight, girl? Your head's not here." Frank says through the window as I load up my tray.

"Sorry, there's a lot on my mind. I'll try to be quicker." I sigh. He's as sweaty as ever- the air conditioner in the kitchen hasn't ever worked, as far as I'm aware, but despite the heat, he's jolly.

"What's going on? You know I'm always here to talk."

"It's too much and too messy to get into tonight, Frank. Besides, the last time we 'talked', I had to call out of work because I was so hungover. Remember that?" I retort, but there's no malice in it.

He laughs; a big belly laugh that almost makes me feel better. "Whatever. You're just upset an old man like me can drink you under the table."

I chuckle, rolling my eyes at him as I hoist the tray of food onto my shoulder and start for the table. My feet are killing me, I can feel my hair tangling in knots, and I swear if one more guy at table four calls me 'sweetheart', I might dump his drink in his lap just to see if he keeps smiling. I smother the irritation as I approach the table to deliver the food.

"One order of nachos, one chicken quesadilla, and one house salad. Can I get you anything else?"

The guy with the salad barely glances up. "Ketchup."

"For your *salad?*" slips out before I can stop myself.

He blinks. I grin, stifling a laugh.

"Coming right up."

I don't have time to make it back to the kitchen before a body crashes against the glass door and slumps forward.

The girl at the table I'm serving screams, seeing the trail of red now smeared down the door, and cowers into the boy sitting next to her in the booth. He screams too, almost louder than she does, and scrambles under the table, leaving his date wide open.

I roll my eyes, but I'm scared too- I just hide it better. *They must not be from around here.*

This is a typical sight in this part of Oakridge, but it ruins business- as soon as blood spills anywhere, we have to shut down all operations while the cops process the scene, and it really puts a damper on my tips. *Shit, and I thought this was going to be a good night for me.*

I've learned not to startle at death.

Don't get me wrong- the sight of a body is never something you really get comfortable with, but I've seen enough for something like this not to ruin my night that easily. Visions of Isaac flash through my mind- his lifeless eyes, his pale skin. *All the blood.*

Before I can process what happened, the body is pushed aside and a man burst through the door.

I tense- I've never seen this man before, but there's no telling who *he* could've hired to find me. He's tall, really tall, and looks like sex on legs, with his sandy brown hair falling into his eyes and a million-dollar smile across his face. If this were any other night and any other man, I'd be fawning over him instantly- he's exactly my type, and I *really* need to get laid. But this is dangerous territory- too dangerous for someone in my situation, and besides- it's a bit below me to get in bed with a murderer. *Again.*

"Sorry folks, didn't mean to disturb your meal. Unfortunately, you'll have to find somewhere else to eat, as we've got some, uh, housekeeping to take care of." He says, nodding his head towards the body with a smirk, now slumped against the window next to the door. "I'd appreciate it if you moved quickly- oh, and tip your waitress." He says with a wink directed towards me.

That small gesture makes my knees weak, and I can't look away as the once-full diner empties out onto the street, running to their cars, anxious to get away from whatever is about to unfold here.

I don't know this man from Adam, and I just got away from men like this- I shouldn't stick around to find out if the reason he's here is to bring me back to that hell.

I start to head towards the door myself, slowly so as to not startle him, but as I start moving past him, he grabs my elbow.

"Not you, gorgeous. You stay." He murmurs. *Oh hell no.*

"Excuse me? I'd like to walk away from whatever or whoever you just put against that door." I bite back, ripping my arm away from him and continuing my path to the door.

Anger is my best defense here- if I look and act like a bitch, they're much less likely to grab me. I cannot let him know that I'm terrified of him and what he might do to me. Just as quickly as he lost it, he grabs my arm again, harder this time.

"I said you stay. Now you can either sit down quietly and wait for the boss, or we can play. Either way, you're not going anywhere."

My blood runs cold. *He's found me.* I start to back away, as far as I can with his iron grip still around my wrist, going through every possible escape route I can- none seeming like a good option. I feel like a caged animal, and I'm almost ready to chew my own arm off to get away from the bear trap of a man holding me hostage right now.

"You've lost your mind." I laugh, taking another small step away from him.

As soon as I move, his arms are around my waist, lifting me off the ground and throwing me down into a booth. My head bounces off the pleather cushion of the seat, and I sit up on my elbows to find him leaning over me, staring a hole into me. Fear has me in an iron grip, and I have to beg my body not to start trembling. It doesn't listen.

"You want to play? I've got all night."

He leans into me, and I can smell him. He smells like cigarette smoke and cologne, the expensive kind that doesn't normally grace this side of town. I feel the familiar panic start to claw up my throat as I see visions of *him* leaning over me. I check every available inch of visible skin for a tattoo, *the* tattoo, but I don't see one. If he's not a Brother, then why is he forcing me to stay? I didn't see anything more than anyone else tonight, but still, he's holding me here? He must be hired help, some merc from another town Sykes sent. Every instinct in me is telling me to fight, to swing and hit him anywhere I possibly can and get away, to run home and lock myself in forever, but I'm frozen in place, captive in this booth, and putty in his hands.

"Good girl." he murmurs, and it makes my stomach turn, and I'm not sure it's out of fear. "It's much more fun if you fight, but so much easier if you behave. Boss'll be here soon, and he's been dying to meet you."

His sentence is ended abruptly by a ringing in his pocket. He spares another glance towards me and sits up, trapping me in the booth next to him. He wants to *meet* me? If this is really one of Sykes' guys, they would surely know who I am- right?

"Yeah?" he answers. "I've got her, just waiting on you. Hurry the fuck up, she's feisty. Any longer and I'm sure I'll leave with a black eye." He chuckles, locking eyes with me.

"Don't get any ideas." He murmurs and taps the screen to end the call.

"What the hell is going on? Look, I don't know anything and didn't see anything, so can I go? I don't know who you are or who you work for, and I don't want to know. Can I just go home?" I plead, my hands shaking in my lap under the table.

Nice one Georgia, that tough-girl act really lasted a while. Under normal circumstances, I would love to take him home and play whatever games he has in mind, but I can't take any chances, not with a target still on my back.

My vision is starting to turn black around the edges as a panic attack creeps up on me when I hear the familiar chimes of the bell above the door.

Another man walks in, and his gaze locks on me immediately. I'm relieved for a moment- it's not Sykes or anyone else I would've recognized, but still, I want nothing more than to curl myself into a ball and escape the searing eyes of these men. I barely get a good look at the other man as he barks an order at his friend in the booth.

"That's her. Grab her and let's go. We need to get the fuck out of here before the cops show up."

The rage in his voice forces my eyes downward, as I close them and pretend I don't hear him. Just because I didn't see any tattoos doesn't mean they're not there, and I could be taken back, confirming everything I've been scared of for the past year. *He finally found me.*

The man turns and walks out, just as quickly as he came. I scan the back of his head, his clothing- anything I could use to possibly clue me in to what's going on. I'm so confused- one thing I know for sure is that if I leave the diner with this man, I will no longer be safe, and I can't risk it. I need to find a way out.

His friend reaches into his pocket and produces a rag and grips my head before I can even try to slide under the table and make my escape. I thrash against his hold, but he is strong and has the upper hand, pushing me down and against the wall of the booth, climbing on top of me and pinning my arms with his knees, rendering me defenseless against him.

I try to scream, hoping one of the patrons from earlier hears me and comes to my aid, but any attempts are futile as he pushes the rag against my face, hard enough to make the leather creak underneath my head from the force. The rag is coated in something that has a sickly-sweet smell, and given that it covers both my nose and mouth, I can't help but breathe it in.

"I really am sorry, gorgeous. Have a good nap." The last thing I see before I pass out is his smile, looking down at me. *Fuck.*

Soren

"What the fuck, Beck?" I snarl, staring at him through the rolled-down passenger window of his Nissan GT-R. "You didn't have to kill that guy. We knew where she was, it was an easy in and out. Did you not remember the fucking plan?"

Beck looks back at me with a lopsided grin, his blue eyes squinting, almost closed.

"Sorry Sor, I couldn't help it. He was in the way, and I needed to get in. Besides, what are we going to do with a low-level dealer, anyway? We already have the best of the best- he was useless, if you really think about it." He shrugs.

I roll my eyes. "You could've, I don't know, asked him to move? Didn't anyone ever teach you to use your words instead of your fucking gun?"

He gives me a pointed look. "No. You know that. I needed in, he was in the way, end of story. Easier to tie up at least one loose end, right?"

I turn away from the car. "We just got cleared of that investigation. There's no way we can move on anything else for at least a few weeks. We just got back in the game, and you already fucked it up." *This is the last time I send his ass out to do a job for me.*

I take a few steps forward, running my hands through my hair and pulling. Beck is always performative and sloppy on his jobs. Sure, he gets the work done, but he always leaves a mess to clean up afterwards and costs us a ton of favors making sure nothing can be traced back to us. A month ago, I sent him to make our presence known on that side of town- nothing major, just rough some people up, put our name out there. The idiot went in with stolen guns covered in our prints and ditched them in an alley when the cops were called by a local business owner. His fuck up landed us a full-blown RICO investigation, the charges of which were just dropped a week ago, no thanks to his help.

"You need to be more careful next time, though I feel I say this to you *every* time." I bite out, turning back towards him.

Beck barks out a laugh and shakes his head, leaning back against the headrest, allowing the adrenaline of tonight's events to subside. He's lucky we're family, or I would've put a bullet between his eyes ages ago for the constant messes he leaves in his wake.

We may not be blood, but Beck has been in my life for as long as I can remember. Our fathers created The Vipers together and turned it over to us when they felt we were ready- despite how ready we actually felt. We learned everything we know together. He was molded to be my second from the moment

he held a gun for the first time, just like his father was
to mine.

I turn back towards the car, and my eyes
wander to the unconscious girl haphazardly draped
over the backseats. To an untrained eye, she would
look asleep- peaceful, almost. But I know what Beck
did to get her subdued enough to drag her to his car,
and she'll feel every bit of it when she wakes up,
whenever that is. *Nothing peaceful about chloroform.* It
can't be long now, as she's been knocked out since
the diner, and stayed out cold the whole thirty-minute
drive back to the compound.

"We need to move her inside. She'll be awake
soon, and I don't want the trouble of fighting to get
her inside." I jerk my head, signaling Beck to get out
and help me move her.

She's a tiny thing, small and frail looking.
*Just like any other Oakridge whore, probably a junkie
working for her next fix.* I don't need another one of
those to add to my collection.

I open the back door and grab her ankles,
sliding her gently across the back seats towards me so
that I can lift her easier. I lift her limp body into my
arms like she weighs nothing- she practically does-
and note how beautiful she is. *No wonder they kept her
locked away for so long, I'm sure anything with a brain is dying
to get a piece of this.*

Her long, blonde hair falls across my arm and hangs down, nearly dragging the floor as I close the car door with my hip. Beck locks the car and closes the large, industrial-style garage door leading to the compound with a remote he pulls from his pocket.

The Vipers' compound is as secure as an old warehouse can get, and one can never be too careful with the constant turmoil waiting for us outside. We start towards the door, and he jogs ahead to open it for me. We pass Axel and Devin on our way inside, two of my men who are on shift tonight to watch the door. They nod their heads as we pass, but I don't miss the look of confusion on their faces as they take stock of our little blond house guest passed out in my arms. I ignore the questions their eyes pose and step inside the door, Beck following me closely.

The compound isn't much to look at- an old tobacco warehouse that we've slowly made into our home. The floors are original to the building, dark wood that still slightly smells like the product that was housed here. Concrete pillars span across the main floor, dressed in string lights that provide some source of illumination, given the overhead lights rarely function anymore. We've established a bar in the center of the room, fashioned out of old palettes found inside when we bought it. Old couches sit against the walls, with mismatched tables and chairs surrounding the bar. Old tin tobacco and alcohol signs line the walls, and in the center of the back wall behind the bar, a collage of everyone's mugshots from stints in jail.

It's a Viper's rite of passage, getting picked up, and you can't be considered made until you've spent at least two nights inside- or done something that would've landed you worse.

A metal staircase sits to our left, leading to the bunks of my men, and an old elevator sits to the right, leading to our quarters and holding cells. I make a beeline for the elevator, not wanting any of the lingering Vipers inside to get a look at the girl and ask questions. Plus, I know I'll find Jax and Kain down there, and I'll need all the help I can get with her if she's as fiery as Beck claims she is.

We step inside the elevator, and Beck jabs the button for the basement. As soon as the doors close, he turns to me, eyes like a kicked puppy. He can barely look at me and stands as far away from me as he can get in the small elevator.

"Look man, I'm really sorry. I know I fucked up. I'll clean up whatever I need to."

He can barely meet my eyes as he gives his apology, which is always how this goes. The line between boss and second is blurred with us, considering our closeness, and the minute he sees the reverence I'm met with when entering the compound, he remembers who I am and retreats into apology.

"Like I could ever stay angry with you, Beck. Just don't let it happen again. We're cool." I scoff and look over to him still staring at the floor.

"Beck." I press, and his head jerks upwards, his eyes meeting mine. "We're good. Drop it."

He smiles sheepishly, the smile not quite meeting his eyes, and stares back at the door of the elevator.

I know his nerves are not just about my scolding outside- he's worried about what kind of state we're going to find Jaxon in when we get downstairs. We've been gone for a few hours, and there's no telling what kind of trouble he might've gotten himself into while we were away.

The ding of the elevator sounds, and the doors finally creak open. We step into a long hallway, lit with barn lights, and lined with heavy metal doors. Beck walks ahead to open the first door we pass, leading to a holding cell, and we step inside. The room is barren, with a cot and dirty mattress in one corner of the room, and a table secured to the floor in the other. The walls and floor are concrete, rendering it virtually soundproof; we can never be too careful, and sometimes our guests scream so loud it wakes the guys.

I deposit the still-passed-out girl onto the cot, and head to the table to grab the cuffs the guys left for me. I turn to look at Beck, who is standing at the door, holding it open with his boot.

"Go and grab Kain and check on Jaxon while you're out. Bring him if he's up for it."

He nods once and leaves the room, the door shutting with a clang.

I take the cuffs and stalk back over to the sleeping form on the cot, taking in everything I missed before. She really is beautiful, with a thin, upturned nose and long, dark eyelashes that fan across her cheeks. She is hardly wearing makeup, though she doesn't need it, and is dressed in a white tank top and denim shorts so short her ass is falling out of them. Her shoes have been discarded, presumably in Beck's car, and her feet are bare.

I grab one of her wrists and secure one cuff, before attaching the other to the frame of the cot, tugging on the chain connecting the two once to ensure they'll hold. I have the urge to reach out and trace her features, dying to know what she feels like, but before I make contact, the door bangs open, and Beck walks in with Kain in tow. I look towards them, noting a missing Jax, and raise an eyebrow towards Kain.

"Probably not a good idea for him to be here right now. Let him come down and go see him, he'll need it. It's bad tonight"

That last part was pointed at Beck, who stares at the ground with a look of disdain all over his face. He can't stand Jax when he's like this, but he loves him too much to stay away from him and is the first to rush in after a bad night to check in on him. I shake my head, filing that issue away to be dealt with later, and turn back towards the girl.

"She'll be awake any minute now. Are you ready to go?" I ask Kain, my eyes not leaving her frame.

She's starting to twitch, and I slip into the persona of the leader of the notorious Vipers, leaving behind any remnants of my former softness towards the girl behind. I hear Kain's knuckles crack behind me, and the tell-tale sound of his knife sliding out of its holster, right as her eyes begin to open. *It's time for answers.*

Her eyes jerk open, and she looks up at me with sheer panic, her mouth open in a silent scream.

"Good morning, beautiful."

Georgia

I'm dead. Maybe not yet, but I'm about to be. I'm staring into the cold, dead, eyes of the man from the diner, the one who terrifies me so badly that I feel it in my bones. My throat is raw, like I haven't had water in days- maybe I haven't. *How long was I out? What the hell did they do to me?*

"Good morning, beautiful."

Those three words amplify the panic that was already running through my body, and I move to curl my body towards itself. My right arm jerks against something cold, metal biting into my flesh. *They cuffed me to the fucking bed.* I pull on it frantically, trying to force it to give, and hear a throaty chuckle from behind my captor.

My blood runs cold as I realize how outnumbered I truly am, and I stop my thrashing and squeeze my eyes shut.

"It's okay, we just want to talk. Open your eyes." My captor commands, and my body complies, going against any instincts I have.

It's like his words are law, and I have no choice but to do everything he says. I'm lying flat on my back, staring at a concrete ceiling. The air is thick with the scent of mildew and blood, intensifying the sense of danger in this room to the point where it's hard to catch my breath.

He's staring at me, his green eyes moving over every inch of my body, as if he's trying to figure me out by looks alone. His black hair is slicked back but looks mussed, like his hands have been in it one too many times today, with pieces falling out as he looms over me. He's covered in tattoos, with a dagger inked on the side of his face, running from his hairline to the bottom of his ear. He looks dangerous, but I don't recognize him as a Brother.

Don't they know who I am? Sykes will have their head for touching me like this. They must be prospects, doing Sykes' dirty work for him until he feels like coming down himself. I've spent too many nights in a basement to be stupid enough to expect Sykes to sit out of a training session- it's only a matter of time before he shows up, too.

I tilt my head as much as my body will allow and take note of the friend from The Lucky Plate leaning casually against the door. *I guess this is a normal Thursday for him. Just took a girl hostage, no big deal.*

His brown hair looks as though he just rolled out of bed, but he pulls it off. Like my captor, every inch of visible skin is inked, and the pull of the muscles in his arms contort the art in ways that keep my attention. He locks eyes with me and immediately looks away at his hands, picking at his nails, as if even looking at me is too boring for him.

He's standing next to the biggest man I have ever seen in my life- at least 6'8" and also inked all over, with a nasty scar that carves his face from his left eye to the corner of his mouth. His black hair is buzzed, and he wears a tight, stoic expression that makes it impossible to tell what he's thinking. He stands statue-still, twirling a knife with a wicked curve in his hand.

I'm frozen to the bed, not that I could move much anyway, and completely at the mercy of these assholes. "Let's start with the basics, shall we? What's your name, pretty girl?" my captor asks, unmoving from his position above me.

"Fuck you." I grunt, barely able to get out two words without my throat feeling as though it's closing in on itself. *I need water, bad.* The large man chuckles behind him, and he grins down at me, but there's no humor in it.

"That's not very lady-like. Didn't your parents raise you not to swear at strangers?"

In truth, no, they didn't. They didn't give two shits about me growing up, and the second I told them I was involved with a member of The Iron Brotherhood, I came home to all my shit in black trash bags on the lawn and changed locks. I haven't spoken to them since I left, not for a lack of trying, which is almost four years ago now. Tears burn the backs of my eyes at the thought of them- in this moment, I want nothing more than for them to come bursting through the door and take me in their arms, taking me home and away from these awful men and all the shit I've had to endure over the past few years. That'll never happen, and I almost laugh at the delusion. *I'm losing it.* No way in hell I'm going to let these bastards know that, though.

"Fuck. You." I manage, followed by a coughing fit that leaves me feeling like I swallowed tacks.

A low whistle leaves my captor's mouth, and he speaks to the friend on the wall.

"Damn, Beck, you weren't lying about this one. She's got a mouth on her. Maybe one of us should fill it for her?"

His words are like ice water over me; there's no way these are Sykes' men. They know the consequences of touching me without his permission, and no Brother would be stupid enough to go against his word.

I tense and shut my eyes again, trying to block out the hell that surrounds me. The tears in my eyes threaten to spill over as I try and soothe myself in

hopes a panic attack doesn't come. *It's okay, Georgia.
Just stay alive.*

The man called Beck grunts out in agreement,
and my captor grins wider.

"Look, we know who you are. We've been
keeping tabs on you since you left your little
clubhouse. We've seen you out at bars, surrounded by
leather and those ugly patches. We know who you've
been in bed with, we just don't know where it is you
came from. We know where you live, where you
work, what time you leave and come home, who
you're running with, and we know there's no one
coming for you or anyone who gives a shit that you're
in this room with us right now. If you don't talk,
you're not going home- it's as simple as that. It's not
often those idiots let people go, which means you're a
very useful tool for us. So, you can open your mouth
and tell us where the fuck The Iron Brotherhood is
hiding, or my friend over there is going to start
cutting, and mommy and daddy never taught him
how to play nice." He snarls, gesturing with his head
to the large man behind him.

Wait. Are they really not Brothers?

At the sound of his name, the big guy
advances towards me, and I thrash against the cuffs
again. I feel a trickle of blood down my arm from the
cuff slicing into my wrist, but it only makes me fight

harder. The fear is back and stronger, now that I know these men are not the usual group that I find myself trapped by. The larger man is standing next to my captor now, his black eyes resembling a soulless void as he looks down at me.

"Last chance, princess. Tell us what we want to know, and no one will get hurt." He taunts, giving me room to reply.

I shudder at the name. Only one person has ever called me that, and hearing it again makes me want to vomit.

This is it, I think to myself. If I'm going to die here, they need to know exactly how I feel about it. I swallow as much fear as I can muster and look him in the eye for the first time since I've been here.

"Fine." I manage to get out. "But come closer, I can barely talk. My throat is on fire."

A triumphant glint flashes across his face as he leans in closer, but I seize the moment and spit directly at him. My spittle hits its target and lands right on his cheek, sliding down and just barely missing his mouth. I smirk as he slowly lifts his hand to his face, wiping my saliva from his cheek. He nods once to the others, and in an instant, Big Guy grips my hair and yanks me up, pressing his knife to my neck so hard that I'm sure it's cut me.

"What the fuck are you thinking, bitch?" He hisses, yanking me further off the bed using my hair.

Every single hair in his hold feels as though it's on fire, and I know he's probably ripping a good number of them out at the roots. I scream and struggle against his hold, only making him tighten his grip. He pushes the knife harder against my skin, and I feel the moment the skin breaks, and blood begins to leak out of the wound. My captor straightens himself out and puts a hand on Big Guy's shoulder, halting his assault.

"I'm not sure who the fuck you think you are, little girl, but you've just dug your own grave. Enjoy that thought tonight- hopefully the rats don't get you before I do."

With that, he jerks his head towards Big Guy, and he rips the knife away from my throat, as if it causes him physical pain to show any kind of restraint towards me. My captor must be someone of importance if he can make this asshole heel at his command.

My hair is released, and I drop with thud back onto the cot, the springs in the mattress squeaking under my weight. They turn on their heels and walk out of the room, Beck following closely behind them, looking back at me as he leaves.

The door slams shut, and I'm left cold and alone in total darkness. The tears that have been brewing finally fall, and all that can be heard is the loud, ragged sobs leaving my body.

I fall in and out of consciousness, only being able to sob while awake, both out of anger and of fear, then fall right back into the blissful numbness of sleep, taking me away from reality. I don't dream, but my comatose state is better than what I wake up to, and that fact only makes me cry harder.

I'm not sure how long I've been crying, but my tears stop instantly as I hear the door being opened and the lights flicking on, assaulting my unadjusted eyes. I instantly curl into my cuffed arm, tucking my legs into my body to appear as small as possible. I'm running on overdrive, and with the fear and exhaustion coursing through me, I'm relying on primal instinct to keep me safe.

I squeeze my eyes shut in preparation of another attack, but it never comes. Instead, I hear something dragging across the ground, stopping only when it reaches somewhere close to my bed. Silence.

Against my better judgment, I open my eyes slightly to see who and what has just been placed in front of me. To my surprise, Beck sits in a metal chair to the side of my bed, holding a bottle of water. My eyes zero in on the bottle, and he notices instantly, and I see the corners of his lips twitch, a flash of a smirk across his face before the mask of stoicism is replaced.

"Hello again, gorgeous." He says softly, crossing his ankle over his knee and leaning back in his chair. "How's your neck?"

As if I'm possessed, I lift my head slightly to give him a better look at the parting gift his friend left me with. It stings as the skin stretches, and I hiss as the pain registers. He sucks his teeth as he moves closer to get a better look.

"Damn, he got you good. Does it hurt?" I glare up at him, and he chuckles. "I figured it did."

A serious look passes his face, and he leans in, his eyes staring straight into mine. "Listen, you have to talk to him. Soren will not stop until he gets the answers he wants, and if they don't come from you, you'll end up like the last Brother that was in here, and we'll move on to the next. We don't want to hurt a club whore; we get your position. But Soren's desperate, baby girl, and if you want to make it out of this alive, you've got to start talking."

He almost sounds like he cares. What a fucking joke.

"I'm not a whore." I manage, the familiar sting of tears back behind my eyes.

"Sure, whatever you want to call it. All we know is that you've had to see something, and we need to find out everything you know about The Iron Brotherhood. He's not going to make it easy for you, and you've only seen a taste of how bad they can hurt you."

Tears slip out onto my cheeks at his words, and at the threat of something worse than they've already given me. Before I can react, he leans in and swipes his thumb across my cheek through my tears, wiping them away. From this close, I can see he's been crying too, his eyes rimmed in red. Without thinking, I reach up with my free hand for his face.

"You've been crying, too." At my comment, he rips his hand from my face, any kindness he's shown gone.

"That's none of your fucking business, whore. Talk or don't, I don't fucking care. Either way you're going to end up dead- by our hands or those assholes you're protecting."

He stands abruptly, causing his chair to clatter to the ground and throws the water bottle at me, hitting me in the stomach with it hard, nearly knocking the breath out of me. He stares at me and spits on the ground, storming out of the room, slamming the door behind him.

The lights turn off again, and the room goes silent. I fumble around the cot, trying to find the water bottle he left behind, and when my fingers finally brush the cold plastic, I almost weep with joy. I use my teeth to crack the seal and take small sips, relishing in the feeling of cold liquid coating my gravelly throat, and allow my eyes to close once more.

I am so confused. I thought he'd finally found me, that I was taken back to him, and I can't help but think I'll see his face every time the door opens. Is this a test? Is he making sure I truly will not sell him out?

These men are nothing like the ones I've escaped from- they're ruthless and take no issue with causing me pain. If they were truly Sykes' men, they would not have cut me, never drawn blood. That was his one rule- never mar my skin, as that was his job. My free hand wanders up to rub my sore scalp, the burning sensation slowly leaving, and down to my neck to feel how badly I'm cut. When I realize the blood has clotted, I drop my hand and allow the tears to flow freely.

I have to get out of here. The only way I'm going to make it out of here is to talk. If it is a test, I'll deal with the consequences and beg Sykes to let me back upstairs, to take me out of here. Fuck my dignity, I just want this to stop. When they come back, I'll tell them anything they want to know, anything I know. Feeling content with my plan, I drift back into a dreamless state of unconsciousness and pray that they'll listen to me when they come back.

Beck

I should have left her alone. I knew I needed a minute when Soren asked me to go in and play 'good cop' with her, and after my most recent fuck up, I didn't want to piss him off any further by declining the task, so I went in anyway. That's how I found myself with my fingers to her face, softly tracing the contours of her cheek, wiping her tears away.

She's gorgeous, probably the most beautiful girl I've ever seen. She's staring up at me with eyes so blue they rival Jax's, and her dark lashes flutter against her cheek. If we were in different circumstances, I would be trying every trick I know to get her into my bed and keep her there for at least a week, until all she knows how to say is my name. For some reason, being around her in my current state feels okay.

Normally, our prisoners don't make it this long, especially after that stunt she pulled with Soren, but he's kept her alive. I stare at her, trying to memorize every feature because I know it's only a matter of time before Soren gets tired of her and moves on to the next one.

She's got some balls on her, I'll give her that- I knew she was a spitfire at the diner, but she really showed out. I mean, spitting in the face of the enemy? Literally? I'd never tell her, but I was impressed.

I hesitate to look her in the eyes, considering the breakdown I had before coming in here, but they hold me captive in a way that I can't do anything but stare. I'm not crying anymore, but the evidence is all over my face. When she mentioned it, it made me so sick I almost threw up right there in front of her. I can do nothing but slip back into comfortable cruelty and get out of that cell as fast as possible.

When the door finally slams behind me, I run down the hall into the bathroom connected to my bedroom and empty the contents of my stomach until there is nothing left. I sit back from the toilet and lean against the cold tile wall, running my hands through my hair.

I can't let them see me like this. I shouldn't have let *her* see me like this. I'm supposed to be a Turner- the coveted second of The Vipers, not some pussy who can't control his emotions.

If Dad could see me now. If my dad could see me now, he'd backhand me and tell me to shove it down, get back to work. I laugh dryly at the thought, fingers itching for my phone to call him for a pep-talk. I don't, only because I know it's late and I need to handle my shit alone, and I'm startled from my thoughts by the sound of the bathroom door opening.

Kain steps in, shutting the door behind him, and looks me over, leaning against the bathroom sink. The fluorescent lighting of the bathroom glints against his scar, and I'm sure anyone else would be cowering in the corner at the mere sight of him, but I'm comforted by the sight of him and not Soren standing there.

"Did you see him?" he asks quietly, and I don't have to question who he's referencing.

"Yeah, I went in for a second after we saw the girl. I couldn't stay, not when he's like this." I pull my knees against my chest and lean my head back against the wall.

"I assumed that's what's got you worked up like this. Listen, he'll be fine. He should be good soo-"

I cut him off, getting to my feet in record time, despite my shaky legs. "Is it fine, Kain? He was pacing around his room and could barely hold my eyes. That doesn't sound fucking fine to me." I scrub a hand down my face. "Sorry. I didn't mean to yell at you; I'm just pissed at him. We need to get him clean."

He nods his head in agreement, staring at the floor, and I know I fucked up again by getting loud with him. Jax is beginning to be a problem- since his parents died, he's developed unhealthy coping mechanisms.

He runs drugs, and he's excellent at what he does, but recently he's taken to sampling just about everything that we import, export, or stock at our club. He's high most of the time, and it bothers me more than it does the others.

I have a history with this shit that the others don't. Every time I look at him, I see my mom, and I'm terrified that he's going to end up the same way that she did. Unfortunately, that makes me the first line of defense to scrape him off the pavement when he needs it. It doesn't help that Jax and I are… involved, for lack of a better term. I shake my head- regardless of my feelings for him or my idiotic willingness to help him come down, it's bad business for him to be so fucked up all the time.

"How long has he been awake?" I ask, knowing I won't like the answer.

"About two days now. He hasn't been working either- he's been off doing god knows what. I told you it was bad." He confesses. *Shit.*

"Fuck, man." I whine, scrubbing a hand over my face. Alright, I'll go back."

I move past Kain, reaching to lay my hand on his shoulder, but I reconsider before it makes contact, and drop my hand to my side. *Probably not a good idea right now.* He looks up at me, and I offer a half-smile.

"It'll be fine. I'll fix it." *Again. Goddamn it, Jax.*

The walk to Jax's bedroom feels like a walk to the executioner's chamber, and I drag my feet the entire way. When I reach the door, I press my ear to it, hearing nothing, and feel a wave of relief wash over me. Silence is good when it comes to Jax- it's how I know he's coming down. I crack the door and find darkness. I hope he's asleep.

I slip inside and latch the door behind me, noting the state of disarray I see in the brief glow of the hallway light. A creaky wooden bed frame stands in the middle of the room against the back wall, and an old, worn-out black sofa sits at the end of his bed. The glow of his television, mounted on the wall facing the bed is the only source of light I have to make sure I don't trip on his shit. Various dressers and tables scatter the remaining three walls, their drawers haphazardly open and clothes flowing out of them. I scan the room for him, and I find a lump of blankets in the center of his bed. *Perfect.*

I cautiously step towards the bed, almost like I expect him to jump out at me. When I reach the edge of the bed, I see a mess of blonde hair poking out of the sheets, and I reach down and lay my hand on the top of his head, shaking him gently.

"Jax?" I whisper. He tenses at the sound of
his name and begins to shake.

"W-what, Beck? Did you come in here to give
me a lecture, too? I fucking know I m-messed up.
Leave me alone." He gruffs from under the covers.

"No, I didn't, but I can if you want me to."
He groans from under the covers and rolls over,
facing away from me, and I chuckle quietly. "I came
to see if you were okay. Kain says you've been up for
a while. I've barely seen you here. What's going on?" I
sit carefully on the edge of his bed, taking up the
space he vacated.

"Nothin'. I'm fine."

"You don't look fine to me." He scoffs,
scooting further away from me, my hand falling away
from him and on to the mattress. "Don't do that, Jax.
Don't shut me out."

I feel tears burning at the back of my eyes
again, and I blink hard to push them away. He sits up,
looking at me for the first time since I walked in. His
eyes are rimmed in red, but not for the same reason
mine are. His pupils are still blown, making his blue
eyes look almost black. He's shirtless and sweating,
glints of moisture visible in the glow of the TV light.

"I said I'm fine, Beck. Leave. I'm not a
fucking kid, I don't need you or anyone to babysit me.
I've got this under control."

"Sure looks like it." I scoff, and he looks away from me. I reach out and grip his chin, forcing his eyes back to mine.

"I said don't, Jax. Don't fucking look away from me right now. Do you know how much of a wreck I've been since I saw you earlier?"

He jerks his head out of my hold, and I exhale, rolling my eyes. *Whatever.*

"Fine. I'm gone." I stand and my trek back to his door through the warzone he inhabits, and I'm stopped by the shaky sound of his voice.

"Beck?"

I don't respond, but I stop walking, not moving to look at him.

"I'm sorry. I'll work on it."

I've heard that before. I turn back to face him and nod my head, stepping back towards his bed.

"I know you will, Eight Ball." I say with a wink, using his nickname to lighten the mood because if I don't, I'm afraid I'll break down again.

I don't believe him, but that's a problem for tomorrow. It'll take something big to get him to finally stop, and I have no idea where to start.

I kick my boots off and pull my gun out of the back of my jeans, setting it down on his nightstand and sitting back down on the bed, stretching my legs out in front of me.

"Come here."

He shuffles closer to me and my hand finds his hair again, rubbing the top of his head in a way I know will soothe him to sleep. When I finally hear his soft snoring, I lean my head against the headboard behind me and allow my own eyes to close, seeing visions of the tiny blonde girl that I allowed to see a side of me that only my brothers have ever seen.

I wake to an inferno. My body is so hot that I feel lightheaded, and I quickly realize the source. Jax is still shirtless, pressed against my side with his head buried in my neck, his arm draped over my stomach and his leg sprawled over mine. His skin is still wet with sweat, and as uncomfortable as I am with his oppressive body heat, I am content knowing we made it through the night without much trouble.

I peel his limbs away from me, and he grunts at the loss of contact, but doesn't stir. He'll be asleep for a while longer, considering how long he'd been up, and I have shit to do.

I slide my feet back into my boots and tuck my gun back into my waistband, grabbing my phone out of my pocket to check the time. *11:00. Fuck. Soren's going to kill me.*

I spare one final glance at Jax, now curled into a ball beneath the covers, and smile at him. I dance around the piles on the floor and make it to the door, opening it slowly and slipping out, closing it softly so as to not disturb the sleeping man behind it. *I need a shower.*

I head down the hallway to my bedroom and step inside, flicking on the lights. My space is the complete opposite of Jax's- clean, orderly, and bright. My bed sits in the corner of the room, with the linens still perfectly intact from my absence last night. There's a tall dresser across from the bed, with very little personal touches. I have a brown leather armchair positioned in the corner opposite the bed, and a black rug lines almost the entire room. My furniture is sparse but intentionally placed- I take pride in having a space that is clean and organized, a stark contrast to the rest of the compound. I step into the adjoining bathroom and turn on the shower, waiting for it to heat up. I strip, leaving my clothes in a heap on the floor, and once I see the beginnings of condensation around the edges of the mirror over the sink, I step into the shower. The hot water is reminiscent of waking up next to Jax, and I brace my arms against the wall, leaning my head forward and letting the water pound against the back of my neck. I can't stop thinking about her, that girl in the cell, and I want nothing more than to go back in and see her, but I also want to crawl back into bed with Jax and lock him away from the world. Hell, I don't even know her name, and even still I feel so pulled to her.

The thought of her blue eyes and pink lips make my cock jerk, and I resist the urge to reach down and run my hand along my length, with nothing but the thought of her driving me.

I shake my head and methodically move through my shower, rinsing the sweat and dirt from last night away. I turn the water off and step out of the shower, grabbing a towel and roughly drying my skin and shoving a toothbrush into my mouth. I step out into my bedroom to grab a change of clothes and jump when I see Soren sitting on my bed, waiting for me.

"What the fuck, man?" I manage through my mouthful of toothpaste.

"How is he?" Soren asks, picking mindlessly at his nails.

I roll my eyes and grab a fresh pair of boxers, jeans, and a black T-Shirt, stepping back into the bathroom. I spit the toothpaste into the sink and rinse my mouth out, scrubbing a hand over my face when I've finished. "He's okay. Nothing out of the norm."

"Did you stay with him?"

I pause, glancing over to where he's perched on the end of my bed. I don't know what I'd call whatever I have with Jax, and I've sure as hell never discussed it with Soren.

"Um- yeah, I did. Just to make sure he didn't OD or some shit. We need him for tonight." I respond, leaving out the part where I got him to sleep and woke up tangled up with him.

"Good. We've got a lot of money on him; I need him awake." He stands and looks over at me. "Get dressed. We need to go and see her. Some time alone probably did her good, and a day without food or a bathroom will get her talking."

He walks out of the room. That has my attention, and I nearly fall on my face pulling on my clothes and tucking my gun into my waistband, rushing out of my bedroom and towards her cell. I wrench my phone out of my pocket and fire off a quick text to Kain, letting him know that it's time. In typical fashion, he doesn't reply.

I meet up with Kain and Soren outside of her door, anxious to get in and see what state she's in. Soren turns and spares us a glance over his shoulder, and turns back, opening the door and flicking the lights on.

We're met with an icy glare, as the girl sits up on the cot, clutching the water bottle I left her last night in her free hand. It's still halfway full, which I don't miss. My face flashes with confusion- I figured she would've chugged the whole thing straight away. *This must not be her first time.*

"Hello there, beautiful." Soren coos, his voice dripping with venom as he steps towards her. "Are you ready to talk?" She hesitates, her glare trained on Kain, and after a beat nods her head.

"Good girl." Soren simpers, stepping towards her. My chair from last night is still discarded on the floor, and he sets it upright and turns it around, sitting in it backwards facing her.

"What's your name?" He starts.

"Georgia." She bites back, eyes not moving from Kain.

Georgia. Her name is almost as beautiful as she is. I ache to know how my mouth feels saying it aloud, but I repress it and keep quiet.

"Pretty name for a pretty girl. Are you ready to talk?" He repeats, and she nods.

I feel a rush of comfort knowing I won't have to watch Kain hurt her again.

"Good. Start from the beginning."

Georgia

It's time. I know this is a test, but I need to pee so badly that my bladder might just rupture inside of me, and I'm starving, so I'll bite. "What do you want to know?" I ask the man called Soren, his unwavering stare never leaving my face.

"Everything." He replies coolly, and I roll my eyes.

Here goes nothing.

"I was their prisoner for three years. Rowan Sykes kept me in their clubhouse for the entire time and was grooming me to be his wife. I know every single member of their inner circle, at least by face. I don't know where it is, or how to get there, or I would've told you by now. Is that enough? I need to pee." I feel all three of their eyes on me, with their brows furrowed in confusion. "What? You thought I wanted to be there?" I laugh, but there's no humor behind it.

My time spent with The Iron Brotherhood was nothing short of my own personal hell- I was beaten, starved, and violated in more ways that I can count, all in the name of Rowan Sykes' *love*. On the day I escaped, I was so sure he would find me. I've spent the last year in complete fear, and when I was abducted from the diner, I knew I was going to die. I wasn't scared of death, though. I was scared of the horrors Sykes would have subjected me to before he finally killed me. I'm still not convinced that I'm not being tested, so I don't say more in fear of being beaten again, meeting Soren's eyes with a hesitant glance.

"You're telling me you're *not* a club whore?" Soren looks the most confused of the three of them, looking at me like he doesn't know whether to believe me.

"No, at least not willingly. I was dating one of the Brothers, and when he died Sykes kept me for himself. Why the fuck do you think I haven't gone back, dipshit? If you've been keeping tabs on me like you say you have been, you should know exactly where I've been, and it's sure as hell not back with those animals." I bite out. "And for the record, they didn't *let me go*. I ran. On my own. I did that. I'm not helpless, and I'm not stupid."

"How do I know you're not lying? Downplaying your involvement so he," Soren gestures to Big Guy behind him, "doesn't kill you?"

"I'm going to die regardless, Beck made that very clear last night. Believe me or don't, I don't really give a shit anymore, but I'm tired of waiting around in here for you to come back." I turn my head away from him, and he reaches out and grips my jaw, forcing my head back towards him.

His touch against my jaw brings heat to my core and I silently curse my body for the reaction it has towards him. He's gorgeous, anyone would be blind to not see that. His dark hair is artfully slicked back with no sign of last night's disarray, and his tight black t-shirt shows off more of his arms that I didn't see before. He's toned and tall, not huge like Big Guy behind him, but I know he would be lethal in a fight, considering his wingspan. His muscular thighs rest on either side of the metal chair Beck brought in earlier, and I can't help but think about how they would feel in my hands. *Get your head out of the gutter, Georgia. He could and probably will kill you.*

He notices my staring and smirks at me.

"See something you like?" I half-groan and roll my eyes, but it's all for show, because *yes*, I really do.

"No assshole, I don't. Look, I really need to pee, and unless you want to clean my piss off these floors, I would like to be taken to the bathroom." I look over to Beck, and see a twitch of his lips, quickly replaced with his usual stoic expression.

Soren looks back to Beck as well and then turns back towards me. When he hesitates, I purse my lips like I'm going to spit again, sending him a clear reminder not to fuck with me. I don't miss the twitch in his face and the slight flutter of his eyes, like he expected me to do it.

"Fine." he resigns. "But you're not going alone. You're too useful to me now, pretty girl, and I can't have you running from us."

He looks back towards Beck once more, jerking his head towards the door and producing a small key from his pocket, which he hands to him. Beck rolls his eyes and snatches the key and strides over to me. He roughly takes hold of my arm, jerking it backwards so he can unlock the cuff holding me in place.

As soon as my wrist has been released, the pain from the sores the cuffs left washes over me, and I reach over to rub some feeling besides pain into it. It's covered in dried blood from my struggles, and the sores are still fresh and weeping, and I'm sure they're infected. *What does a girl have to do to get a first aid kit around here?*

Beck grabs my elbow and hauls me up off the cot, and I nearly collapse on my shaky legs. I haven't stood for as long as I've been here, and my legs turn to jelly as soon as I try to use them. He catches me and hauls me up once more, half-leading half-dragging me out of the room. This is the first time I've left this room, and my head is on a swivel taking in everything I missed while I was unconscious. The hallway outside the room is barren, with doors lining both walls. Beck drags me down to the second-to-last door and opens it wide, revealing a sparsely decorated bedroom. *Where am I?*

"Don't fucking touch anything. The bathroom's through there." Beck sneers, gesturing to the door with his head.

Is this his space? I don't meet his eyes as a mumble a thanks and head towards the door.

"You have two minutes. No longer." His voice stops me in my tracks, but I don't linger too long.

I hurry into the adjoining bathroom and rush to sit down on the toilet. I could almost cry at the release of my bladder. It smells like *him* in here, the same cologne from the diner filling my nose, and I find myself wishing I could be interrogated in this bathroom instead.

I finish up and step over to the sink, looking in the mirror for the first time since I was taken from the diner. The gash Big Guy left me is red and angry, with dried blood covering my neck and staining the straps of my white tank top. My eyes are swollen, yet sunken in from crying for hours and being left in the dark, and my blonde hair is stringy and is in knots. I don't look like myself at all, and panic overtakes my body, replacing the false-confidence I mustered for my previous interaction with the men.

I run the water and frantically try and wash off the blood that coats my neck and my wrist, getting most of it off. I splash some water on my face, feeling slightly better and cup my hands to drink as much as I can before my two minutes is up. My desperate attempts at hydrating myself are interrupted as Beck bangs on the other side of the door.

"Time's up, Georgia. Let's go."

I pause, trying to ignore what the sound of my name on his lips is doing to me. *What the fuck is wrong with me?* I spent my time in the cell ogling Soren, barely paying attention to anything that was said to me, and now I'm clenching my thighs all over again at the sound of Beck's voice. *I need to get the fuck out of here.*

I look in the mirror one final time and open the door. He's standing in the middle of the room, eyes locked on the door frame, looking anywhere but at me. We stay like this for a moment, me looking at him and him looking everywhere but back at me.

"Who are you?" I ask softly, the previous paranoia of being tested creeping back in. "Is this a trick?"

He finally looks at me, a puzzled expression on his face. "A trick?"

"You know what I mean. Are you going to take me back to him?"

I can't help the way my voice cracks, and I catch a brief look of pity in Beck's eyes. My eyes well up with tears, and they fall down my cheeks in rapid succession.

He steps towards me, reaching his hand up to my face like he had in the cell, when it was just the two of us. He was kinder then, and I silently hope for that same kindness now. He pauses right before he makes contact, finally locking eyes with me.

"You telling the truth, baby girl?" He questions, his hand hovering over my cheek. I nod my head furiously, desperate for him to believe me.

"Yes," I sob. "I promise, they didn't let me leave, a-and I tried, I swear, but I couldn't get away. I promise, I'm not lying to you." I rush out, breaking out into full-body sobs.

I'm crying so hard that I've doubled over, bracing my hands on my knees to try and catch my breath. My vision starts to darken around the edge, and I know I'm nearing the point of no return. I know I shouldn't let him see me fall apart like this, that it makes me look weak, like everything I said I *wasn't*. I can't help it.

He leans forward and grabs my face, forcing me back up to look at him. "If you're lying to me -

lying to us- he will kill you without hesitation. You know that don't you?" He grits. I nod, and his hold on my face tightens. "I don't think you understand, Georgia. I've seen it happen, helped him do it. Soren will put a bullet in your head and feel absolutely nothing. Do. Not. Lie. We need to know everything. There's no way we're going to let you go now, but we can make it so much more comfortable for you if you work with us."

My tears have started back up, and I ache to jump into his arms and cry into his shirt. As if he can read my mind, he drops his hold on my face and wraps his arms around my shoulders, petting my hair as I sob into him. He smells the same as he did in the diner, the same smell that lingers in his bathroom, and it's almost comforting now.

His shoulder is firm, and I want to bite into it, partially to hurt him, maybe gain an advantage and escape, but also because I know in my gut he'll like it, but the shock of his embrace has me frozen in place, and the only thing I can do is cry.

"You want out of that cell, don't you baby?" He murmurs into my ear, and I can only nod in response. "Then talk, and it better be the truth." He pushes me away at arm's length, any tenderness he had in his embrace gone, replaced quickly by his typical blank stare.

"Good. Let's go."

In the same fashion we came in, he grips my arm and drags me out of the room, back in the direction of my cell, and back towards the others. We reach the cell door, and he opens it and pushes me inside.

"I need to have a word with my brothers. Wait here." He says towards me, jerking his head towards the two men.

What else am I supposed to do?

They hesitate to move from their positions, no doubt considering restraining me again, but the look Beck gives them has them starting for the door, with Beck hot on their heels. The door opens, and before he leaves, he looks back at me. *Be good*, he mouths, and I nod. The door slams behind them, and I'm left alone.

I collapse onto the cot, thankful to have both my arms at my disposal, and stare at the ceiling, numb. *I think this is what shock must feel like,* I think to myself. Not only have I found myself in another goddamn basement in captivity, I'm also being kept here by the most gorgeous men I have ever laid eyes on.

I think back to Soren's slender, muscular frame, and how his thighs gripped the side of the chair. How his hair fell in his face when he leaned over me, and how desperately I wanted to reach up and pull it. I think about Beck, and how intoxicating my name from his mouth was. How it felt to be held by him, to feel his body against mine. I think about how badly I wanted to spread myself out on his bed like a four-course meal and let him devour me. Even the Big Guy, who makes me flinch the second he walks in the room, makes my thighs clench. He's huge, not only tall but stacked like a house, and I know he could throw me around in all the ways I need him to. I wonder what it would feel like to trace his scar, to be that close to someone who could kill me in a second. *I'm going fucking crazy in here.*

How can I think about these men this way? They've been nothing but predatory, using me solely for information, and inflicting nothing but pain. I should not fantasize about them in any capacity, but I cannot stop my mind from wandering.

I'm jolted from my thoughts by the room darkening, the lights going off with a click. *I guess they're not coming back.*

I huff and throw my arm over my eyes, trying to ignore the pains of hunger in my stomach. I'm used to not eating regularly, either because I wasn't allowed food or because I couldn't afford it, but this long without it is criminal, even for them. I pray for sleep soon, or something to quell the ache I feel everywhere. Soon enough, my body gives, and I drift into unconsciousness again.

Soren

I'm furious as we stand in the hallway, arms crossed in front of my chest. My fingers itch to hit Beck in the face for dragging us out of there without securing her first, but I take a deep breath and push it down. If he pulled us out here, it would be important. *It fucking better be.* He closes and locks the door behind himself, flipping the light switch next to the door off, joining Kain and I in the hallway, and I glare at him.

"What in the fuck is so important that we had to leave her completely unsecured?" I bite out. "What could you possibly need right now?"

I feel the rage bubbling up again, begging for an outlet.

"Listen, she's telling the truth. I believe her. She doesn't know where they are." He lets out, scrubbing a hand over his face.

Kain stares him down, and glances over to me.

"I don't know, they were in there for a while. He probably fucked her and doesn't want to lose his new plaything."

Beck shoves Kain into the wall, with his hands on his shoulders. Kain stays put, not because

Beck is stronger or even capable of holding him there, but because he allows him to.

"I didn't fuck her." Beck growls, and I roll my eyes. *It's always something with these two.* "You weren't in that room, Kain. She's not fucking lying."

Kain stares straight at him, not moving a muscle. I can see his jaw ticking, and I know he wants to hit Beck as much as I do right now, but he doesn't move.

Kain has come a long way since we picked him up; before, he wouldn't hesitate to kill anyone who came this close to him, but now, he shows practiced, calculated restraint.

I almost swell with pride, watching him stare a hole in Beck, and think back to the day he came to us all those years ago.

He showed up at the compound, bleeding from a gash in his face and hands stained with ash. He pounded on the garage door for hours until my men ran out with guns drawn. He didn't bat an eye at the number of weapons in his face and calmly asked to talk to whoever was in charge. I let him into my office, and he told me his story- about his parents, what he did to them. We got through two bottles of whiskey that night, and by the end of the conversation, he had a room with us and a job to do the next morning. Kain's the type who needs to belong to something or someone- if he's left to his own devices for too long, the path of destruction that follows him is too much for one man to handle alone. He's ruthless, and the best goddamn enforcer this organization has ever seen.

Kain's got his demons just like everyone else, and the closer we get to him, the more they rear their ugly head. I almost laughed when I'd heard him mention how long Jax had been awake and wanted to ask him how long it's been since *he'd* had a proper night's sleep. *Years, probably,* I think to myself, shaking my head and focusing back on the snarling Beck, who still has Kain pushed against the wall.

"Knock it off." I bark, and Beck backs off, with Kain chuckling under his breath. "What the fuck are you talking about, Beck?"

"Look, man, I've been around enough liars to know when someone's putting on a show. She wasn't. The way she froze up- like she expected me to snap her neck on the spot- people don't fake that. Her hands were shaking so bad she couldn't have held her own water. I'm telling you, she's scared, not scheming. I think we should let her out. We give her a little breathing room, she'll talk. Think about it, Sor- we've got lineup photos of all the Brothers from the database. If she can tell us who they are, we can find 'em and end this shit for good. She's useful, but not locked in that cell like an animal. She's feisty, sure, but right now she's a wreck, and she won't survive much more of that without her mind breaking. She won't be of any use to us then." He rubs the back of his neck and looks at the ground, refusing to meet my eyes.

"So, you're telling me we should let her out? Give her free reign of the compound, let her do whatever the fuck she wants? We might as well give her a fucking gun so she can take us all out while we're at it, because that's exactly where that plan is heading." I scoff, turning away from him.

Beck's thinking with his dick right now, and I'm not going to let his hard on for her ruin everything I've worked to build. Everything our fathers worked to build. *Even though I want her under me just as badly as he does.*

"Soren, listen to me. She's terrified. She's not going to fucking kill us, and I'm not saying she has the freedom to do whatever she wants. She'll stay with one of us at all times and doesn't leave the compound on her own for anything at all. We can even fit her with a tracker, if that makes you feel better. She'll open up, man, and we need her. She's the closest we've been to The Iron Brotherhood since this shit all started. Are you really going to pass that up?"

He has a point. We haven't been able to get close to them since we got Jax, after we found one of their bars that we were sure would be crawling with Brothers. We blew it up, but it was a setup- the building was empty, and they followed us back to his parents' house. They surrounded the house, taking Beck and I outside at gunpoint, shooting any men we had with us, and murdering Jax's parents.

The fuckers held him with a knife to his throat and made him watch the entire thing.

The Iron Brotherhood is a gang in Shadeview Heights, made up of ex-cons and bikers who have nothing better to do than sell hard drugs on *our* corners and pussy for cheap. They never used to bother us much, maybe a few crossed wires here and there, but nothing like it is now.

We're at war and have been ever since Rowan fucking Sykes took over. He's a power-hungry son of bitch, and steps on any and everybody he can to get ahead.

After everything went down with Jax's folks, an unforgivable line was crossed, and they all need to die for it. They all *will* die for it. They've ruined one of my men, taken the lives of part of our family, and the consequences of that will be bloodshed. I exhale and pinch the bridge of my nose. *He's right. Goddamn it.*

"Fine." I bark out, not missing the look of surprise on Beck's face. "Let her out. Get her a change of clothes and set her up down here. But let me make myself clear," I get in his face, our noses almost touching. "One slip up, one wrong move, one inkling that she's fucked us over, and she's dead. You will not fraternize with her, you will not take her out of here without my approval, and no one fucks her, or anything remotely close to it. I will not jeopardize everything for this."

Beck nods, swallowing hard, and takes a step backwards, creating distance between us. "Understood, boss." He can't meet my eyes, and I instantly feel like shit.

"Beck, look, I-"

"I'm going to go get Jax, it's almost time. We need to leave soon." He cuts me off, pushing past me and heading down the hall towards Jax's bedroom, hitting my shoulder with his as he passes.

I look over at Kain, who's shaking his head, a smirk playing on his lips. "What?" I snap, and he barks out a laugh.

"She's just as much up your ass as she's up his. God, you two need to get laid."

"I said no, Kain, and I-" I shout, but he's already turned away from me and is walking the other direction, shaking his head as he strides towards his own bedroom, and I'm left standing alone in the hallway.

Fucking hell.

I fire off a few texts to the Viper wives and girlfriends, scrounging up whatever I can for our houseguest, and considering I have no idea how long she'll be with us, I check the empty bedroom between Beck's and my own to make sure it's ready. I don't know why I care enough to check- something about what Beck said about her having a panic attack made me feel… guilt? *No, that can't be right.*

Regardless, I mindlessly move through checking the room, ensuring the bed is made and there are towels in the bathroom. The bedroom resembles a hotel, with white linens on the bed, a nightstand, and one chest of drawers across from the bed. It has an adjoining bathroom similar to ours, fitted with a standing shower, tub, and vanity-style sink. It's not much, but it's better than the holding cell. My phone dings, and I see a confirmation that the clothes I requested are being sent down, so I head to the elevator to retrieve them. The elevator dings, and the doors open to reveal several shopping bags full of clothes, but nothing and no one else. I chuckle, amused at the empty space. No one in the compound has been to the basement with us before, and it appears as if they don't plan to come down here any time soon.

I hurry back to the empty bedroom I've deemed hers and drop the bags on the bed. I take one final look around, and head down the hallway to her cell. I flick the lights on before unlocking and opening the door, finding her laying down with her arm over her eyes, knees bent in front of her. I still haven't gotten used to her being here, and it makes my dick jump in my pants every time I see her. From this angle, I can see the bottom of her ass poking out of her tiny shorts, and I want to sink my teeth into it. My cock presses angrily against my zipper, in agreement with my head, and I almost walk back out, just to get away from her and the way she makes- no, *forces* me to feel.

"Get up." I bark, watching her jump from her relaxed position. "It appears you're more useful than I first thought. I'm moving you, so get up and let's go." I don't miss the panic in her eyes at my words, so I try another approach. "Don't worry, it's more comfortable. I won't hurt you again." *Lie.*

That seems to soothe her enough to get her legs working, and she shakily stands and follows me out of the cell, keeping distance between us as if she's scared I'll change my mind and shove her back in. I shake my head and lead her down the hallway to the bedroom.

"I got shit for you in there. I didn't know your sizes, so make it work, and don't complain about it. Take a shower and get dressed, we have somewhere to be tonight, and I don't like to be late."

Her mouth opens as if to ask me a question, but I turn on my heel and head into my own bedroom before she can get a word in.

She is going to ruin me.

Georgia

What the hell? First, I was being cuffed to a bed, cut up and starved, and now they're taking me out? *Talk about whiplash.*

I stand in the center of the bedroom, taking in the fresh smell and crisp-looking linens. My body is screaming to get into the bed and sleep for the next three days, but I have a feeling that Soren is not one that likes to be pushed, so I head for the bags on the bed instead. I pull out the clothes, smelling another woman's perfume on each item, and feeling a hint of unjustified jealousy in my chest. *Do these belong to their girlfriends? Wives?*

The clothes differ greatly from my normal style, which consists of anything I can get for less than five dollars at the thrift store. These are dark, strappy, and low-cut, but when I check the labels, they're all expensive brands that I could only dream of affording.

Any other time, I would be freaking out over this kind of stuff, trying every last bit of it on and planning a night out to show myself off, but these clothes make me afraid here. I don't want to be exposed to these men- there's no telling what they will do to me, and even though Soren claims he won't hurt me, I don't believe it.

I try to push the thoughts of impending danger aside as I set the clothes down on the bed, and my eyes catch on another bag, paper and small. I open it carefully, and inside, there is a to-go box of chicken fingers and fries, still warm, and a bottle of water. My eyes well up with tears, and I immediately tear into the food, barely tasting it as it goes down, thanking whoever or whatever is watching over me for the meal. I down the bottle of water in two gulps and take a step back. The ache in my stomach is slowly subsiding, and my throat feels less like I've eaten sand. It's not nearly enough to satisfy the hunger that has grown from not eating this long, but it's enough to take my mind away from my stomach.

Crumpling the paper bag and setting it inside the to-go container, I wander through to the bathroom, locking my gaze on the shower. *Oh, fuck yes.*

I run into the glass stall and crank it on, the water beginning to heat up instantly. I strip, leaving my clothes piled in the corner, and step inside. The hot water against my skin makes me groan, and I tilt my head back and let the water cascade down my body. *Can someone live in a shower? Because I really want to live in this shower.*

I notice the shelf built into the wall is already stocked with bath products, and I pour a generous amount of shampoo into my hands, scrubbing it into my hair to rid myself of the dirt, blood, and sweat that cling to me. I moan again at the contact of my fingers in my hair and rinse the shampoo out. I gather up enough soap to wash a car and begin to clean myself.

My hands brush over my nipples, and my breath catches in my throat. They wander through the valley between my breasts, leaving a trail of bubbles, past my navel, and end between my thighs. *I really shouldn't do this,* I think to myself. I'm sure any therapist would tell me to lay off until I've had a moment to process everything that's happened, but all I can think about are Soren and Beck, and my fingers slide easily over my folds.

I brush against my clit, and exhale at the familiar feeling of my own touch. I start working it in slow circles, guiding myself towards release, thinking of Beck's embrace. How his shoulder feels against my face, and how badly I wanted to leave scratches down his back. I think of the muscles in Soren's arms, and how with every pull the ink in his arms seems to paint a new picture, one that I could get lost in for hours. I wonder what they would look like flexed as he laid over me, giving me everything I was too scared to ask for myself. My circles grow faster and sloppier, and I'm so close that I lose my breath. As I finally reach my peak, a pounding at the door forces my hand to fly away from my clit and I let out a string of curses, losing my orgasm almost as fast as I achieved it. *Motherfucker.*

"Ten minutes, Georgia! I will not be late." I hear Soren yell through the door, and I groan, letting my head fall against the tile.

I quickly rinse the soap from my body and turn the water off, grabbing a fluffy white towel from the bar hanging next to the shower and wrapping myself up.

I walk back to the bedroom and dump the bags out on the bed, looking through the mass amounts of things Soren's left for me. I settle on a black cut-off wife beater and a pair of jeans. I pull on the tank top, and it fits me like a glove, hugging my tits in an almost-pornographic way. The jeans are next, fitting a little big around the hips, but I find a black belt with a gold buckle in the bag and secure it around my waist. *This'll have to work. Don't complain.*

On the floor at the end of the bed, I find my black sneakers, discarded somewhere between the diner and here. I sag as I kneel down, clutching them to my chest. They are the only thing I have left of home, and I give silent thanks to whichever one of them left them in here for me.

My parents bought them for me for the last birthday I spent at home, and I've worn them almost every day since I got them. Especially now, they give me a small tether to the life I had before.

I slide them on and head to the bathroom, using the towel to begin drying my hair. I don't have any make up here, so I leave my face bare, but find ponytail holders in one of the drawers of the vanity. *There is for sure a girlfriend.*

I run my fingers through my damp hair to get out as many knots as I can and quickly style it into two braids hanging over my shoulder. I stare in the mirror, and for the first time in days, I feel a bit like me again.

I tilt my head back a bit to look at the cut that runs along my neck. Now that the blood is gone, it's turned a greenish-yellow color and has scabbed over. *Nice,* I think to myself. *Really fucking hot, I look almost decapitated.* I mentally curse the Big Guy for this, and take one final look in the mirror before turning and leaving the room.

I open the bedroom door to find Soren staring furiously at his phone, and Beck leaning against the wall with his ankles crossed, wearing a shit-eating grin. Soren's dressed in a pair of black fitted cargo pants and his signature black t-shirt, and a pair of shit kickers that I'm sure have met a body one too many times, with Beck in a baggy band t-shirt and ripped jeans, completed with a pair of blown out Vans.

The hallway smells like their combined scents, cologne and fire and cigarette smoke and *sex*. I take a second to pick my jaw off the ground and compose myself before I speak.

"I'm ready. Where are we going?" I question, directing the last part at Soren.

"Out." He replies, not looking up from his phone. He curses under his breath and shoves his phone in his pocket. "You're late. Don't make this a habit unless you want to be locked up again. I already know I'm making a mistake by bringing you along, don't rub my nose in it." He growls, turning on his heel and heading down the hallway.

Beck pushes off the wall, chuckling under his breath. I don't miss the way his eyes linger on me for longer than normal, and the slight flush of his cheeks when he looks away. I eye the hallway cautiously, looking for the Big Fucker, and Beck catches on quickly.

"Kain went ahead, he took our friend with him. We'll see him there." He says with smirk, turning and heading in the direction Soren went.

Kain. That's fitting.

"Come on, baby girl. We don't want to piss him off anymore."

I scurry off after Beck, dread taking over my body as I step into an elevator with the two, completely at their mercy with nowhere to run if things take a turn. The doors close, and I squeeze my eyes shut, expecting the worst. The ride up is silent, though I can feel the buzz of electricity between myself and the two men I am stuck between. The doors open and we step into a bustling factory, with men covering the main floor. Rap music blares through speakers, and there are barely clothed women writhing against men sitting in chairs and on couches against the wall. *Is this what they brought me up for? No fucking way.* I barely have a moment to look around before I'm being shoved into a garage.

I turn around and see the same car as Beck drove that night at the diner, and I begin to panic. "What are you doing?" I ask him slowly, backing away from the car until my back hits the door that just closed behind me.

Soren gives me a pointed look and slides into the passenger seat of the blacked-out Nissan GT-R, slamming the door behind him. Beck winces at the slam and shakes his head, focusing his gaze back onto me.

"Relax, Georgia. We have to drive to get where we're going. Or would you rather walk?" Beck's lips twitch in the ghost of a grin, but I stay put.

"I'm not getting in that car, Beck. It's not happening." He frowns at me, his brow furrowing, seemingly forgetting the events that brought me here.

"Georgia, get in. Now. I'm not going to hurt you."

He opens the back door of the car for me, and I take a shaky step forward.

They let me out of my cell, they let me shower, gave me a change of clothes, and allowed me to eat. If they wanted to kill me, or bring me back to Sykes, they would've already.

I take a deep breath and slide into the backseat as Beck closes my door behind me. Soren angrily taps his phone screen and doesn't look up at me as I settle in and pull my seatbelt across my chest. The driver's door opens, and Beck slides in, pushing the ignition button, and the car roars to life.

It's obvious that this car is modified, and not legally, as the sound of the idle shakes the entire garage, and I feel it in my bones. I stay quiet, staring out the window as the men in the front seats exchange words, and Beck reaches up to press a button on a remote clipped to his sun visor. The garage door in front of us creaks open and the illumination of the streetlights floods the garage. He revs the engine twice, the sound nearly blowing out my eardrums, and without warning, Beck floors it and sends us sailing out of the garage, leaving me breathless. *God help me.*

Jax

It's evening by the time I wake, according to the clock on my phone screen. I'm curled up under the blankets alone, my sweat staining the sheets beneath me. I faintly remember Beck coming in at some point, but I was so out of it that it could've been a dream.

I stretch, groaning at the ache that's settled in my joints, and cover my face with my hands. They shake, and I can't control it, knowing the only thing that will stop it is sitting in the pocket of my discarded jeans. *Not yet.*

I hear a knock on my door, and Beck cracks the door open. "It's almost time. Get dressed, we're leaving in an hour."

He closes the door softly, and I push up onto my elbows. I know what tonight is, and I need to be focused. I can't afford to piss Soren off anymore, considering my falling behind these past few days, and I know there's a ton riding on me tonight.

I climb out of bed, stretching my arms above my head as I stand, and fumble around my room for a clean pair of sweats and a t-shirt. I dig in a drawer lying on the ground and find what I'm looking for, hopping in place as I pull my sweats on and throw my t-shirt over my head. *Only one thing missing.*

I search the ground, favoring the flashlight on my phone over the big light in my bedroom. I locate my jeans from last night and reach into the front pocket, producing a small plastic bag of white powder. I flick it a few times, gauging how much it contains, before sliding it in the pocket of my sweatpants.

I stretch once more, feeling a breeze on my stomach as the hem of my t-shirt slips up, and drop my arms, shaking my shoulders. *It's go time.*

I open my bedroom door, finding Kain walking out at the same time as me. He offers me a half smile, and I jog to catch up with him as he heads to the elevator. "What's up, Eight Ball? Are you ready for tonight?" He asks, bumping shoulders with me as I reach his side.

This is as much physical contact as I've ever had with Kain, but I don't complain. I don't like many people touching me either- that, we can relate on. "Can I ride with you? I don't feel like sitting in a car for half an hour with Soren and Beck after last night. I'm not really up for another intervention."

He chuckles, pushing the button for the elevator. "Yeah, man, whatever. I'm leaving now though, you ready to go?"

I nod my head, and we step inside the elevator.

"I've got a lot to fill you in on."

We slide into Kain's Escalade, and he cranks the engine and pushes the button for the garage door. As he pulls out of the compound and onto the street, I reach into the center console and pull out his pack of smokes, ducking the smack he aims at the back of my head.

"Get your own."

I chuckle, pulling a cigarette out and lighting it. I take a long drag and lean my head against the headrest.

"They have a girl downstairs; you know that right?" Kain says, glancing at me out of the corner of his eye.

What?

"What do you mean, a girl? Someone Beck's fucking, or what?" I try not to let the pang of jealousy I feel seep into the response, but I'm not sure I'm successful, because Kain backtracks quickly.

"No, nothing like that. She came from The Brotherhood."

My blood runs cold at his words, and I say nothing. The car is silent for a few moments, the only sound that can be heard is the soft hum of the engine as we drive. My hand slides over the pocket of my sweats. There's only a tiny piece of fabric separating me from relief from the panic I feel. *Not. Yet.*

"She's going to lead us straight to them. Apparently, she's some kind of hostage Sykes kept there for a while, and she probably wants him dead as much as we do. Beck's hopeful, but Soren's pissed she's here. It's hilarious, watching them bicker over it."

I can tell he's trying to lighten the mood, but my nerves are already shot. I stay silent as he fills me in on the rest of the recent developments, staring straight ahead, and lifting the cigarette to my lips, taking another drag.

"She's coming tonight. I didn't want you to be blind-sided, y'know? Seeing her sitting there with them." He glances towards me again, and this time I meet his eyes.

"Why? What's the point in that- parading the captive around like the flavor of the week?"

"Honestly, I'm not sure. Take it up with the boss, I guess." Kain says with a shrug.

"Whatever man." I scowl, turning my head to stare out the window.

I can tell he notices how short I am with him now, and I hope he doesn't think it's because I'm angry with him. Any mention of The Iron Brotherhood sends me into a bender, and I'll be coked out of my mind for at least two days. I can't think about that night without throwing up anymore, and the only thing that helps is the drugs.

I know they hate it, the guys. I know it makes me look weak, like a liability, but it's the only thing that makes me feel like me again. *Fucking coward.*

They took everything from me. My fingers absentmindedly brush against my neck, where their knife sat. If I close my eyes, I can still feel the cold, sharp metal pressing into my neck. I can smell the blood and the gunpowder, and I can see my mother, with her eyes gouged out and a bullet in the back of her head. I can hear my father screaming as they violated him with the end of the same knife they used to hurt my mother, and I can feel his blood splash against my face as they finally put him out of his misery. I reach into the center console and pull out another cigarette, noting Kain's lack of protest this time.

For the rest of the drive, I relive that night over and over again until my stomach turns and I'm close to vomiting.

Kain's voice pulls me out of my head, alerting me of our arrival to the warehouse.

"Jax, you good?" I half-nod, but he doesn't move. "Are you going to be okay tonight? You don't have to do this if you don't want to."

Yes, I do. "I'm fine. Let's go." I open the door and jump out of the car, shutting the door on Kain's concerned face.

I toss the remnants of my cigarette onto the concrete, snuff it out with my foot, and walk over the entrance, opening the door to the warehouse and taking it all in. Every time I come in here, it's like I see it again for the first time.

The warehouse has been completely transformed into an underground arena, being used mainly for our fight nights- one of our biggest earners as an organization. On the days I fight, we bring in an easy fifty thousand from bets and covers, and that's not the kind of cash we can pass up on. We have mouths to feed and bills to pay, and an hour of taking punches is nothing if it means The Vipers thrive.

I step inside the warehouse, making sure everything is set up correctly. There's a make-shift ring in the center of the long room, lined with reinforced chain link fencing. The mats on the floor have worn down over time, and are all stained in various places with blood. Chairs surround the ring, and work lights point at it from all directions, for optimal visibility. There is a creaky wooden staircase leading to the top floor, where there is more arena-style seating, for the casual or more squeamish viewers.

I head straight, past the ring, to a gym door where an old locker room has been constructed. There are two in the building, at opposite ends of the first floor, most likely so that the opponents wouldn't kill each other- at least not without an audience present.

I enter the locker room and move to sit on the wooden bench situated in the center of the room. I let my head hang forward, staring at my trembling hands, thinking about what Kain said to me in the car. I don't want any part in finding The Iron Brotherhood, unless it means I get to kill the men who tortured and murdered my folks. I fantasize about it, what it would feel like to slit their throats. To make them hurt the way they hurt me, hurt my parents. If she's even slightly a part of it, I want her dead just as badly. *Fuck this shit.*

I shake my head, trying to dissipate any lingering thoughts I have about them. They do not deserve to occupy my mind right now. I have a fight to get ready for, and there's no way in hell I'm going to lose tonight.

After a quick warm up and a lap around the warehouse, I'm ready to go. I'm filled with anxious energy, not only from the fight, but also knowing that *she's* here. I don't even know what she looks like, but I can't help but shake the feeling that this is all a really bad idea. I'm terrified that somehow, they'll find us-they'll find me. *They can finally kill me, too.* I don't fucking trust her, and I can't wrap my head around why my brothers trust her either.

I pull my phone out of my sweats, checking the time. *Nine already.* I need to finish getting ready before the crowd arrives, and before *she* gets here with Soren and Beck.

I jog out of the locker room, in search of Kain. I find him talking with one of the staff in the middle of a row of chairs, going over details of the match. Here, we don't play by the traditional rules, and the only way you leave the ring is if you can't move anymore, or if your opponent manages to kill you. I've lost my fair share of fights, but ever since my parents' passing, I've been on a winning streak, and tonight will be no different.

They never share the details of the bets with me beforehand, for the sake of not giving me any more reason to be anxious, but from the buzz around the compound the last few days, I know if I can get my shit together, the payday from this one night is going to double anything we've made all month.

I stand awkwardly to the side, allowing Kain to finish his conversation, looking at my shoes. Once I hear him dismiss the staff, I step over to him, mustering as much of a smile as I can.

"I left something in the car. Can I grab your keys to go get it?"

I don't know why I always insist on lying to him about this. I ask the same thing every time, and every time he knows I came with nothing but the shit in my pockets. He usually throws the keys to me, mumbling something about being quick, not wanting to pull his head out of whatever he was preparing. This time, though, he stares back at me.

"Do you think I'm an idiot, Jax?" *Shit.* "Do you think I don't know what you do with my keys? Or did you think I just don't care enough to enable you forever?"

His face is blank, and per usual it's hard to read him. I know he's mad, and I know last night was not a good look for me, but there's no way I'm getting into that ring without a fix.

"Kain, please, I really nee-"

"I don't care. You didn't see him last night, did you? Not really. He was a mess, crying and shit, thinking you were in too deep. You know what that shit does to him, and you continue to do it. You were up for two fucking days, Jax, and you want to do that again? I'm not dealing with it anymore. You need a fix, fucking figure it out yourself." With that, he storms off towards the stairs, leaving me alone and shell shocked.

Motherfucker. I check the time again, and it's almost 9:30 now, meaning the match will be starting soon, and I run back into the locker room. *Guess I'll do this the old-fashioned way.*

I step into one of the toilet stalls and shut and lock the door behind me. I sit down on the toilet, angling myself towards the bulky, plastic, toilet paper holder mounted to the stall, and fish my wallet and the bag out of my pocket. I pull out my ID, discarding the rest of the wallet, and dump a bit of the powder out onto the top of the holder. Using my ID to create three neat lines, I put my nose directly to the dirty plastic and sniff hard. I pull back, sniffing again, blinking my eyes a few times. *I'm going to get a fucking cold after this, if not something worse.*

I feel the immediate effects, euphoria overtaking my body and smile, hearing the music boom through the warehouse.

"Insanely Illegal Cage Fight" by Dal Av blares through the speakers, and I know it's time. I gather my belongings and head back out into the main locker room, jumping in place, anticipation and adrenaline coursing through my body.

Let's fucking do this.

Beck

The warehouse is packed, more so than usual, considering who Jax is fighting tonight. Sure, they come for him, but they're used to his wins now. Tonight, I guarantee over half of the people in here have placed bets *against* Jax, but I hope their money is where their mouth is, because he doesn't lose. Not anymore.

We step inside, and I feel adrenaline coursing through me at the thought of watching him. I haven't seen him since I left his bed because he came early with Kain, and I hope he's cleaned himself up before coming.

I shudder internally at what I saw last night, how broken he was. I know he'll be keyed up tonight again, and I'll want to keep my distance afterwards, but I find myself missing him already. I don't deal with it well, not after my mom, but I can't fault Jax for his coping mechanisms either.

My mom passed when I was sixteen, after a nasty car accident left her with a dependency on pain pills. When her scripts ran out, she turned to shit from the street, and one day it went bad. A tale as old as time- simple yet devastating.

We've all seen some bad shit, though, and lived through worse. We have to find ways to deal with it, and as long as he's alive and breathing, I guess I can't be too hard on him, but that doesn't stop me from constantly urging him to get clean. I don't want to lose another person I care about to a bad batch.

Soren pulls me out of my head, bumping my shoulder as he pushes past me, walking in front of me. I bring up the rear, pushing Georgia in front of me, sandwiched between us, with a possessive hand on her lower back. The demographic of men gathered here would kill each other without question just to get a taste of her, and I need to stake my claim from the moment we walk in. *She's ours.*

Soren walks quickly, not stopping to talk or acknowledge anyone on the way, finding our usual row of seats directly in front of the ring. From here, Jax can hear everything we say and can see us the entire match. Soren has a nasty habit of coaching him from the sidelines and insists we sit as close as possible- it's like a little league game to him, I guess, but to his credit, his guidance has gotten Jax out of a few hairy situations inside the chain-link.

We can see everything that happens, while Jax is laser-focused on his opponent. We can see every time a wooden plank is thrown into the ring, every glint of metal on fingers, and have learned to anticipate every next move where he can't. It also helps calm him down, having us so close to him while he fights. It's brutal, and more often than not, the men in this ring leave in body bags instead of the cars they came in.

Soren continues down the aisle, claiming the chair next to the aisle seat. The spot closest to the aisle is always reserved for Kain, so he can jump in to help Jax between rounds, giving him water and applying extra Vaseline to his forehead and around his eyes.

I usher Georgia into my usual seat next to Soren, continuing to keep her between us. I park myself in the spot next to her, sliding my hand onto her knee. She tenses, and I can hear Soren scoff next to her, but I don't remove my hand. Sure, I can pass the gesture off as a way to keep her here, but in reality, I've been dying to feel her in my hands, and this is as close as I can get right now. I can hear Soren's voice in my head- *always pushing the envelope, Turner.* I almost laugh.

I lean over to her, taking in her smell- it's like an aphrodisiac to me, but maybe that's because I haven't been with a woman in a while.

"Behave yourself tonight, baby girl. Soren's already on edge, and Kain will be too. I'd hate to see you get hurt again." I whisper in her ear.
Her eyes widen for just a second, but I don't miss the

tiny bob in her throat as she swallows. I make her nervous. *Good.*

While my warning stands, I mean every bit of what I said. I don't want to see her hurt again, especially not by the hands of my brothers. I'm incredibly attracted to this girl; she's fiery and loud when she wants to be, but she also knows when to shut up and listen, something that a lot of the girls I've tried before never knew. On top of all of that, completing the whole package, she's drop-dead gorgeous. Her choice of outfit tonight doesn't allow my eyes to travel above her neck, and I know I'm not being polite about my staring, but I can't help it. Her tits are practically spilling out of her shirt, showing off the perfect amount of cleavage. I want to leave bruises all over them, like a dog marking his territory, and the thought of seeing her topless has me adjusting in my seat.

The lights dim and the music starts, and I feel her tense again. I see the gym doors open on either end of the warehouse, and the two men walk out. Jax is shirtless, only in tapered sweatpants and his black boots. *God, I hope that idiot remembered his mouth guard.*

The other man is what makes my jaw tick and sets me on edge.

Lucas Freeman, a dealer from our newly acquired territory that includes The Lucky Plate, is a big motherfucker. He's got at least thirty pounds on Jax, and four inches in height. I'm worried- Jax hasn't lost in a while, and I know Lucas knows that, so he's going to be ruthless in trying to snatch the crown from the king's head.

The announcer introduces them both, and they meet in the middle of the ring and touch their bare knuckles together in one final act of cordiality, before retreating to their corners. *Showtime.*

The bell rings and Lucas quickly strides towards Jax, trying to corner him against the fence. Jax might be smaller, but he's faster, dodging his advance with ease and sidestepping him, moving towards the center of the ring. Lucas makes up the lost ground quickly, swinging hard straight at Jax's face. He steps backwards, effectively dodging the punch, and Lucas stumbles forward. He recognizes the hole and swings himself, making contact with Lucas's temple, sending him to his knees.

Instead of going in for the kill, Jax steps backwards, jumping up and down and flicking his hands in anticipation of Lucas standing, ready for more.

That's the thing about his fighting style- he realizes that the audience came for a show, and while he is capable of killing him in the first round, he toys with his opponent, allowing him to get up and start after him again.

"Stop fucking playing with him, Jax! Kill him!" Soren yells, sitting on the very edge of his chair, elbows braced on his knees.

I spare a glance at Georgia, watching her press herself against the back of her chair. Her fingernails are digging into her thighs, and her eyes are wide. She doesn't look scared, though- she looks interested, awe-struck, almost. I smirk, squeezing her knee once. She briefly glances towards me, heat flashing across her face, followed by a frown, crossing her arms over her chest and locking her eyes back on to the fight, but I don't miss her blush. *She likes it.*

I look back towards the ring, and Lucas is standing now, and running towards Jax. He fakes him out, and Jax doesn't have time to dodge before Lucas's fist makes contact with his nose, blood flying as his head snaps backwards. I hiss and resist the urge to get in there and finish it myself.

Jax puts a hand to his nose, taking stock of the injury, and looks up at Lucas with dark eyes, grinning like a vandal, showing his teeth which are now covered in blood. I narrow my eyes- no mouthguard.

"You hit like a bitch, bro." Jax spits, and closes the distance easily, ducking a blow and delivering a sharp punch to the other man's liver.

Lucas groans, and his hand finds Jax's hair, wrenching him up and hitting him again in the face. *Get it together.*

Jax kicks out, the toe of his boot striking Lucas in the groin, and his grip on the smaller man's hair releases as he doubles over, almost falling to his knees. Jax moves quickly, following Soren's instruction, and pulls Lucas's head into his knee, crushing his cheekbone.

He throws him to the ground, straddling his waist and delivering unforgiving blows to his face, hitting him again and again until the referee steps in and pulls him from Lucas.

The round is over, and Jax retreats to his corner, while part of Lucas's team jumps the fence and helps him to the other. Kain's up in a flash, jumping onto the platform and leaning over the chain-link, saying something in Jax's ear. He nods, and Kain produces a tube of Vaseline from his pocket, warmed up with his body heat for easy application, and slathers it over his eyebrows and the bridge of his nose, smearing the blood covering his face into his skin.

The ref steps back, signifying the start of the second round, and Jax jumps up, moving back towards the center of the ring. Lucas meets him there, and the two circle around each other for a moment, gauging how injured the other is and where to strike to end it. Lucas is slower this time, most likely due to a concussion forming, and Jax quickly picks up on his handicap.

He dives for him, wrapping his arms around his midsection, and pushes him to the mat, getting him on the ground once again. This time, Jax is bloodthirsty, pinning his arms with his knees and promptly begins to wail on his face again, delivering fast blows to his face, blood splattering onto the mats with every swing of his fist.

Soren's on his feet now, hands behind his head as he yells. "Fuck him up, Jax!"

Being this close, we can see him grin, and the blows come faster. *He's going to kill him.*

However, as if he's expecting the next punch, Lucas jerks his head away at the last second, and the momentum of Jax's fist flying has him falling forward over the other man's shoulder. They flip over, Lucas using his hips to push Jax off, and he begins delivering his own blows to the smaller man's face and body, and I swear I hear a rib crack. I jump to my feet now, my hand flying from Georgia's knee. She remains seated, eyes wide, taking in everything as if she's photographing it with her mind. She's breathing heavily- I can see her chest rising and falling.

"Get him off, Jax, use your hips!" Soren's screaming now, using his hands when he yells.

At that exact moment, we hear the *clink* of a pipe being thrown into the ring, and both men's eyes lock on the weapon. I follow the path it was thrown from and find two seedy-looking guys, sitting front row on the opposite end of the ring. They cackle as Lucas jumps off Jax to scramble towards it, but Jax is quicker, crawling on his stomach towards the pipe, and wraps his hand around it. I turn back towards the men and smirk- they're not laughing anymore.

He turns over onto his back, swinging the pipe upwards towards where Lucas is leaning over him, and catches the larger man under the jaw with a sickening *crack*, sending him flying backwards to the ground.

For a second, the noise of the crowd fades. Jax just stares at him- at the blood pooling under Lucas's chin, beginning to drip onto his chest. He knows what a hit like that can do, and I know he's probably freaking out inside at the thought of actually killing Lucas. But he can't. Not right now, not with this much riding on him. We'll face the consequences later.

"Do it, Jax! Hit him again!" I'm yelling now, bending slightly at my waist and leaning towards the ring.

Jax stands shakily, and wields the pipe, swinging it again, making contact with Lucas's ribs. He curls in on himself, trying to protect his midsection from any further assault, but Jax doesn't let up, swinging it once more and clocking him in the head with it. Lucas goes limp, and I know it's over.

I exhale the breath I didn't realize that I was holding, relieved that Jax is still standing. The ref runs in, kneeling next to Lucas and checking his pulse. He nods, and I'm assuming he found one, although probably faint, as his team doesn't rush in and no one makes a move to drag his body away.

The ref approaches Jax and holds his arm in the air, signaling him the victor, and the warehouse erupts in cheers- the king keeps his crown tonight.

Jax can hardly stand, but he has a look of pride on his face as he looks over to me. I grin at him, but watch his face falter as he catches sight of Georgia.

Fuck, I should've probably mentioned that.

As if he can read my mind, Kain motions me over, and I sit back down, pushing Georgia forward so I can lean behind her to talk to him. She protests, but bends forward at the waist, her chest practically touching her knees.

"He knows." Kain yells above the screaming and the music. "He's not happy about it, but I told him everything on the way here."

I exhale sharply and let Georgia up, leaning back in my chair. I know she heard what Kain said, but she seems unfazed by his words, leaning back and resuming her previous position of crossed arm and a frown. *That'll be a fun conversation later.*

I look back to the ring and notice Jax has retreated to the locker room, and Lucas's team is crouching beside him, trying to wake him up. I slide my hand back onto her knee and pull her towards me so that I have unrestricted access to her ear.

"What'd you think? Too much?" I murmur into her, and I swear I can feel her thighs clench.

She shakes her head and leans back towards me. "That was intense. Are they okay? Which one was yours- the little one, right?"

Mine. I nod. "The blonde one, Jax." He'd lose his shit if he ever heard what she called him.

I stand, reaching my hand out for hers, but she brushes me off and stands on her own. She looks around nervously, noticing all of the other viewers starting to file out, and I'm sure she's anxious about what happens next.

Soren is wearing a rare, genuine smile next to her, clapping a man on the shoulder as he passes. "That kid just made us so much fucking money."

He's proud, and I am too, but I'm also nervous about what happens now. I saw how he was up there, jerky and all over the place at times, and I know it's because he's wired right now. I know he's going to snap when he sees Georgia at the compound, no thanks to Kain's loud ass mouth, and I don't know that I'm going to be able to hold him back on my own.

I sigh and shake my head, jerking it towards the door.

"Let's go. Soren'll catch a ride back with Kain."

I push her in front of me, guiding her out of the row and down the aisle, leading to the exit. I replace my hand at the small of her back, glaring at anyone who got too close. When we reach the exit, I open the door for her and usher her out into the night, grabbing her arm and leading her towards my car.

I'm street-parked right in front of the warehouse, and I open the passenger door for her and wait for her to slide in, bracing for another argument. She doesn't hesitate this time, and slides in, buckling her seatbelt behind her.

It's clear she's feeling an adrenaline high from tonight, but she seems much more confident than she was yesterday, and I send Soren a telepathic *I told you so*. I'm sure getting out of her cell helped things along nicely.

I jump into the driver's seat and crank the engine, closing my eyes as soon as I feel the first of the vibrations from the engine come through the car.

I spent my life savings getting this thing completely modded out, and it still gives me a hard on every time I hear it come to life. I look over at Georgia, who's staring out the windshield, eyebrows still raised.

"Hungry?" I ask her, and I swear I can hear her stomach growl in response.

"I could eat. We should probably go back to the basement; I don't want to make anyone else angry." She says in mock sweetness.

Fuck it, I've already pissed Soren off.

"I was thinking I could take you somewhere to get some food. We don't have shit back at home, and I didn't think the chicken tenders were enough. Besides, I need to make a stop before we head back anyways."

What the fuck are you thinking, Beck? I know that Soren's going to probably kill me for real this time, but I can't help it. I have an annoying urge to take care of her and make sure she's okay, especially after seeing her almost break down in front of me. I know I should be treating her more like he does, but that's just not who I am. I know I can get more out of her if I take her out, but I won't be mean with her- it's not in me like it is in him. Besides, my dad always taught me to treat girls with respect, and considering I spent most of the night staring down her shirt, I've got some making up to do.

"It's not a trick?" She asks, eyeing me warily.

I flash a smile and slide my hand back onto her knee, feeling her tense again. "Not a trick, baby girl. We'll only go if you want to."

She pauses, trying to read my face for any sign of deception. After a beat, she exhales and shakes her head in exasperation, looking at the floor.

"Fine, whatever. But it's your ass if he gets mad about it."

I grin at her and press the gas and floor it out of my parking space and down the street, her screams making my cock grow in my jeans. *God, I want her bad.*

Georgia

I've lost it, officially this time. This man kidnapped me, held me in a basement, forced me to watch two men beat the daylights out of each other, and now I've agreed to go to dinner with him? When this is all over, I'm going to need to get some serious psychiatric intervention.

His hand's on my leg. Oh my god, his hand is back on my leg. Every rational thought in my brain is yelling at me to push his hand off and cease all physical contact with him, but the space between my thighs is telling me to lean into him and never let him take his hand away from me. *I'm so fucked.*

I want to ask him a million questions, like why the hell Soren moved me out of the cell, and what the hell he just made me watch, but all I can do is sit and focus on the heat of his hand on my leg. The weight of it has me squirming in my seat, and the hard squeeze he gives tells me he knows what I'm doing.

He growls under his breath, and cuts his eyes to me, his gaze darkening as we lock eyes.

"Behave, Georgia. I mean it."

I turn my head and stare out the window, closing my eyes and taking a deep breath. I still have a headrush from watching the fight, so *not* in control of my situation, and I know I'm not thinking clearly

when I realize that I *don't* want to behave, not for
him. I shudder. *I'm a fucking headcase.*

The fear makes the intense lust that floods all
my senses that much stronger- knowing a snake is so
poisonous it could kill you makes it even more
desirable, I suppose.

I think back to the diner, and how I would've
been so willing to take him home that night. I
would've done anything he asked of me, just to get
him into bed, to know what he feels like.

But now, everything is different.

I flinch every time he touches me, afraid of
what he'll do to me, afraid of what he'll say to the
others, and what punishment might be waiting for
me. It's funny how things can change so quickly.

Despite my fear, and despite what these men
have done to me, I can't help but to want them. The
idea of finding myself underneath them consumes my
waking thoughts, and being this close to Beck tricks
my body into thinking my fantasies can be a reality.

I squirm again, pushing my thighs together at
some desperate attempt for friction where I need it
most. Suddenly, Beck yanks the car to the shoulder of
the road and throws it in park. Without missing a
beat, his hand is around my throat, pushing me
against the headrest.

It's not enough to cut off any air- I'm still breathing hard, but it's enough to establish control. He tests my limit by squeezing slightly, and I almost moan, feeling a flush climb up my chest and bloom across my cheeks.

"I've tried very hard to be nice tonight, Georgia. I don't think you understand the level of restraint I have to maintain when it comes to you. I'm supposed to hate you." He moves closer, leaning over the center console, our noses almost touching.

"I'm supposed to treat you as a tool. Something I use to get information, and nothing more. But goddamn it, you make my dick so hard I can't focus when I'm in the same room as you. Soren'll kill me for telling you this, but I want to pull you out and fuck you over the hood of my car until you cannot say anything but my name, and I *can't*. I don't want to be nice with you. I don't want to be gentle, and if you don't stop squeezing your fucking thighs when you know I can feel it, I won't be."

Holy. Shit.

I can't muster a response and his closeness has me doing the exact opposite of what he's asked of me. I move to cross my legs, and he locks a hand around my thigh, keeping them apart.

"Don't. Push. Me." He growls, one hand still locked around my throat. "I will hurt you, and not in the way you want."

"How do you know what I want?" I whisper back, longing to lean forward and close the millimeters of distance between us.

He breathes a throaty laugh and tightens his grip on my throat. "I would break you. I want to, you know? I want to destroy you, shatter you into a million pieces and rebuild you into my perfect little doll. Is that what you want?" When I don't say anything, he gets closer, and I swear he's going to kiss me.

"That's what you what, huh? You *want* someone to break you? You want me to hurt you?" Before I can respond, he rips his hand away and leans back in his seat, smirk on his face, shaking his head.

"Too fucking bad, baby girl. You'll have to earn that one." *Fucker.*

He can say whatever he wants, but one glance to his lap contradicts his words. He's painfully hard from the looks of it, and I'm glad I'm not the only one who has to suffer. My thighs are slick inside my jeans, and fuck him for getting me this wound up without getting me off.

"Let's eat, I'm starving."

He puts the car in drive and takes off again, and the sound of the acceleration can probably be heard in three counties. I instinctively reach up and grab the assist handle, and he barks out a laugh.

"Relax, Georgia. I'm not going to fucking wreck it, I've got way too much invested in her to be too reckless."

I nod my head, but don't release my hold on the handle. He glances over to me, realizing I am *not* relaxing, and shakes his head.

"You're fine. I've got you."

I feel his hand slide back onto my knee, squeezing it a few times, and my head starts to spin. *I am so fucked.*

The rest of the drive is silent, the only sound heard is my heavy breathing and the noise from Beck's car. We pull up to a run-down building, and Beck parallel parks across the street from it.

Before I can even look over at him, he's out of the car, and I can't see where he goes because of the dark tint on every window.

I gasp, jumping in my seat as he yanks open my door for me and leans in to unbuckle my seatbelt, grabbing my upper arm and pulling me out of the car to my feet. *Who said chivalry is dead?*

"I could've done that myself."

"Yeah, and run off on me? I don't think so." He scoffs.

"I wouldn't have run. Your car is fast."

He chuckles, grinning as he looks over his car. "Damn right it is."

He leads me across the street and into the building, and I lose my breath when I walk inside. While the outside of the building is dark, grimy, and nondescript, the inside is the complete opposite. It is a fully functioning night club, with a huge dance floor in the center and two full bars lining the walls, facing each other. There is a stage on the back wall with a state-of-the-art DJ booth, and multicolored stage lights pointed at it.

Bodies writhe together on the dance floor, and the music is so loud that I can barely hear my own thoughts. This is the sort of place I would frequent before, getting lost in the music and the liquor to forget how fucked up my life is.

"Welcome to Afterglow."

I flinch, not realizing Beck had gotten so close to me. He's leaning into me, his mouth nearly touching my ear. He tightens his grip on my arm and shifts me to his other side, away from the crowd and closer to the wall. A man comes up to us, just as gorgeous and muscular as the three I'm used to.

"What's up, boss? I didn't expect you tonight. Do you want your usual booth?"

Beck pulls him into a one-armed hug, dropping his hold on my arm. "Good to see you, man. I'm going to head to the back; I'm not staying for long. Could you get Danny to put in two burgers and fries for me? Oh, and bring me a drink back to the office. I need one."

The man nods, and I can feel the second his eyes drift over to me. His brows hit his hairline, and even in the dark I can read his confused expression. Beck picks up on it too, returning his hand to my arm.

"Cargo. Keep it in your pants, Elijah." He warns, tightening his grip and pulling me into him.

Elijah continues to stare but slowly nods his head. I can hear Beck growl under his breath, and he pulls me even closer. I am so close to him that my arm is behind his back, my hip pressing into his thigh, and the charge between us nearly shocks me. He clears his throat, eyes remaining locked on the other man.

"Understood. I'll get everything taken care of."

He turns on his heel and heads off towards the bar, not sparing a second glance backwards. Beck smirks, looking down at me, and starts for a back hallway next to the DJ booth.

We weave in and out of people, but his grip never falters on my arm. He leads me down the hallway to a thick wooden door, and he drops his hand to fish a set of keys out of his pocket.

Once he finds the one he's looking for, he unlocks the door and pushes it open, revealing a neatly decorated office, and pushes me inside, closing the door behind me. The walls are painted black with matching paneling, and a large wooden desk sits in the center of the room, with a dual monitor set up and an oversized office chair behind it. There are two plush leather sofas on either wall, and two conversation chairs facing the desk, the dark opulence of this room a strong contrast from what I've seen in the basement.

It smells strongly of marijuana smoke, so much so that I can almost see it lingering in the air. Beck walks in like he owns the place- he probably does- and plops down in the office chair behind the desk.

"Sit."

My body is on autopilot, and I gingerly drop into one of the conversation chairs facing him. There's a tension in the air and both of us can feel it.

Neither of us speaks for a moment, but he's got his eyes on mine, brow slightly furrowed in the center.

"Tell me, are you feeling better? Now that Soren's let you out of that cell."

"Much better. I really needed that shower."

He breathes out a laugh and pulls open one of the desk drawers, producing a small wooden box and a lighter. He opens and pulls out a tightly wrapped joint, placing it between his lips and lighting it, the cherry glowing strong as he inhales. He holds it for a moment, and tips his head back, exhaling through his nose. He holds it out to me, but I put my hand up in silent refusal.

"Good. Smoking's bad for you."

I raise an eyebrow at him, and he smirks at me.

"I've gotta know, Georgia, what's your angle here? Would it not be so much simpler for you to just talk?"

I pause, because on the surface, I'm sure that's how it seems, but he doesn't understand. He doesn't fully understand that the concept of keeping quiet about the secrets of The Brotherhood has been beaten into me, and that I'm terrified that if I talk, I'm going to die.

"I'm scared."

"You shouldn't be." He leans forward on his elbows, his hair falling slightly in his face. "If you talk, Soren and Kain will leave you alone. It's that simple."

"It's not them I'm scared of."

My words make him pause, and he raises the joint to his lips again, taking another drag. I wish I could tell him what they did to me. What they'll do to me if they ever find out what I've said. But I can't-even if I did, I doubt he'd really believe me.

"Jesus, they fucked you up good, didn't they? They don't even know where you are and you're *still* tightlipped. I guess there is something we can learn from The Brotherhood after all."

I scowl at him, and he chuckles under his breath.

"Sorry, bad timing. But seriously, what'd they do to you anyway? It must've been worse than the usual black eyes their whores leave with."

"They hurt me, yes. But it's so much more than that." I stop myself from spilling my guts right away and focus on what I *can* say. "If I help you and they go down, I'm still dead. I'm the only one they'd suspect of selling them out. I'd rather die at the hands of someone who doesn't care enough to drag it out. There's no history with Soren, and I know with him, the minute I'm not of use, he'll make it quick. If I'm going to die, I want it to be on my own terms, the way I want it to be."

"Fucking Christ, morbid much?"

I'm glad he doesn't press me for more.

"Who says Soren's going to kill you anyhow?"

"Why wouldn't he? I'm nothing to him. I'm a tool, remember? You said it yourself."

"That's where you're wrong, baby girl. I think you have an effect on Soren, just like me. If I had to bet money on it, I'd say he wants you just as much as I do." He stands, dropping the joint in an ashtray and walking around the desk and stopping in front of me.

"I'm sure he's pictured all the ways he wants to break you, too. There's a reason you're still alive, and I can bet it's because he hasn't had his way with you yet. He might be a raging asshole, but there's always a reason behind it."

He puts his hands on either side of the chair I'm sitting in and pushes it backwards, the legs scraping against the wooden floors. He leans over me, and on instinct I cross my legs to give myself some friction. He senses my movement instantly and locks his hands around my thighs, forcing them apart.

"What did I say about that?" He says through clenched teeth, his eyes darkening as he stares down at me.

I don't respond, I can't. I gape at him, the words not coming to me.

"That was a question, Georgia. What did I say about that?"

"Y-you said not to do it." My voice comes out hoarse and full of need. *Please fucking touch me or go sit back down.*

I can't deal with him this close to me, and I long to reach out and close the small gap between us.

"That's right, I did say that. Listening isn't your strong suit, is it?"

When I don't respond again, he shoves my legs open and drops to his knees in front of me.

"Do you need me that badly, baby girl? Is your cunt so desperate for my attention that you're ignoring what I say on purpose?"

"N-no, I'm sorry. I won't do it again."

"No, you won't, and I'm going to make sure of that."

His fingers find my belt, and he yanks it open and rips it off my waist. I feel the bite of the leather as it leaves my waist, my too-big jeans pooling around my stomach. He wrenches the button of jeans open, and shoves his hand inside, quickly finding my pussy through my panties. I can't move, nor do I want to, though I know I should.

"Already fucking soaked for me. You filthy girl."

I have no time to be embarrassed of my body's reaction to him before he starts slow circles over my clit through my panties. My brain is on overdrive with the sensation of his hands on me. He's not gentle, but I didn't expect him to be.

"I'm not going to fuck you, Georgia, because once I get inside you, there's no going back. But I know what you need, and I'm going to make sure you don't squirm in your seat again tonight. Take these off."

I don't think, I just obey, lifting my hips and sliding my jeans down my hips. He removes his hand from me, helping me get them down, and replaces it instantly once my jeans are sitting around my ankles. His circles are getting faster, as is my breath, and I can't look away from him. I'm close, so close, and I'm praying to every god known to man that he doesn't stop and realize what he's doing. He's applying brutal pressure, and it's enough to push me over the edge. I come hard, biting my lip to stop my moan from escaping.

"Good girl, Georgia. I knew you'd be so pretty when you come."

Beck reaches into his back pocket and pulls out a knife, not quite as scary as the one Kain had to my throat, but still big enough to make me shiver. He slices through the side of my panties, makes quick work of cutting through the flimsy material and ripping them off me. My skin stings as the fabric flies from my hip, and as soon as the scraps hit the floor, he plunges two fingers inside without warning.

"Give me one more, baby. Just one more. You can do that for me, can't you?"

I nod my head, and he begins to pump his fingers in and out at a brutal pace. I can't help the moan that escapes, and it only seems to make him go faster.

"Fuck, do that again. Let me hear you."

He's fucking me hard with his fingers, curling them inside every time his knuckles reach my opening.

This isn't sensual or romantic. No, this is full of primal need and lust- there is no love here.

He finds my g-spot with ease and focuses his attention there, applying delicious pleasure with every thrust of his fingers. I'm moaning loudly now, but it doesn't seem to be enough for him. He leans forward, his fingers never slowing, and sucks my clit into his mouth, swirling his tongue around the needy bud. I scream, clenching around his fingers as I come. He slowly removes his fingers, bringing them to his mouth and sucking my juices from them.

"Goddamn, you taste good, G."

Holy fucking shit. That visual makes me wet all over again and ready for more, but he rises to his feet, adjusting his clearly hard cock in his jeans.

"Feel better, baby girl?" He says with a smirk. "Get dressed."

I scramble to yank my jeans back up and search the ground for my belt, finding it thrown onto one of the sofas, and fasten it back around my waist. My face is flushed and I'm sweating, my previously neat braids now wild with hair sticking out of them.

Suddenly, there's a knock at the door, and I'm jumping out of my skin, dropping back into my chair and staring straight ahead. My hands start to shake in my lap, and I'm bouncing my leg to try and quell the anxiety. *What the hell did we just do?* Beck glances at me, smirking and shaking his head.

"Come in, Eli."

The man in question enters, carrying a tray of food, setting it down on the desk. He hands Beck a glass of amber liquid and walks out, his eyes never meeting mine.

"Eat. You need it. We have to leave soon, and Soren's going to lose his shit when he realizes we left him."

As I cautiously tuck into my food, I realize the consequences of tonight. He was never supposed to bring me here, and he made me *come*. I know I'm going to get punished for it, so I savor the meal. *Who knows when I'm going to be able to eat again.*

Beck's already halfway done with his food as I finally look over at him, and he grins at me, picking up his glass and slamming the contents.

"I have to say Georgia, of anything I could've done to sign my death warrant, that was so fucking worth it."

We are so fucked.

Soren

I'm on a high after Jax's win. After the crowd thinned, I followed our bookie to the back and collected the earnings from the bets and cover charges. It totaled out to just over sixty grand, and I nearly cried when he handed me the duffle bag overflowing with cash.

I walk out of the office with a huge smile on my face, bag in hand, in search of Beck and the girl. I want nothing more than to go home and pull down a bottle of something and celebrate, and I'm ready to leave *now*.

I scan the near-empty warehouse and find Kain deep in conversation standing the ring. I walk towards him, jumping the fence and dropping the bag to the ground. The other man takes one look at me and scurries off. *That was easy.*

"Hey man, good shit tonight.' I grasp his waiting hand and pull him into a hug. "I'm ready to celebrate. Where did Beck run off to?"

Kain doesn't reply and stares down at his boots. I instantly feel uneasy; he's not one to dodge my questions like this, and the only reason he would is if he was covering for someone. *Or someones.*

"Kain. Where the fuck is Beck? Where is the girl?"

"Listen, Soren, don't freak out. I'll give you a ride home."

Fuck that. If they split, I'm going to find and kill him within the hour. I knew it was a risk taking her with us, but I couldn't leave her to her own devices in the compound, and Beck had me convinced that she should be allowed out of her cell. *Did he want her for himself?*

"Kain, you have five seconds to start talking before I start swinging. Where are they?"

"They left about an hour ago. I don't know where they went, but he took her and split as soon as the fight ended." He sighs and runs a hand over his buzzed head.

I can feel the rage seeping in, and I know if I don't move now, I'm going to black out. I take a step away from him and turn my back, taking a deep breath.

Kain doesn't do well with yelling, and I don't think I could take him in a fight right now. I push the rage down as far as I can before turning back to him.

"Why didn't you say something when they left? Is that not information that you think I should know?" My teeth are clenched, and I'm trying not to lose my shit.

"I thought they were going to wait for you by the car, but I heard Beck's car take off. I was checking on Jax afterwards in the locker room, I didn't know where you were."

"Pull his fucking tracker and get the goddamn car. I'm going to get the kid. We roll out in five." I spit, turning on my heel and walking away from him.

I grab the cash and hop the fence again, heading in the direction of the locker room. I burst through the door, finding Jax sitting on the bench, hair wet from a shower.

"Get your shit, we're going. Beck went fucking AWOL and I'm two seconds from snapping."

He can sense the anger radiating off me, and scrambles to throw his shirt over his head before running after me.

"What? Where is he?"

I stop in my tracks and whirl around to face him.

"If I knew that, do you think I would be standing here right now? I have no idea where he is, but he has the goddamn girl with him."

I can see him tense up at the mention of her. *I guess Kain filled him in.*

"I'm sure you understand that this is a big fucking problem, Jax, so fall in line and let's go. Kain's pulling his tracker now."

I turn and start towards the door, ignoring the congratulatory remarks thrown towards Jax and I.

When I took over The Vipers, I made sure that the three of us were fitted with trackers, just in case. They're small tubes, no bigger than a grain of rice, that were placed under the skin at the base of our necks. They connect to software installed on our phones, so if a job goes wrong and we lose comms, we'll always be able to find each other. I thank God for that now, because I am desperate to find Beck and the girl. I know she's a hot piece of ass, but if he ran off with her, he's a dead man.

I get to the Escalade just as Kain's pulling it around. I jump in the passenger seat, slamming the door, and settle once I hear Jax climb in behind me.

"Please tell me you found something."

I don't think Beck would've disabled his tracker, but I don't trust that girl. She could've convinced him, or hell, she could've cut it out of his damn neck herself.

"Yeah, Boss. I've got him. He's, uh… He just left Afterglow. Seems like he's on the way back home now. He should beat us there."

You're fucking joking.

For a second, I think I've misheard- Beck wouldn't. He *couldn't*. Then it lands cold, hard- like a punch to my gut. He's gone. With her.

The one thing I asked of them- the one thing he, of all people, should've understood- and he still went against me. Maybe this was his plan from the start- he put this fucking bug in my head that it would speed things up if we let her out, but the second I loosen the leash, he takes full advantage. If I find him... No, *when* I find him, he's going to regret ever speaking this stupid idea into existence.

"Unbelievable." I mutter. "Thank you for checking. Take us home."

The ride back to the compound is quiet, both of them not wanting to stir up any more shit with me, not with what's waiting for me at home.

The second the car pulls into the garage, I'm out, busting through the door and heading straight for our elevator. I slam my hand against the panel, hoping I triggered the right button, not waiting for Kain and Jax.

The elevator dings, and I rush out into the hallway and straight for Beck's bedroom. I open the door, and it's dark, but I can hear the shower running. *Got you, motherfucker.* I wrench the bathroom door open and find a fully clothed Beck standing over the sink. I swing instantly and catch him off-guard, my fist striking him across the jaw, snapping his head sideways.

"Have you lost your goddamn mind!?" I growl, fighting the urge to shake out my hand after the contact. He's fucking solid, I'll give him that.

I swing again and he dodges, but my fist still lands across the side of his face.

"Fucking stop, Soren! Let me explain, will you?"

"No, Beck, the time for explanation is over."

I move to hit him again, but he's faster, catching my fist and pulling me forward, and pushing me against the edge of the sink, pinning my arm behind my back. I try to jerk my arm free, but at the angle he's got me twisted into, I have no advantage.

"Let me go, now Beck. I mean it. You fucked something up for the last time."

He laughs, but there's no humor in it. "Real nice, *Conner*." He sneers. "You want to beat me into submission? I thought you'd turn out to be different than that."

"Don't you dare bring my fucking father into this." I get out, struggling against his hold. My eyes stray to the side, and I see Kain and Jax standing in the doorway.

Fucking awesome, we have an audience.

Beck drops his hold on my arms, and I shake him off and stagger backwards. My fingers itch to hit him again. I've never been this angry with Beck. This girl has only been here a few days, and she's already tearing us apart.

"What the fuck were you thinking, taking her into the city like that, huh?"

"I got her talking. That was the whole point, right? You wanted to get her to sell them out?"

"I could've gotten her to talk. *We* could've gotten her to talk without ever taking her out. I should've never listened to you!" I'm screaming at him now, and I hear Kain suck in a sharp breath and step backwards. "I should've kept her locked in that fucking cell. You showed her everything, Beck. She knows where the club is now. She knows where we live. How the fuck am I ever supposed to let her go now, huh?" I move towards him, getting in his face.

He stays put, standing his ground and puffing his chest out. *Weird.* Typically, when I yell at him, he cowers, accepting whatever I give him and retreating into himself. Not now, though- he's got his eyes on mine, and anger is written all over his face.

"Here's the deal- if we let her go now, we're dead. Because of you. You never fucking listen to me, Beck. If she ever leaves this goddamn compound again, she is going to lead them *straight* back to us and everything we've built, and we're all fucking dead!" I'm screaming so hard, my throat is raw.

I turn and look at Jax, half hiding behind Kain, who also looks pale at the scene unfolding in front of them.

"You want to put Jaxon on a fucking platter for them, huh? Hand him right back and let them kill him too?" I gesture towards him with an open palm.

"Soren, that's too far." he murmurs from his spot behind Kain. I look towards him. His face is nearly pale- I can tell my words are making him panic, reliving everything they did to him, but I can't let up. I need to make sure they really understand the weight of what's been done. I'll apologize for it later.

"Is it, Jax? Because that's exactly what he's doing." I scoff, and turn my back to Beck, who braces himself on the sink with his hands, his head hanging low.

Suddenly, his head snaps up, and he reaches out and punches the mirror, shattering it into shards that fly across the bathroom.

"You think I fucking want that, Soren?!"

It's his turn to scream at me now, his hands starting to shake as blood seeps out of his knuckles. There must be glass stuck in there, and I know it hurts, but he makes no move to check his wounds.

"I would *never* do anything to put my family's lives at risk. I've given everything for you, for The Vipers. I've done everything you've ever asked of me. I'm sorry that's not fucking good enough." He scoffs, shaking his head. "I took her out for our benefit. We're so close, Soren. We are so close to taking back everything and getting rid of them. Georgia is the key to doing that."

"I don't agree. I'm making the call; she's going back to the cell. Kain and I will handle everything from here on out. You are not to interact with her. I'm not sure what the fuck happened between you two, but you're obviously in too deep with her already and her pussy is blinding you to what's really going on here."

"Soren, I promise you, it'll work. Just give it time-" His breath is coming in shallow bursts, and I can tell he's on the verge of breaking down.

"No." I cut him off, putting my hand on his arm. "You tried, brother, I know. But you failed. And with something like this, failure is not an option. You're done. We can't afford another mistake."

He pauses, staring at me with a world of hurt and confusion in his eyes. He shrugs my hand from his arm and shakes his head, like he can't believe the words coming out of my mouth.

"Fuck you. You're just like your dad, Soren. I thought you were different, but you're just another fucking tyrant. Fuck. You."

With that, he pushes past me, bumping his shoulder against mine hard enough to almost knock me over, and leaves the bedroom. Jax stares at me, mouth half open in shock, and turns to follow him, rushing out of the room as well.

I think back to when we were kids. I was always the golden child- everyone knew I was going to be something special. Beck was content to live in my shadow, proud to be the one beside me. He never seemed to mind that the light hit me first.

Our parents used to say we came into the world like a set. They kept us in the same crib, side by side, because we wouldn't sleep otherwise. We learned to walk together, to fight together. Every scrape, every bruise, every punishment- we earned them as one. If I bled, he bled. If I laughed, he laughed harder.

Beck's two months and four days younger than me, and the I swear I can remember the day he was born. Even though it's impossible, I swear I remember how he cried- how his mother laid him next to me like he was mine to protect.

And now he's the one who's defied me. The one who looked me in the eye and did exactly what I told him *not* to do. He took her and made a choice that could unravel everything we've built. After all that history, all that loyalty, he still couldn't follow me this once.

The thing about brothers, blood or not, is that they always know the best ways to wound you.

When I finally pull myself out of my thoughts and make my way out of the bathroom, Kain is sitting on the bed with his head in his hands. *Shit.*

"I'm sorry. I didn't mean for you to see that. You could've left, we were fine."

"I didn't want to leave you. I feel like shit about tonight. I should've told you they were gone right away. It's my fault this happened."

"Stop. It's his fault. He shouldn't have taken her to Afterglow. This doesn't blow back on you, Kain."

He looks up at me, and I can tell it's going to be a long night for him. His eyes are bloodshot, and there's a slight shake to his hands. *Jesus, when was the last time he slept?*

"Go work out or something, take your mind off it. I really am sorry, man. Walk away next time, I don't want to scare you."

I stand, stretching my arms above my head. I need to go find the girl and fix this shit before it escalates again.

I leave Beck's room and open the neighboring door to the guest room we've got Georgia situated in. The room is dark, and she's lying in bed under the covers. As soon as she hears the door open, she jumps, and I can see the silhouette of her body tense up. I walk in, closing the door behind me, and stand at the end of the bed.

Her blonde hair is sprawled out over the pillow, loose from the braids she wore it in this evening. I want nothing more than to sit at the edge of her bed and console her, to get rid of whatever fear she has, even though I'm probably the cause of a lot of it.

The thought sickens me. While I'm fucking pissed at Beck right now, I also understand the reasoning behind what he did. He can lie to me and say that he did it for information, but I know truthfully, he wanted to get close to her. She is so different from any of the girls we have at our disposal. She's authentically herself, and a woman who is not afraid to spit in my face, even when faced with brutality, earns my respect. She's more beautiful than any woman I've ever met- I dream of what she would feel like, what my name would sound like on her lips.

I don't want her to be afraid of me, but I don't know how to be gentle. I do want to hurt her, at least a little bit. She is supposed to be the enemy. I should want to shoot her on sight simply for the place she came from, but I don't feel that way about her anymore. *I'm a fucking coward.*

My father would've had this handled from the start. There wouldn't have been room for errors like tonight, because he would've gotten everything he needed and discarded her. He was a brutal man, and Beck's right, he was a tyrant. His rage was uncontrollable, but he was efficient, and he struck fear into every single person that looked his way, including me. He was an effective leader; one I thought I should try to emulate. I know Beck thinks we're alike, and I know the way I acted tonight probably proves him right. But inside, I couldn't be any more different from my father.

When I was a kid, I wanted to be just like him. As a child, the fear looked like respect. I thought the training meant he wanted to spend time with me, and I idolized him. It wasn't until I was a made man that I realized who he truly was.

Conner Bishop was a monster, and his legacy follows me like a long shadow. I'm cursed just for bearing his name. I don't want to be like him anymore, but I don't know how to lead without fear, without the brutality that my father had- something that was ingrained in me from the time my fist could fully wrap around the handle of a gun.

But Georgia is making me realize my mistakes. I feel awful for the way I've been with her, but I'll be fucked if I ever let her know that.

"I know you're awake, Georgia."

When she doesn't respond, I step closer to the bed. "What happened tonight cannot happen again."

"I don't know what the fuck you're talking about."

"Georgia. Do you not think I know where you were? I know where he took you. I know everything. It can't happen again. It *won't* happen again."

"In case you've forgotten, I'm not really calling the shots here. You should be talking to him about this."

"Trust me, I did."

At that, she sits up, looking right at me. I don't know why I'm even discussing this anymore. The longer I look at her, the more it's going to hurt me to have to put her back in that cell. *Get it over with, pussy.*

"What did you do to him?" Her voice is shaky, but I can tell she tries to put some fire behind it.

"Don't worry about that, Georgia. I'm going to move you back. That was too much of a risk." I wait for her to get up on her own, like a good little captive, but she stays put, frozen.

"Please, Soren, I'm sorry. Please don't make me go back in there." I can hear the tears forming in her voice.

"It's not a discussion. Let's go." I speak softly to her now, but I don't know why. It's a stark contrast from how I've been with her in the past, and I know she picks up on it.

"Please, I'll do anything. I don't want to go back, please don't put me back."

She's crying now, her words laced with sobs. She jumps out of bed and stands in front of me. Even in the dark, I can make out the way her shoulders shake with sobs, and I can hear the way her breath hitches after every one. Suddenly, she drops to her knees at my feet and wraps her arms around my calves. I'm shocked, my body going rigid.

This is the first time she's touched me, and the first time I've been touched by a woman in a long time. My back is ramrod straight, and my hands are balled at my sides. She's crying even harder now, her nose pressed into my thigh.

"P-please, Soren. I'll help, I'll talk- I'll do whatever you want, I swear. Don't do this to me again."

I lose control of my body, and my hand finds her hair. I can hear her breath hitch in her throat, and her crying stops. I start to gently scratch her scalp, trying to bring her some form of comfort where I can. My head is empty- I can't think right now, or I'll hurt her. My instincts are telling me to yank her up and drag her back into the cell, to get it over with and move on.

I shut my eyes, tilting my head backwards and taking in the way her hair feels in my hand. I know she hasn't brushed it in days, but even so, the strands are soft, grounding me as they move in my grip.

I am not my father.

"Get up." My voice is hoarse, and I'm on overdrive. I'm not acting on reason or falling back on any of my training. I'm acting on feeling alone. When she doesn't move, I urge her again.

"Get up. Please, Georgia." I rasp.

She shakily stands, standing so close to me I can smell her. My mouth waters. If I weren't a decent man, I'd have her bent over the bed before she took her next breath. *Fuck, I want her.*

Her eyes are wide, and her whole-body shakes. I reach out and brush her cheek with the tips of my fingers, afraid of touching her anymore, and I swear I feel her lean into it.

"What are you doing to me, pretty girl?"

I open my palm and cup her face, pushing myself even further. *I don't want to hurt her. I don't need to hurt her.* I'm repeating that mantra in my head, blocking out any thoughts of doing the opposite.

Beck's right, watching her break like this changes things. She looks fragile, like the slightest push in the wrong direction will shatter her.

"Can you work with me? Will you help me?"

She pauses, surely confused about my sudden softness.

"If I do, they'll kill me. I can't, Soren. It's better if you get it over with."

I growl under my breath. They won't touch her, not if I have anything to do with it, and I've made up my mind about her fate here. This girl will not die by my hand. I can't do it, even if that's what I truly wanted. *It never was.*

"I will not let that happen, Georgia. You tell me what you know, and I will make sure nothing happens to you."

She gasps, and I feel her body go slack at my words.

"Is this a trick?" She whispers.

"No. I mean what I say. I'll keep you safe."

She's sobbing again and can barely stand. I drop my hand from her face and guide her gently back to the bed, sitting her down on the edge. I stand in front of her, between her legs, and press her head to my stomach, my hand finding her hair again. Her arms slowly circle my waist, and she buries her face into my shirt, soaking it with tears. Now that I've gotten a taste of what it's like to touch her, I'm addicted. I cannot let her go.

"I need your words, pretty girl. Tell me you'll help me."

"Yes. I'll help you. Whatever you need."

Her words are barely a whisper, but their weight rings out like a scream. I continue to hold her until I feel her sobs subside, and her small frame begins to slump. I know she's close to sleep, so I move her backwards, until she's laying down. I gently place the covers back over her body and turn to leave. As my hand finds the doorknob, I hear a small voice.

"I knew you weren't all bad. Thank you, Soren."

My lips twitch upwards, and I ache to turn around and kiss her. I don't- I *can't*-, instead opening the door and slipping out into the quiet hallway. When the door closes behind me, I sag against it, breathing heavy.

I made the right call tonight. I did the right thing. I could've gone in there and forced her to bend to my will, but I didn't. I didn't hurt her.

I am not my father.

Kain

I'm still sitting on Beck's bed when I hear the door to the guest suite close. When I don't hear footsteps, I move towards the bedroom door, opening it a crack and peering out into the hallway.

Soren is slumped against *her* door, his head in his hands, but the girl is nowhere to be seen. I open it wider, stepping out into the hallway. Soren's head jerks towards me, and he sighs when he realizes I'm alone. I walk towards him, standing in front of him, leaning against the wall.

"I couldn't do it. I couldn't put her back in there."

I can tell he's battling his own head right now, a feeling I know all too well. I push off the wall and set a hand on his shoulder, feeling his body jerk in response to my touch. It's rare for me to touch others, and I'd lose my shit if someone tried to touch me. In the six years I've been with The Vipers, I can count on one hand the number of times that I've touched someone the way I'm touching Soren.

"Does that make me a coward? A weak-willed man, blinded by a woman?"

I shake my head, looking down at him. "It makes you a good leader. You made the right choice."

Lie.

I would rather her be locked away, somewhere far from my family. I'd prefer we get this shit over with and kill her already, but I won't tell him that.

He laughs bitterly, shaking his head. "My dad is rolling in his grave right now."

"Your dad was a dick."

He nods, laughing again. "Yeah, he was." He stands, my hand dropping from his shoulder. "I'm going to bed, I'm drained. Are you good?"

No.

"Yeah man, I'm good. Good night."

He walks off towards his own bedroom, and I stand there until I hear his door close. I pull my phone from my pocket, checking the time. *Two-thirty.* I don't feel tired at all, though. I'm wired, and hearing Soren scream at Beck like that didn't help anything. *Beck.* I have no idea where he went after the fight, but I need to put my eyes on him and make sure he's okay.

I protect my people, and those three are the closest thing I've ever had to a family. I never had one growing up, and I latched onto them as soon as I could.

My parents, if you could even call them that, hated me, and made sure I knew it. My entire life before them was a nightmare. I've had almost every bone in my body broken by the time I was fifteen, and I've been ruined in ways unimaginable. My parents were addicts, and when they finally had their very own crack baby to raise, they did everything they could to make sure I would befall the same fate as them. In hindsight, I don't think any of it was ever on purpose. They raised me the only way they knew how to live themselves- full of hate and rot. A gutter rat from the wrong side of the highway, like they were, and like their parents were.

I rarely talk about my childhood. Suffice to say, I learned quickly that people will take whatever they can from you if it keeps them comfortable.

I hate being touched. Sleep doesn't come easy, and caffeine has become a constant companion. I can endure being shouted at by anyone- anyone except my brothers. When it comes from them, my body shuts down. It drags me back to voices I thought I'd left behind.

Still, that isn't the worst of it.

The worst is what I never had- an education. I never went to school. I was the one keeping the lights on. By the time I could have learned, I was too ashamed to try.

I'm twenty-six, and I can barely read a fucking sentence.

Soren's the only one who knows. We were preparing for a job once, and my task was to read through some documents he'd dug up. I stared at them for almost nine hours and managed maybe three words. Eventually, I went to him, ready for him to call me a liability and cut me loose.

But he didn't.

He just nodded, like it was no big deal. From then on, he had photo maps ready for me- visuals, instead of reports. Somehow, it worked. I can memorize every street, every exit, every face. As it turns out, my brain learned to absorb pictures where the words don't stick.

I made sure my parents got what they deserved, though. The first chance I got, I set the house on fire, with my parents in it, and I relished watching it. They burned for everything they did to me- the only regret I felt was that I didn't get to watch them die myself.

I split before the cops showed up, and I assume they think I died, too, but I didn't stick around long enough to find out.

After the fire, I came straight to the compound and went dark. I'd heard stories of The Vipers, and I knew I couldn't make it alone without ending up in prison. I was bloodthirsty when I burned my old life to the ground, and I wanted to find and kill every single woman who ever laid a hand on me. To get retribution for the things they did to me.

Soren showed me a better way, though, and I was able to find an outlet in people who wronged others. I was able to push my shit aside and focus on a job. *My* job. I love being an enforcer. It allows me to slip into a persona that I wish I could embody all the time- strong, brave, and unwavering. That's not who I am, though. *I'm a fucking traumatized freak.*

I shake my head, pulling myself out of my thoughts and head towards the elevator. I refrain from checking Beck and Jax's trackers, trusting my ability to find them without checking.

When I get to the main floor of the compound, it's mostly empty, save for a few of our girls keeping a few of our men company.

My eyes catch on our usual table in the corner behind the bar, and I find the man I was looking for. Beck is sitting sideways in a chair, leaning against the wall and nursing a bottle of something clear, and Jax is sitting next to him, with his head down on the table, resting on his arm, facing Beck. I walk over and pull up the seat across from them.

"Hey man, you okay?"

Beck grins at me, a streak of blood still present across his mouth from the previous onslaught. His eyes are empty and glazed over though, and I can tell he's drunk.

"Yeah, man, I'm aaalll good."

Jax sits up, turning in his chair to face me and shakes his head, instantly negating what Beck said. I look him in the eyes and find his pupils almost normal sized. His hands tremble in front of him, and I know he's coming down from earlier.

"I was just tryin' to help, y'know?" Beck slurs, his head lolling against the wall. "I just wanted to… to do somethin' right, you know? Just… somethin'."

"I know. I'm sure Soren knows that too." I sigh. I can smell the booze on him from here. *This is going to be a long night.*

Beck's head rolls forward, as if his neck can't support the weight of it. His hair is wild, more so than usual, and his t-shirt is wrinkled and riding up as he slumps further against the wall.

"Does he, though? Because every fuckin' thing I do, man… Not. Good. Enough. It was a fucking problem when I brought her here for him, a problem when I wanted her out of the cell, a problem when I do this, a problem when I do that. Every fuckin' thing, man."

"Look, I know Soren gives you a lot of shit. But he's coming around. He left her in her room tonight, I guess she got through to him in whatever way she did you."

He starts laughing, sighing audibly as he catches his breath.

"I fuckin' doubt it, Kain. Like, I really, really fuckin' doubt it." He hiccups and laughs again.

"Because if he did get through to her like I did, you woulda heard it from up here."

Shit.

"Beck. Please tell me you didn't fuck her."

He rolls his head over his shoulder, leaning it back against the wall with a hard thump.

"Not yet, brother, but I almost did. I had her coming all over my fuckin' hand, though, I'll tell you that much. She's different, dude, and she's not gonna sell *us* out, I know that for sure."

I don't miss the way Jax bristles at his words. I don't know what's going on between these two, but they're closer than the rest of us. Beck's the only person willing to take care of Jax when he's using, and Jax in turn follows him around like a lost puppy. I've seen Beck leaving his room more times than I can count, thinking no one noticed, and it's never fully clothed.

"Alright Trigger, I think we should get you to bed." I stand, moving towards him.

Jax jumps up, waving a hand at me to sit back
down, and grabs Beck under one arm, hoisting him
up from his chair.

"I got it. I'll take him."

I nod, digging in my pocket for my cigarettes.
"Make sure he doesn't choke on his own vomit."

I watch as Jax half-carries and half-drags him
towards the elevator, Beck singing something off-key
the whole way across the floor, and I turn back
towards the table as soon as I see the doors close. I
pull a cigarette out and light it, taking a long drag.

We are a family, but we're nothing if not a
little fucked up. Between Jax's shit, and now this rift
between Soren and Beck, I know we've got to fix
what happened, and fast. I can't have any of them
killing themselves over the bullshit we're dealing with.
I don't agree with any of what Soren's doing, and as
angry as I am about it, I can't fault him too much. I
doubt he really knew what he was getting himself into
with all of this.

I've chain smoked half of my fresh pack of
smokes before deciding to head back downstairs. I
board the elevator, relishing in the silence of the short
ride down. When the door opens, it's quiet. I start
towards Beck's bedroom door, putting my ear against
it. I don't want to walk in on something I shouldn't
see, but I also want to make sure he's okay before I

leave them for the night. I hear hushed voices, and then Jax's laugh, so I know they're alright.

I start to walk past his door to get to the offices, but I pause when I reach the guest suite.

What is it about her?

Before I realize what I'm doing, I'm pressing down on the handle and cracking the door open, slipping inside silently. I press the door closed, gliding the handle back into place so that the door doesn't click shut. She's asleep, burrowed in the center of the bed, covers pulled tightly around her neck. I stare down at her, observing every way her body twitches and moves in her sleep.

Objectively, she is gorgeous, but that doesn't mean I trust her. I like the way her hair fans out around her, like a blonde halo. *Ironic, considering who she is.*

There's a chair in the corner of the room, and I silently sink down into it, leaning forward on my elbows. I don't understand my brothers' fascination with her. I can't understand why we've taken her out of the cell, and why we've made her so comfortable here. This is not what we do. We interrogate, get information, and move on. We've never kept someone here for more than 48 hours, and she's been here for almost four days. She is the enemy, and now

Beck's gotten into bed with her. I wanted to hit him after that confession upstairs.

I have a gnawing feeling that he will try to keep her here permanently, and now that Soren's made the call to keep her in the room, I'm sure he won't disagree with him. We can't let anything get in the middle of us. She could be the one to ruin my brothers, and I have to make sure that never happens.

I stay watching her for what seems like hours, marking every tiny move she makes and every sound her body produces, as if even in her sleep I'll be able to pick up on some kind of deception. I don't. She sleeps almost peacefully, and it upsets me. *She should not be here.*

After a while, I pull my phone out, clicking on the screen. It's nearly five-thirty now, and I know Soren will be awake soon. He's a very predictable man with his habits, waking up at exactly the same time every day. He chalks it up to relieving his men, but I know it's because he enjoys the peace and quiet of the morning before the chaos begins- namely, Beck waking up.

Not waiting around to be caught watching her, I slip back out of the room, as quietly as I came, and head towards the kitchen. We've transformed the basement level of our compound into a complete apartment, with four bedrooms and bathrooms, a kitchen, a gym, a movie room, and three holding cells. At first glance, it just looks like a barren hallway, but that's by design. The kitchen is through a door at the end of the hall, adjacent to Jax's bedroom.

Pushing the door open, I step into the open space and walk over to the coffee maker. The kitchen isn't much to look at, truly, but we built it ourselves. The cabinets are wooden and painted black, with cheap laminate countertops. An island sits in the middle of the space, with barstools pulled up to it. The appliances are white, the cheapest we could find, and half of them are used.

Not my coffee machine, though. Once I got enough payout from jobs here, this was the first thing I bought. It's nothing fancy, just a regular drip coffee machine, but it's *mine* and it works. I pull the red canister out from next to the machine and start a fresh pot, the smell of the grounds making me close my eyes.

This is my favorite part of every day. I've gotten a bit better about my habit- I used to drink nearly three pots of the stuff by five o'clock every day, but I've reduced it to one and a half- two on really bad days. *This feels like a two-pot day.*

As soon as I hear the gurgles begin, the door opens, and a groggy Soren walks in, rubbing his eyes.

He's shirtless, his vast amount of ink on display, and has got a massive case of bedhead.

"Morning." He rasps, stretching his arms over his head and scrubbing his hand over his face when they come back down.

"Morning. Coffee's on." I offer, just to be polite. I hope he refuses it.

He barks out a laugh, shaking his head and opening the fridge. "I've learned my lesson with that one, man. Remember the last time? I won't touch it anymore."

"Good call, Boss."

Once, Soren drank the last of the pot without starting a new one, and I didn't speak to him for nearly two days. While he learned his lesson, he refuses to drink *any* coffee anymore, even on the rare occasions I offer it- works for me. The others have transitioned to energy drinks, which are arguably worse for you, but it keeps me agreeable.

"You good? Did you sleep at all?" He asks me, cracking open a colorful can of something only likened to lighter fluid.

"No, but I kept busy. Sat with Beck's drunk ass for a while. He was really messed up about everything."

He doesn't respond, just slowly nods his head. It's clear he's still angry with Beck, and as much as I am too, I know I need to at least attempt to patch things up between them- at least for my own mental's sake.

"You should probably talk to him. See where his head's at today. Maybe apologize for decking him, if you're feeling generous this morning."

His groans stop me from saying anything else. He throws his head back in resignation, and I can hear his can slightly crush from his tightened grip.

"It's not even six yet, Kain. Do you have to play peacekeeper already?"

"It's kind of my job, Boss."

"Fuck it. Fine. I'll talk to him, as soon as he decides to grace the world with his presence."

I pour my cup of coffee and lean against the counter behind me. "Can I ask something?"

"Sure."

"What's going on with the girl? I thought we were going to move her back. We can't keep her here forever, Boss."

His body tenses, and he lowers himself onto one of the barstools. "I know we can't. Do you not trust me?" He bites, his eyes hardening.

My eyes widen at his harsh tone- was this not the plan? Surely *he* doesn't want to keep her here for longer than we need to.

"Of course I trust you. I just thought-"

"Don't think about it. Just do what I tell you to do when it comes to her. I will decide how long she stays, and if and when I'm ready to let her go, I will decide that, too. Trust that I'm making the right decision for us, for The Vipers. Would I ever do anything to intentionally hurt us?"

No. Not intentionally, at least. I trust Soren with my life, but something about his tone makes me uneasy. *I don't want her here.*

"No, Boss. My mistake. I apologize for stepping out of line."

Soren scrubs a hand over his face and groans again. "Goddamn it, Kain, you're worse than Beck. Don't shut down like that, it makes me feel like more of a dick than I already do. Look, I'm figuring it out. This is new territory for me, keeping someone here for a long period of time. But we need her, and Beck has a point with all of this."

He stands, turning towards the door.

"Don't ever fucking tell him I said that. I'm handling it."

He walks out, leaving me alone and speechless in the kitchen, my hands beginning to shake around my coffee mug.

I trust Soren to make the right decision with everything. For six years, my life has been in his hands. I'm a *good* soldier. But now, I can't help but doubt his choices. This girl is not good for us. She will rip us and everything we've built apart at the seams, and we'll never be able to repair it. But I trust Soren. He won't let that happen.

Right?

Georgia

I can't sleep. I know it must be morning, or close to it, by the voices in the hallway, but I haven't really slept at all. When Soren came into the room last night, it felt like all the air left as soon as the door opened. I knew it was him the second the handle turned. A chill came over me, and my vision started to darken in preparation for more violence. What I didn't know was that the man had a softer side. What I expected to be chaos and torture was the opposite. He was almost kind to me. It was almost...
Comforting?

Something in the way he held me told my body it was okay to stop crying. His presence, at least in that small moment, made me feel somewhat safe. His smell dug its way into my nervous system and wrapped itself around it, momentarily quelling the anxiety and fear I felt.

I see him differently now. The hard front that he presents is part of him- probably the biggest part-, but he's layered. A truly evil man wouldn't have been that way with me, wouldn't have promised to protect me. I'm not sure what Sykes did to these men, but for some reason, they want retribution almost as badly as I do, and I know I can help them. I have no choice but to trust Soren's promise- I have to talk, and that conversation needs to happen now.

I stand, stretching my arms above my head, and start for the adjoining bathroom. I take a quick shower, brush my teeth, and step back into the bedroom in search of the bag of clothing Soren left for me. I pull out a pair of cut-off denim shorts and an oversized t-shirt that smells like cologne. I pull the shirt to my face, inhaling. *I know that smell.* It dawns on me- this is Beck's shirt. He must've slipped it into the pile while I wasn't paying attention.

I fight the twitch of my lips and swallow my smile, remembering what we did in that office. I wonder if he's told anyone- surely not, considering the fact that Soren was so gentle with me, and I'd like to keep it that way.

Not that it mattered- he did me a favor, nothing more to it, but it does mean at least one of them doesn't hate me as much as I thought.

I discard Beck's shirt, deciding to keep the peace today, and opt for a dark-brown cropped tee with a faded Viper printed onto it. Once I'm dressed, I tie my still-wet hair into a knot at the top of my head and move towards the door.

Should I wait for someone to come and get me? I still don't know really the layout of this place, and I don't know if I want to be caught on my own down here.

I'm not sure if anyone else sleeps on this level, or what to even *do* once I've left the room.

But the idea of sitting patiently like a slave brings back horrible memories- moments in time I've sworn to myself to never repeat. I may not be here of my own free will, and truthfully, I may never get to leave this place alive. But as long as I'm breathing, I will *not* allow myself to become that again- no, if I'm stuck here, I will be angry. I won't live in fear. I'll do what I need to stay alive, but I will not be the scared, weak woman they think I am.

I shake my shoulders, trying to relieve some of the anxiety I feel about leaving the sanctuary of the room, but allowing the resolve of my newly turned page to wash over me. I nearly smile.

I take a deep breath and turn the handle, peeking my head out. The hallway is void of men- *thank god-*, and I hear the faint clink of pots and pans. I walk out, closing the door silently behind me, and heading towards the noise. When I reach the sound, I open the door and am faced with a kitchen, and The Big Fucker is standing at the stove with his back to me. *Of course.*

I almost turn around and leave, but the gravelly sound of his voice stops me in my tracks and turns my blood to ice.

"Morning. Are you hungry?"

What. The. Fuck. Am I still asleep? Is this not the same man who cut my neck like, two days ago?

"Um, morning. No, I'm good." I turn to leave, confusion and irritation written all over my face.

"Sit. We have a lot to discuss today."

"I think I'm good. I'm not trying to add to my collection of cuts you've given me- I'm sure you can understand."

"Sit."

I huff and roll my eyes, dropping into one of the three barstools lining the island in the center of the kitchen. As much as I want to give him the finger and walk out, I am still afraid of him. He's already shown me that he has no issue with spilling a little blood when he feels like it, and I don't want to find out how much worse he can be.

The big asshole pauses for a moment and abandons what he was doing at the stove to turn and look at me.

I've never really looked at him before, and he is terrifying. A deep scar takes up almost his entire face, but it does nothing to take away from his looks. He's huge. I knew he was tall before, but being this close to him really proves it. He's built like a tank, his hand dwarfing the coffee mug he's holding, and the muscles in his arms bulging in a way that makes me think he could crush it as easily as if it were made of paper.

"I'm Kain."

"Cool. Sorry, I don't feel like chatting it up with someone who had a blade to my neck. I think we had a good enough introduction, dickwad, let's not continue." I bite back, lifting my chin and showing off the cut on my neck. It's healed some, the nasty green fading to a dull but angry red. It'll scar for sure, and I hate him even more for that. He looks at me, and I swear I can see a twitch of a smile on his lips.

"Sorry about that, little one."

Like hell you are. "I need to talk to Soren. Where is he?"

"The boss ran upstairs to handle some things. He'll be back. You'll sit and wait for him here." Kain's face is completely stoic, void of emotion, and leaves no room for me to argue. I want to be scared of him, of the sternness that rests on his brow. My instincts are telling me to back down, tuck my tail between my legs and retreat to the bedroom. I don't. Too bad.

I roll my eyes at him, but I don't move from my stool. "Whatever, man."

He turns back to the stove and continues what he was doing. I scan the countertops, taking in the things sitting on them. It's strange sitting here, knowing how brutal they were towards me, knowing how they want to kill me, and seeing the domesticity. The same man who held a knife to my throat is scrambling eggs, and I'm sure the others will be in here soon to eat. The scene makes my heart sag in the smallest way, and I feel a bit softer for them than I did before. They aren't all rage and violence.

I saw that in Beck, when he had his hands on me, and I've seen it in Soren now, too, and maybe-just maybe, I have a shot of making it out of this alive.

The sound of the door slamming open jerks me out of my thoughts, and the man I watched the night before shuffles in, shirtless and disheveled. He's tall, though not as tall as the others, and is noticeably bare of ink, with only a few tattoos littering his chest and arms. He looks like a kid compared to the other men I've met, lanky with sandy blonde hair that falls in his eyes. From the angle I'm sitting, I can't see his face in full, but I notice the myriads of bruises and cuts littering his body from the fight.

He trudges over to the fridge and yanks it open, bottles clinking together in the door as the seal is ripped apart, and pulls out a brightly colored can, cracking it open and draining most of it before slamming it onto the counter. He scrubs a hand over his face, not once looking in my direction.

I notice a shake in his hands, a violent tremble that makes me wonder how he managed to hold that can. Kain looks towards him with something that looks like pity and shakes his head, turning back towards the stove.

"Morning, Eight Ball." He chuckles under his breath.

The other man grunts a response and grabs the handle of the fridge, using the leverage of his body weight to stretch out his back.

"Where's Beck?" Kain asks.

"Still asleep." He grunts. "He was fucking trashed, dude. He'll be sleeping that shit off for a while."

"Great. Soren will be so glad to hear that." Kain says sarcastically. "This is our house guest, Georgia." He gestures towards me with a jerk of his head.

The other man looks at me, and I can finally get a good look at his face. His eyes are a brilliant blue, like the ocean, but the sadness behind them stops me in my tracks. They're rimmed in red and sunken in, and they're empty- no spark, no sign of life. This one has a story; he's been through some shit- I know from experience of seeing my own eyes like that. He is damaged, and I mentally note that he is not to be fucked with. *I definitely won't be spitting in this one's face.*

"Jaxon." He introduces himself. "Why are you here?"

"Jax, relax man, Soren-" Kain starts, but I hold up a hand to stop him.

"I was held captive by The Iron Brotherhood, and I am going to help you kill Rowan Sykes."

My breath catches in my throat. I've gone over those words a thousand times in my head, mulling over some poetic way to say them, but... finally saying them out loud feels like I've stepped over a ledge I can't claw my way back up. This is the first time I've really said it- what I wanted to do. I do want him dead. I want to watch the life leave his eyes, the way he took the life out of mine with everything he did to me. If they're the ones who can help me do it, then I guess I'll need to start talking.

"Yeah, right." Jax claps slowly, glaring at me. "Take your bow, girl, that was an award-winning performance. You really said that with your chest, huh?"

He turns towards Kain, an accusatory look in his eye. "You're good with this, right? Just bringing enemy number one right where we sleep?"

"No. But it wasn't my call."

He laughs, out loud this time, and looks back at me. "Look. I don't want you here, and I'd like to make that clear from the start." He steps closer to me, our noses almost touching. I can feel the anger vibrating off him. "I have a nasty feeling in my gut that one of my brothers is going to end up dead because of you and make no mistake- I will not hesitate to kill you before I let anything happen to one of them."

He takes a step backwards, his eyes never leaving mine. A grin tips the corner of his mouth upwards, but there's no humor in it. His eyes are still dark, still deadly serious. The air in the room shifts to something that begins to make me afraid for my life again.

"I want every single one of those motherfuckers dead, and the way I see it, you fall into that same group. If you're smart, you'll tell them what you know and get the fuck away from us- before you get hurt."

With that, he turns and moves to storm out of the kitchen.

"Jax, where are you going?" Kain calls out behind him.

"I'm going to find Soren. This is fucked, man." He snaps; his words almost cut off by the sound of the door slamming closed behind him.

Kain turns towards me, a grim look on his face. "He's never killed anyone before. You won't be his first."

Gee, thanks. You really know how to put a girl's mind at ease.

"I'm not worried."

Kain huffs softly and chuckles under his breath, turning back towards his cooking.

"No, actually, you big fucking freak, I'm. Not. Worried. If you all really wanted me dead, I would've been already, and to be quite goddamn honest, I don't care if you kill me or not anymore. Now where the hell is Soren? I would rather get this show on the road so that I can finally get the fuck away from you." I'm surprised at how steady my words come out. I nearly swell with pride. If only my younger self could see me now.

He turns back towards me and stares, not saying anything.

"Well?" I question. "Where the fuck is he?"

Kain remains quiet, locking his gaze onto mine. I don't miss the way his eyes flicker in surprise, though. *Good.* I'm done cowering to him.

"Hello? Are you fucking dense?"

"Are you done? My eggs are starting to burn."

I glare at him as he turns back around to his eggs. *I should piss in his eggs. Fuck this guy.* I decide that

I'm not going to sit here and be ignored, so I push off of the stool and start towards the door. Before I can fully push the handle down, arms are wrapped around my waist like vice grips, and I'm yanked away from the door and deposited back into the barstool I had previously occupied. I blink a few times and turn around, looking towards Kain, who now stands with his fists balled at his side, breathing heavily.

"I told you to sit."

"Yeah, and I'm not a dog. Goodbye, Big Fucker." I turn and scramble back towards the door, only to be shoved against the wall, my face painfully pressed against the plaster. I can hear Kain's breathing, and he's got a vicious grip on my hair, holding me against the wall. The door creaks open slightly, and I hear a chuckle from the other side.

"I wouldn't push him, pretty girl. His trigger finger gets itchy when people don't listen to him." Soren's voice lilts through the crack in the door. "Can you move, Kain? You're blocking the door." His tone is softer with the other man, and he complies.

Kain lets out a breath and shoves off me, giving my face one last good push into the wall. I right myself and run a hand over the side of my face, feeling the indentation of the plaster in my skin. *Fuck you, dude.*

Soren enters the room and perches on a barstool, beckoning me over to him.

I stay by the wall, partly because I don't want Kain pushing me around again, and partly out of spite, because no way are these men going to order me around when I've already agreed to help them. I shake my head once, feet remaining planted in my spot against the wall, and I can see agitation written all over Soren's face.

"Please don't be difficult. We are not morning people. I'm sure Kain's made that clear enough now."

Okay, he might have a point with that. But also, fuck him and fuck Soren, too.

I saunter over to the island and hop up onto it, perching my ass right where Kain was moving to put the pan of eggs. I hear him snarl behind me, and I have to hold back a laugh.

"Did you have something you wanted to talk about?"

Well, I guess there's no time for small talk today. "Yes, thanks for making time for me in your busy morning." I say sarcastically.

When I see no trace of humor in either of the men's faces, I clear my throat and stare at my lap.

They aren't morning people. Right.

"I can't tell you the exact location of their clubhouse, because they rarely let me leave it, and when they did, it was always with a bag over my head. I can tell you who all of Sykes' inner circle are, what their routines are, and what their legits are, though I don't know where any of the businesses are. They own an ice-cream shop and a dive bar, but I don't know the names of them."

Soren nods his head, like he's taking mental notes. "Go on."

"I know that his second, Emmett Riley, operates the dive bar, and the ice-cream shop is run by innocents, mostly the wives and older kids of Brothers. I think they use it to launder money."

"What are they dealing in?" He asks, leaning forward, bracing his elbows on his knees.

"I don't know for sure, but I think they have a ring. Skin trade. There were always girls at the compound that looked too young and too scared to be there willingly, but I never got confirmation that they were bought."

Soren muses over that for a moment, picking at his nails. "Say we hit the dive bar- would Sykes' second be there?"

"Probably, but I told you, I don't know where it is, so how would you even-"

"Let me figure that out." He cuts me off, dismissing me with a wave of his hand. "We've got that part covered. It has to be somewhere in their territory, right?"

I nod, but anxiety creeps up my spine like a cold embrace. *They're going to find me if they attack.* As if Soren can read my thoughts, he stands and steps closer to me, reaching a handout to touch my shoulder.

I force myself to stay still. *Not cowering, remember?* Every instinct tells me to pull back, but I don't. Instead, I meet his gaze, steady and unflinching. I don't know what it is about him- something dangerous, magnetic- but for the first time, I'm not afraid of it.

"Remember what I told you. I mean what I say, Georgia."

He's going to keep me safe. I need to trust him. I *can* trust him. *Right?*

"Okay." I exhale. "Yes, they'll most likely be there."

His eyes go wide for a moment, the hint of a grin on his lips.

"It's settled, then. We move tonight." He orders, jumping up and turning towards Kain, giving him a nod.

With that, he strides out of the room, leaving me alone, yet again, with my new best friend. Kain sighs audibly and shakes his head, walking away from his eggs and following Soren out the door.

"I hope you know what you're talking about, little one."

I stay in the kitchen, polishing off the pan of eggs left abandoned in record time, feeling somewhat satisfied. I poke around the space, pulling open every drawer and cabinet, getting a glimpse into the lives of the men holding me here. When I don't find anything telling, I gingerly walk out of the kitchen and into the hallway. I'm met with non-descript doors, and push my luck even further, cracking the one closest to me open.

The bedroom is pitch-dark and frankly disgusting, with clothes, dishes, and clutter crowding every available surface and spilling onto the floor. I hear the shower running and turn back, afraid of catching one of them naked and wanting to get away from the mess as soon as possible.

I quietly close the door and move on to the next one, popping it open and finding another dark bedroom- this time, with a sleeping form in the bed in the corner of the room.

I recognize the surroundings as Beck's room from when he brought me in here last, and as soon as the light from the hallway seeps in, the sleeping form stirs and pops up. Beck's face appears from under the covers, eyes still closed, and I almost smile at how innocent he looks.

"Jax?" His voice is raspy with sleep, and I want to dive into the room to get closer to him.

"No, sorry, I got lost. I'll let you sleep." I move to close the door again, but his voice beckons me to stay.

"No, baby girl. Come here." Beck's voice is rough, and it sends heat straight to my core. How can he *sound* like sex? My body moves without instruction, padding over to the side of his bed, taking in his state of undress.

He's shirtless, and the way the sheets are haphazardly draped around his waist, I can see a distinct 'V' that proves he's fully naked. *I guess I'll have to see one of them naked anyway.*

His arm shoots out and grabs my wrist, yanking me down onto the bed next to him.

I freeze, and he takes the opportunity to pull my back to his chest, snaking his arm across my waist in a possessive hold.

"I missed you, Georgia." His breath fans across the back of my neck, and I can smell the alcohol on him.

"No, you didn't. I think you're just hungover, Beck. I should go." I squirm, trying to break away from his hold, but his grip on me tightens, and my breath hitches in my throat.

"Hungover, or still drunk?" He chuckles, pushing his face into my neck. "You don't get to tell me what I feel, baby. I missed you. I only got a small taste last night, and I want more."

His hand slips from my hip and traces the waistband of my shorts, his pinky breaching the surface, rubbing small circles into my skin. I let my eyes close and lean into him. Just for a second, I can allow myself to be vulnerable. For this one moment, I can let him in and feel a sense of normalcy. Beck is the only one here that even tries with me- sure, he only wants my body, but I think I'm okay with that. *It's better than wanting me dead, I guess.*

He slips another finger under my shorts, and his hand is almost where I want it. He peppers soft kisses to the side of my neck, and my skin pebbles. I exhale, relishing in the thought of the orgasm I'm about to receive.

"Beg me." He murmurs.

"What?"

"Beg me to touch you. Beg me to make you come like I did last night."

"Beck, I'm not-"

My words are lost as he pulls his hand away and taps my hip twice as to say, *'time to go'.*

My pussy aches with need, and in this moment, I want nothing more than to give him every inch of me. Any prior notion of being headstrong and doing just enough to stay alive is thrown out of the window.

Fuck that. I'll beg.

"No, no, Beck please. Please." I scramble to find his hand again, wrenching it back towards where I need it most.

His deep chuckle vibrates against my back, and damn it, it only makes me want him more.

"Please what, Georgia?"
He allows me to move his hand to the bottom of my stomach, just below my belly button but still above my shorts but resists when I try to push it further down. I let out a frustrated sigh, and he tries to pull his hand away again. I cling to it like a life raft.

"Please make me come Beck. I need it, please."

"That's all you needed to say, baby girl."

Without warning, he shoves his hand beneath my shorts and plunges a finger inside me. I'm so wet that it slides in easily, and I cry out softly.
"Shhhhh. We have to be quiet, G. If you stay quiet, I'm going to make you feel so good."
I listen, slapping a hand over my mouth to stifle any more sounds.

He works his finger in and out, deliciously slow and deliberate, but I need *more*. The thought barely forms before he moves, pushing a second finger in. The stretch is exactly what I need, and when he curls his fingers, I see stars. My hips begin to rock back in forth, chasing the friction of the heel of his hand against my clit. I'm so close, and when the tips of his fingers find *that* spot, I shatter. My cries are muffled by my hand, but I know I'm not as quiet as he'd like me to be.

He slows his pace but doesn't stop- giving me a second to catch my breath while letting me know he's not near finished with me.
But when the door bangs open and light casts over the bedroom, I'm like a deer caught in headlights. I can't even make a sound; I can only stare straight ahead. Beck's hand stops in its tracks but doesn't move from its place inside of me.

"Are you fucking serious, Trigger?" Soren's voice booms through the doorway.

Well, this is it. I'm dead. Officially.

I'm frozen in place, and my pulse is racing so fast that I feel like my heart might stop.

"Get the fuck up. We need to talk." Soren storms off, and I hear Beck chuckle behind me.

I sit up and look over at him as he pulls his hand away from me, and I gasp at the sight of his face in the light. The area around his left eye is black, and the eye itself is blood red with burst blood vessels. Without thinking, I reach out and touch his face, running my hand over the bruising. He flinches, and I rear back like his skin burnt my hand.

"What happened?" I barely whisper, my eyes wide.

"Don't worry about it, baby girl. Just a little misunderstanding with my brothers, that's all." He manages a grin, and I can see the side of his jaw is swollen too.

"I've had worse, this is nothing. We better get up, though. Daddy Soren doesn't like to be kept waiting."

I scramble out of the bed, getting to my feet. Beck slowly stands behind me, stretching his arms above his head, and I turn my head as the sheets fall away and expose him, a blush creeping up my face. I fight the urge to look at him, to see what I could've had, but instead I head for the door, opening it and slipping out quickly before Beck can call me back again.

I walk back towards the kitchen, where I'm met with the others, all wearing scowls and glaring at me as I enter. They say nothing as I stand in my previous spot by the door and against the wall, and I prepare myself for the worst. I know I've been caught in a trap, and I can't help but to blame myself for it.

I should've walked out of the room, I shouldn't have gotten into bed with him, and I guess while we're at it, I should've called out of my last shift. But guilt and blame do me no good now, as I'm met with three of the meanest men I've ever met, and they're all looking at me like my life won't last much longer.

Jax

When I hear Soren yell in the hallway, I nearly fall out of the shower in my attempts to finish up. I pulled on the first clothes I could find and raced out of my bedroom, tripping over anything and everything blocking my path to the door. My anxiety is high today, especially after my run-in with the girl Soren insists on keeping here. As soon as I saw her at the fight, I tried like hell to avoid her, and it was pretty easy throughout the night. But this morning, the sight of her made my fingers itch for something to take the edge off. *I need to book another fight.*

When I walk into the hallway, Soren is there, barreling towards me like an angry bull.

"I'm going to kill him." He growls, storming past me and heading for the kitchen.

I don't wait around to question what happened, choosing to follow him, almost taking the door to the face with the force of Soren slamming it open. Kain's there already, holding a coffee mug and leaning against the counter.

"You rang?" He quips, a grin playing at the corners of his mouth.

Soren plops down on one of the barstools and leans forward on the island, his head in his hands.

"Trigger's in bed with her. If anyone knows anything, speak."

Kain clears his throat, setting his coffee mug down on the counter and pulling a pack of cigarettes out of his back pocket. He pulls a smoke out and shakes the pack at me, and I graciously accept one, placing it between my lips. He leans forward over the counter and lights mine first, then cups his hands over his and does the same.

"He told me last night that they were… together, at Afterglow."

"He fucked her!?" Soren booms, rising to his feet, the barstool nearly crashing to the floor behind him.

"No, but I guess he got close. He spared me the details, but I got enough."

I almost walk out of the room at Kain's statement, finally being faced with it as the truth after Beck admitted it last night. My jaw ticks, and my fists are itching to strike something. Beck and I have a different kind of relationship- we've never defined it, but we see each other differently than the others. We've never labeled it, so I don't technically have anything to be mad about, but learning that he was with *her* just hours before I was in his bed makes my blood nearly boil over. I can hear my pulse thumping in my ears, and my teeth hurt from how hard I'm clenching them. If I looked in the mirror right now, I'm sure I'd look like a raging bull, nostrils flaring and all.

I thought it was us, that we didn't need anyone else. But hearing what went down, I guess I'm just a warm mouth to him. *Fuck, I need to hit something.*

Soren begins to pace around the kitchen, and I take a long drag from my cigarette, closing my eyes as the nicotine caresses my nervous system and the rush of dopamine hits. This is bad, really bad.

Not only did he prove where he stands with me, but he's bedding the enemy right under our fucking noses. I wonder if the sheets still smelled like me when he laid her down.

"We're moving on The Brotherhood tonight. She gave up a bar, and I've got Nate looking into it as we speak. He'll find it, and we're going to fuck some shit up." Soren explains, and my ears perk at the mention of violence.

I haven't been made yet- never experienced what it's like to take another life, but tonight might be my chance. Once that's done, I can truly become a Viper and earn my place here.

I'm not sure why they keep me around the way they do. The others have to live upstairs in the quarters, but they allowed me down here, and it makes me guilty to be taking up a room without earning it. I want to prove myself, need to prove that I'm more valuable to this organization than just the drugs I oversee.

I'm the best goddamn drug lord this side of Oakridge has ever seen. I sell the best of the best- I should know, I taste just about everything we get in- but as soon as shit hits the fan, I freeze, my mind going back to that night with my parents.

I'm well trained- I can fight well, and it's not like I don't carry a gun. Soren makes sure we're all strapped everywhere we go- I just haven't been able to use it. But since I learned that we may have a real shot at taking out The Iron Brotherhood, I dream about what it will feel like. I have visions of killing them, watching them die by my own hand. *This girl might just be useful after all.*

"We'll take a small team, just us, and once we get the details of the building, we'll plan our entrance and escape routes. I want everyone's heads clear and ready tonight." He turns towards me, his face serious. "Keep your nose clean. I need you present."

I nod slowly, rolling my eyes and walking over to the sink to stub out my smoke. I run the water, washing away the ash, and can hear the door creak open, and none other than the whore of the house steps in, not quite meeting our eyes. Her back is pressed flat against the wall, her eyes shifting from side to side as if she's tracking some invisible threat. A thin sheen of sweat covers her flushed skin, creeping down her neck as her chest rises and falls too quickly.

No one moves or speaks, letting the uncomfortable silence linger in the air. A moment later, the door opens again, and Beck walks in, wearing a pair of gray sweatpants and nothing else. Then all hell breaks loose.

Soren rushes Beck, pinning him against the closed door with his forearm to Beck's throat. Kain runs after him, trying to get in between the two, and I don't move. I can't. Honestly, I think I want to see Soren hit him again- it might quell a bit of the anger I feel towards him.

The girl screams, and I cut my eyes to her, glaring at her and snapping at her to shut up and stay out of it.

"You *want* me to kill you, huh?" Soren snarls through clenched teeth. "You must. Maybe I didn't hit you hard enough last night. Or maybe, you're already in so deep that you willingly go against what I say to you. That has to be it, right? You're so blinded by pussy that you don't give a fuck about orders anymore?"

He slams Beck hard against the wall, and I can hear him struggling to breathe.

"It's not like that." Beck rasps out.

"Liar."

Beck jerks in Soren's hold, his fists swinging wildly, landing blows to Soren's sides and stomach. Soren rears back and Beck swings, catching him right in the nose, and blood immediately starts gushing from it. Kain tries to break it up, but Beck shoves him aside and continues raining punches onto Soren.

It's complete chaos as the two men fight like rabid animals, knocking over the barstools in their wake, but I know they need to get it out or nothing will get done, so I don't intervene. The girl is cowering in the corner, and I almost laugh at her. *Pathetic.*

Soren gets Beck into a chokehold and slams him down onto the island, Beck's chest and ribs connecting with the corner of the counter. He grunts, and tries to twist in Soren's grip, but he's stuck.

"What the fuck is wrong with you?" Soren growls, and Beck laughs, his voice raspy from the assault on his windpipe.

"What's wrong with *you,* brother?"

Soren grabs the back of Beck's head and slams it down onto the counter, earning a whimper of pain.

"We'll settle this later. Get the fuck up." He gives Beck one final shove, and picks up the barstool he previously occupied, sliding into it and using the bottom of his shirt to wipe the blood from his nose.

Beck stands, breathing heavily and clutching his ribs, his face bloody and bruised. I smirk, picking up my own barstool and plopping down next to Soren.

"Now that you're done fucking around-"

"I didn't fuck her." Beck cuts in, earning a nasty glare from Soren.

"Now that you're back," Soren snarls, "We're moving on The Brotherhood tonight. We're leaving as soon as we get intel on where it is, and we'll map out entry and exit points when we get there. We'll stake it out for a while before we move in. I need confirmation that Sykes' second will be in that building, so you," he says, gesturing to Georgia, "will be going with us."

I watch the color drain from her face, though she tries really hard to hide it behind an eye roll and pouty, pursed lips.

Holy. Shit. This is the perfect opportunity to kill two birds with one stone- or bullet, I guess. If he's taking her in, I'm going to kill her. We'll finally be rid of her, and I'll earn my place at the table, saving my family from the thing that will destroy us.

Soren's phone rings about thirty minutes into planning, and he excuses himself to answer it, leaving the three of us in the kitchen to wait.

The tension is high in the room, and I can't even look in Beck's direction, instead staring at a nick in the countertop. I feel a hand on my shoulder, and I look up, finding Beck looking back at me, worry and guilt across his face.

"Jax, listen. This isn't what you think it is. I would never-"

"Save it, Trigger." He tenses at my use of his nickname. He walks around me, stopping directly in front and grabs my jaw, leaning his forehead against mine.

"This changes nothing."

I close my eyes, leaning into the closeness for what may be the last time, and fight the urge to reach out and wrap my arms around him.

"This changes everything."

I gently shove him off me, ignoring the stares from *her*. I can't have him close to me right now. I can't allow him to change my mind about anything. He used me, and I need to see that for what it is. I *can't* let him back in again. He's made it very clear where we stand and what we are, and I don't plan to perpetuate the pain I'm going to feel over this. It's better to rip the bandage off clean than to wait for it to fall off on its own.

Soren breaks the tension as he busts the door open, eyes flying between all of us.

"We've got an address, and Nate's hacked into surveillance. Get strapped and let's move. We roll out in twenty."

Fuck yes. I push past Beck, my shoulder bumping his hard, and rush out of the kitchen and into my bedroom.

I find my Glock on my nightstand and tuck it into the back of my cargo pants and find my Kevlar on the floor. I put it on under my shirt, the material scratchy against my bare chest, and pull on a long-sleeved t-shirt over it. I grab my boots and rush back out of the room, heading towards the elevator, not stopping to wait for anyone else.

As I ride to the top floor, I give myself all of twenty seconds to let the anxiety wash over me. I'm well aware that the events of tonight might change me forever, in ways I may not ever be able to fully repair. But knowing that I might be able to save my family while getting my revenge... It overpowers any fear I feel and leaves me with a clear head- ready to go, ready for it to be done.

When the elevator reaches the top floor, I head straight back past the bar in the center of the room and scan my finger at the door of the armory.

Our weapons are locked down tighter than Fort Knox, and only a select few Vipers have access to them. When the scanner glows green, I push the door open, and my eyes light up. I feel like a kid on Christmas morning. The armory is nothing special- most of the shit in here is stolen anyways, but it is fully stocked with all of the best toys. Cargo containers line the walls, full of weapons, and there are Kevlar vests and various gun holsters in every size on racks by the door for easy access. I grab an ankle holster from a rack right inside the door, propping my leg up on the bottom of it to strap it on, and grab a pistol to tuck into the holster. I find a collection of knives in an equipment case on the floor and slide one into each pocket of my pants. By the time I'm finished, I'm armed to the teeth and ready to go.

I walk out of the armory, securing the door behind me, and find Kain and Beck walking towards me. I don't say anything as I walk past them, but someone grabs my bicep and spins me around. Beck's gaze is full of heat and remorse, and he looks almost as if he'd been crying.

"Please don't do this."

"Do what, Trigger?"

"Fucking stop, will you?" He shouts loud enough to gain the attention of some of the other Vipers taking up space in the common area. He notices the extra eyes on us, and his face flashes with embarrassment. He leans down to my level, speaking softer. "Don't do this, Jax. I can't survive that. I can't lose you." He's begging, and it almost makes me cave. The previous resolve I had begins to crumble, bit by bit, until my hands start to shake again.

"You've made it very clear where I stand. I am not your problem anymore."

"Jax, it's not like that-"

"I think it's *exactly* like that, Beck. You told me yourself. Or did you forget that when you were drunk and buried in my throat last night?"

Kain's head snaps towards us, raising an eyebrow. I wave him off, locking my eyes back onto Beck's.

"I will not be a plaything, or something you do when you get bored. You want to fuck her? Fine. But I'm not going to be there to pick up your pieces when shit goes sideways like I know it will." I surprise myself with my ability to keep my voice steady for the entire exchange.

I turn on my heel and stalk towards the garage.

A few minutes later, Soren strides out, his Kevlar sitting on top of a white wife-beater, and he jerks his head towards one of the Vipers lingering in the garage. He runs off, presumably to pull the car around, and Soren walks over to me.

"You're the only one who's got his head on straight." He breathes a laugh, probably because I'm always the one who *isn't* thinking straight. "Beck's a lost cause. Let's get this shit done."

"Copy that, Boss." I try to sound confident and ready, but my head is fuzzy, and my hands are shaking badly from my unsavory conversation with Beck.

I told Soren I would keep a clear head for this, but I'm not sure how much longer I can keep that promise. I run my hand across my front pocket, feeling the tiny canister I have stashed there. My fingers and nose start to itch.

The car pulls in, and we slide into Kain's blacked-out escalade, Soren taking the passenger's seat and me in one of the captain's chairs in the middle row. *It's now or never.*

"I forgot something inside. I'll be right back." I move to get out of the car, but Soren hits the locks. The child locks are enabled on the back doors, effectively trapping me inside the car.

"Nope. Text the others, they can bring it."

"What? Quit being a dick, just let me-"

"No, Jaxon. I'm not stupid."

I feel like a caged animal, and my skin suddenly feels like it's too tight. Panic claws up my throat, and my thoughts focus only on getting the fuck out of this car. My breathing gets heavy, and I start to tremble.

"Soren." I breathe out, trying my best not to scream at him. "I really need to get out of this car. If you don't unlock it, I'm going to break a window."

"What happened to keeping your-"

"Save it. I fucking know. Now let me out." I cut him off. "Please." I beg, the last part coming out almost as a whimper.

Soren sighs loudly as I hear the click of the locks disengaging.

"Let me be clear." Soren's voice is deadly calm. "I'm *only* letting you out of this car because I don't need you freaking out the whole way there, and I don't want to explain to Kain why his back window's been busted out. I'm disappointed, Jaxon."

I scramble out of the car and back into the garage, throwing my middle finger up at him behind me as I walk away.

"Not a good look." He calls after me. "Don't think this is going to fly every time, Eight Ball."

The second I get back inside, my hand is inside my pocket, retrieving my salvation from my pocket and scooping a bit of powder onto the tiny spoon attached to the lid. I hold it to my nose and take the bump, going back in for seconds. *Okay, and thirds.*

Once the tightness inside my body has loosened, I return the canister to my pocket and shake my now-steady hands. I take a deep breath and start back towards the garage, finding Kain, Beck, and *her* walking out at the same time. Beck's got his hand on the small of her back, ushering her through the compound, and I almost puke.

I shake my head, tailing them and walking back out in the garage, sliding back into the car, this time in the furthest row. Kain is in the driver's seat, and Beck crawls into the back to sit next to me. I roll my eyes at him, turning my knees towards the window and blocking out whatever meaningless conversation they've started with each other.

Soren's hand comes through the gap between the front seats, holding our comms pieces. I lean forward and grab mine and slip it into my ear, tapping it twice to turn it on, making sure I can hear the others before tapping it again to turn it back off.

I stare back out the window, watching the garage door open and the afternoon light stream into the garage, wishing this to be over already and for things to go back to the way they were. I never thought things could change so quickly- just a few days ago, we were a happy family, nothing between us. Now, Beck and Soren can't even remain civil in the same room anymore, Kain's barely sleeping or talking, and I can't function sober. I'm terrified of losing them- without them, without The Vipers, I have nothing. I don't have anything to go back to if shit goes south here.

There's one thing, one catalyst to all of this, one single thing that has driven my bloodlust more than anything I've experienced before.

Her.

Not even the death of my parents makes me feel as murderous as her presence here does. She's begun to dig her claws into my brothers, but I plan to cut her out of them at the root. I let my rage fester as we drive out of Oakridge, knowing I'm going to need to draw on it when we arrive and shit gets real. I almost smile- I can't fucking wait. I'm taking my family back from this bitch, even if it kills me.

We drive for another thirty minutes in complete silence. When we pull up outside of a grimy looking dive bar, my hand instinctively reaches towards Beck. He always calms any nerves I have before we go into a job, acting as a grounding force.

He's relaxed before things like this- he's got blood on his hands, tainted already, and the anxiety seems to have faded away for him, allowing him to take on mine and send it to the same place he sends his. Before I realize it, my fingers graze the side of his hand resting on his leg. I pull my hand away like it's been burned, but he's faster, and envelops my hand with his.

"You're alright, Eight Ball." He whispers to me with a sad smile. "I've got you."

I stiffen my hand in his hold, but he tightens his grip and brings the back of my hand to his lips, placing a feather-light kiss to the skin.

"I'm sorry, Jaxon. I'm so fucking sorry."

"I know." I pull my hand away.

Beck sighs. I can hear his breath hitch in the back of his throat, as if he's holding back tears.

"Everything's fucked, Jax. I want things back to how they were."

"You should've thought about that. Let's focus, I want to get this done."

He shakes his head, but his hand slides onto the tip of my knee, and I don't move it. I'll take the closeness for what it is, knowing I need to be completely calm before I do this. We watch several men walk in and out of the bar, and I pull my phone out of my pocket to check the time. It's nearly four by this point, and as soon as the sun sets and we have confirmation that the man we're looking for is in there, we'll move in.

I lean my head back against the headrest, almost closing my eyes, when I hear the girl's voice ring out from the captain's chair in front of me.

"That's him. White shirt, tattoos."

She points out a greasy-looking man in a stained wife beater striding into the bar with a girl under each arm, and my eyes lock onto him until he disappears behind the door.

Let's go.

"Turn your comms on. Nate's watching the back. We wait a bit longer, and if he doesn't leave by six, we move." Soren orders, and I tap my comms piece twice, Nate's voice coming through.

"We're here, Nate." Soren announces, his voice doubling as I hear it both through the comms and out loud.

"Alright motherfuckers, don't get yourselves shot tonight." Nate's raspy voice comes through, laughing.

He acts as our eyes back at the compound, with years of hacking under his belt. He's our most lethal weapon, even more so than the fire we're packing, because he knows exactly where everyone in that building is at all times. He has access to every single camera they have placed, and if we bribe him enough, he can even tap into the cameras and microphones of the phones of the people inside.

"Don't count on it. Eight Ball's getting his lick back tonight. If shit goes well, we'll come home celebrating new blood."

I swell with pride- he thinks I can do this. I *can* do this. I just don't know how they're going to feel about celebrating when they realize their new toy is my way in.

Georgia

This stakeout has aged me fifteen years. Between the waiting, the deafening silence, and the anxiety of being so close to Emmett, not to mention being pressed against Beck, I feel like my head is going to explode. We've been sitting in the car for nearly three hours, and I nearly cry out of relief when Soren gives the order to move.

We slide out of the vehicle on the driver's side, Soren's large frame struggling to climb over the center console and Beck sliding across the backseat and through the aisle. I go to move, but Beck pushes me back into my seat.

"Not a chance, baby girl."

There's no way he's going to stop me from going in. Sure, I'm so terrified of seeing him again that I can't control my body, but there's one thing I know- if Emmett Riley is going to die tonight, I'm going to be there to watch. I want to look right into his eyes as he realizes that this is it. I want my face to be the last thing he sees, the same way I thought his would be so many times.

"I have a vest on, Beck." I retort, patting my chest where the heavy Kevlar sits. "Plus, you don't know the faces of any of the people in there. I'm an asset here, and you know it." I cross my arms across my chest, and he sighs, knowing I have a point.

"She comes. We'll cover her." Soren barks.

I give Beck a shit-eating grin.

"Yes, daddy." he sneers, and Soren shoves him further into the car, his body falling almost over mine.

"Don't push it tonight, Trigger. I might just leave you in there."

Beck rolls his eyes and climbs back out of the car, and I slide out behind him, the cool, summer night air chilling my face and making me shiver. Beck hands me a hunting knife, and I hold it in my hands, a confused look on my face.

"We're not giving you a gun." He deadpans. The look of confusion is still clear across my face, and he sighs, leaning into me to whisper into my ear. "You might be good enough to eat, but you have to remember where we are- if any of *them*," He gestures to the others, pulling their own gear on, "leave here with any more holes than they came in with, it's lights out for you. I hate to be this way, but I need to make sure you understand. No one trusts you yet, and you can't afford for any of them to get hurt. Besides, I don't want to have to watch them hurt you again."

Oh. I nod slowly, sliding the knife into my waistband, attaching the small clip on the holster to the fabric. Beck looks down at me, pleased that I listened without complaint, and turns on his heel, heading towards the trunk of the Escalade. He's right, as much as I hate to admit it- if any of them were shot, they'd look at me first, probably before they'd even bat an eye at any of the Brothers inside.

A strong hand grips my bicep hard enough to bruise and I startle, my head whipping sideways to find Kain staring at me with cold, calculating eyes.

"You move when we say." He growls in a low voice. "You're going to take five steps towards the hood of the car, press your chest against it, and stay low. On Soren's mark, we're going to move silently towards the entrance. Eight Ball is going in through the front door to act as a diversion, and the rest of us are going around the back, through the kitchen." He doesn't give me enough time to ask who the hell Eight Ball is before he starts again. "Do not allow yourself to get separated from us. If we lose you, you leave the building immediately and wait for us back here, inside the car. We're loosening your leash quite a lot tonight, little one. Don't make us regret it."

I nod at him, and he releases my arm, shoving me forward. I do exactly as he says, creeping towards the hood of the car and leaning over it, pressing my chest against the warm metal and staying flush with the car. I hear the unmistakable click of clips being inserted into guns and the scratch of metal on metal as silencers are screwed on, and everything goes silent.

"Move. Now." Soren whispers, and we start towards the bar.

I try to prepare myself as best I can, but even still, I can feel my bottom lip begin to quiver, my pulse quickening. This is insane- I'm basically unarmed, walking right back into the hornet's nest I escaped from. There's no telling who all is inside, if any of them would recognize me- try to take me back. I shake the thoughts away- I have to trust myself, and *them*.

I stand wide-eyed as I watch Jax stroll in through the front door of the bar like he owns the place. I'm pulled around the corner of the building and match the guys' light jog to reach the back door.

There are two men standing outside, but they're distracted, lounging against the dirty brick passing a joint between them. Soren nods his head towards Beck, who pulls a gun from his waistband and makes quick work of the two Brothers, putting a bullet in the chest of the one closest to us and between the eyes of his friend.

Holy shit. Holy shit. Holy shit. I can't do this. I need to get back to the car- maybe I can run? Surely they'll be too distracted with the scene unfolding to notice my absence.

I pause, just long enough to end up in the back of the convoy. Like a movie, scenes of Rowan Sykes' head rolling across the floor play through my mind. I see Emmett Riley, crying and pissing himself out of fear, staring right at me. I think about how *good* it's going to feel to take everything back- to wake up every day without looking over my shoulder. I swallow any fear I might've felt.

The thought of their slow, painful deaths calms me enough to follow behind Soren, as he storms through the back door, gun drawn and barking orders to the people inside. He's completely focused, face set hard and hands still.

My fingers reach for the hunting knife, but before I can drag it out, I'm pushed over the bodies Beck left and inside the door, blood smearing across my skin, and I'm met with complete chaos.

Two women cower in the corner screaming, and two men with guns in their hands charge towards Soren. Kain rushes forward, the same wicked knife he had to my throat in his grip. He grabs the man closest to him by the hair, yanking him backwards, his back hitting Kain's chest, and brings the blade up, slashing the other man's throat in one quick motion. He drops the body and moves onto the next. My jaw drops, and I hesitate slightly, earning a curse from Soren.

I duck behind the metal island in the center of the kitchen and hear two more pops of someone's gun. I make eye contact with the women, who are huddled together on the floor against the stove. *I'm so sorry,* I mouth, and they can only stare back, eyes wide with shock.

Soren rounds the corner and pulls me back to standing, dragging me out of the kitchen towards more gunfire and shouts. It's clear they were ready for us, with the number of men and weapons that are currently being deployed.

We enter the main room of the bar, and my eyes lock in on Jax, who's pushed up against the bar and taking punches. Soren storms over and shoves the man away from Jax, moving the gun in his right hand across his left side and fires a shot behind him, dropping Jax's attacker. Jax grabs his own gun and follows Soren back into the fray, throwing punches with his free hand and pistol-whipping Brothers with his gun. He doesn't shoot, though, I notice. In fact, he hasn't killed one of them.

Bad boy has a moral compass, I guess.

I remember what Kain said about him never taking a life before- I wonder now if that's because he's afraid or because he refuses.

By the time most of the room is clear, either because of death or because the remaining Brothers fled, it smells like blood and gunpowder. The scent is familiar and makes my stomach turn as I take in the carnage.

There are bodies everywhere, at least five dead in this room alone. I scan each of their faces, not recognizing any. *Shit.*

I make eye contact with Soren and shake my head, earning a roar of frustration.

"Trigger, you're with me." He jerks his chin down a hallway off the main bar area, and they jog towards it, guns drawn. Kain is quick to follow, and before long, Jax and I are left alone in the bar, with only the stench of death and violence to keep us company.

I turn my back to him, staring down the hallway the three men disappeared down, wondering if I should follow, when suddenly a knife is pressed against my throat. I don't move, knowing that if I even slightly flinch, I'll be cut. Strong hands shove me forward and grab one of my arms, spinning me around and shoving me to the ground.

Jax is on me instantly, straddling my waist with the knife back against my neck.

"Brotherhood whore." He bites out between clenched teeth. "I bet you told them we were coming, huh?" He pushes the blade harder against my throat.

"No- I swear." I manage. *How the fuck would I even do that, asshole?* "I haven't had any contact with them. Not since I left."

He laughs darkly, clearly not believing me. "Then where the fuck is Emmett Riley? *You* promised he'd be here. *You* said you saw him walk in, but not out. And now conveniently, he's not here, and my brothers just went off alone into unknown territory." He grips my hair and yanks my head backwards, exposing my neck further. "You broke my family. You die. Tonight."

I can do nothing but stare back at him. His blue eyes that were once glazed over and lifeless are now fiery and angry, and I almost appreciate the life that has found its way back into them. I know he won't back down from this, and he has no reason to- I can't say I would if I was in his position.

Maybe finally dying is better than constantly fearing it. Instead of being scared, I choose to accept my fate. I knew it was coming at some point, right?

"Fine. Do it."

I tilt my head even further backwards and recollect on the conversation Beck and I had at the club. *If I'm going to die, it'll be on my own terms. How I want it to be.*

I'm taking the last bit of control I have and granting him the ability to kill me.

I shut my eyes and think about my apartment back in Oakridge. I think of the Thai food stand that sits outside on Friday nights that always gives me extra spring rolls, and I think of The Lucky Plate and going back and forth with Frank. I think of my parents, and wonder if they're even going to know that I've died. I think about how badly I want my mother, and all the things I would do or endure just to be held by her once again, like she would when I was small. My chest aches and my eyes well up at the thought of her warm embrace, the peace I'd feel as she'd softly sing to me. When things were easier. When she still loved me.

When the pain of the knife doesn't come, I crack an eye open and catch a glimpse of Jax. He's breathing heavily, staring down at me, but the knife doesn't move.

"It's okay." I murmur quietly. "I know. You can do it."

He releases his hold on my hair and grips the sides of my face between his thumb and pointer, squeezing hard. His chest is rising and falling so quickly that he can't really be getting any air, and I can pinpoint the tell-tale sign of a panic attack.

"Fuck." He drops my face and removes the knife from my neck. The blade trails upwards over my cheek and into my hairline as he traces my face with the instrument.

"Goddamn it, why can't I do it?"

His voice cracks slightly at the end, but I don't miss it. I reach a hand up and gingerly bring it to his face, pressing the backs of my fingers against his cheek. He stiffens at my touch, eyes wide with alarm, but he doesn't pull away.

I'm not doing this to plead my case or convince him not to kill me. No, I'm doing this because I know what he's feeling- the panic getting so much that it clouds your vision and consumes you.

He may hate me, but I know exactly what to do to bring him at least a bit of comfort. We're not out of the woods with The Iron Brotherhood, and in the off chance he does let me live, he needs to be able to defend himself.

The quiet is abruptly interrupted by the thundering of footsteps, and none other than Emmett Riley storms into the room. He looks just as I remember him, and it renders me still. His eyes have the same filthy glint they always have- like coins at the bottom of a muddy river, raking up and down my body, searching for some way to hurt me. He smells like cheap cologne, the kind I never wanted to smell again. His hair's thinned substantially since the last time I saw him, leaving his greasy forehead noticeably bare.

My chest tightens until I can barely breath. I was stupid for thinking I could ever look at him again.

Emmett takes one look at our position, and reaches for his gun, but Jax is faster. Before he can get his fist around his weapon, Jax has his own drawn in an instant and fires one shot, the bullet whizzing over my head and hitting Emmett square in the chest. He acts almost out of instinct, and I don't think he even realizes that his bullet made contact until Emmett goes down.

Jax whips his head back towards me, his eyes wide with fear and mouth slightly open, his breath coming out heavy. My ears are ringing so badly it feels as though my eardrums have burst.

"It's okay. You got him. You're alright." I whisper, but it doesn't seem to help.

Jax jumps off me and rushes over to Riley, nudging him a few times with the toe of his boot. Riley groans, and I scramble to my feet to put eyes on him myself. I slowly walk towards them, and Riley's eyes lock onto me as he takes his last few breaths.

"You fucking bitch. I just knew you had something to do with this." Riley gasps, and my blood runs ice cold at the sound of his voice. My knees begin to shake so badly I'm worried I might fall right on top of him.

"Finish it, Jax. Please." My voice cracks, and he stares at me, cocking a brow at Riley's words. "Please." I whisper, turning away from him.

"Once a slut, always a slut, right?" Emmett coughs.

Even with a bullet in his chest, he still manages to make me feel exactly the way he always has. Like nothing. Worthless.

"What, you crawl out of my bed and right into his? You're a fucking joke, Georgia. I should've-" Another gunshot rings out, and I flinch at the sudden noise.

Emmett says nothing else. He can't. It's silent.

A hand falls to the middle of my back, and I stiffen, memories of Riley and the others flooding my body.

For a moment, I forget about the fact that he's lying on the floor in a pool of his own blood, and I'm taken back to that basement. I stand there frozen, waiting for the rough hands that I know are coming to drag me away to my personal hell.

It's not until I hear a familiar voice that I'm pulled out of my head.

"It's done. Relax." Jax murmurs, brushing his thumb across my spine quickly and dropping his hand.

Footsteps down the hallway pull me out of my trance, and Soren and Kain burst into the main room, heads on swivels while they take in the surroundings, their gazes stopping on Riley's body.

"Ho-oly shit." Soren chuckles, whistling low. "What happened?"

"Jax." I breathe out, not sure if any of this is real.

One of the men whose death I've dreamed of, over and over again, is lying dead on the ground. I'm numb- unable to feel anything. Not able to feel the crippling disappointment in myself for not watching him die the way I had rehearsed in my head so many times. Not able to feel the twinge of guilt that Jax had to be the one to finally put him down. Not able to feel the sting of shame his final words left me with.

"Well look at that." Soren says, choking out a fake sob, wiping his eyes dramatically. "Our little Jax finally got his hands dirty. What'd it take, only seven years?" He goads, and Jax chuckles softly.

"Yeah, old man, you keep talking. You're just mad you didn't get to do it yourself. Where the fuck

were you, anyways? Jerking off in the back room?"
Jax fires back, but there's a slight shake to his voice.
He's still scared.

"No, he was jerking *me* off. What happened?"
Beck calls out, striding down the hallway- cool, calm,
and collected. Soren rolls his eyes. He stares at Riley's
body, his eyebrows raised and a slight grimace on his
face.

"Holy shit dude, think you got him?" Beck
drawls, and Jax's face reddens slightly. "I'm just
playing, Eight Ball. Good shit." He leans in, pulling
the smaller man into a one-armed hug, cackling.

My hands begin to tremble as relief washes
over me. *He's never going to hurt me again.*

Strong, familiar hands grip my arms, shaking
me slightly, and I look up to find Kain's void-like eyes
staring back at mine.

He's speaking, barking orders and rapid-firing
questions at me, but my ears are ringing so badly that
I can't register what he's said.

I look past him to see Soren, swelling with
pride and pulling Jax into a hug, with Beck hiding a
smirk, pressing his thumb against the corner of his
mouth.

Jax's words from this morning replay in my
head. *Someone will end up dead because of me.* Figures,
right? All I know how to do is destroy. Hell, I

couldn't even keep my own family together, why the fuck did I think I wouldn't break theirs apart just by being in their presence? It only took me a few days this time- I think that's a new record for me.

My mind begins to shut down, my body moving on autopilot. Kain doesn't let go of my arms, spinning me around in his grip and pushing me out the front door and back towards the car.

I turn back one last time, reassuring myself that Emmett Riley is dead. That it's over- at least, this small part of it.

Soren's speaking into his phone, kicking the body slightly, his lip turned downwards, nose scrunched in disgust.

We reach the car, and the door is opened for me, and as soon as I've slid over to my spot, the door slams closed again. Before I can get comfortable in my solitude, though, the door closest to me opens and Kain is there again, grabbing the seat belt and reaching across my chest to fasten it.

I'm not sure how he got to me so fast, or why he suddenly feels like he needs to take care of me, but I keep my mouth closed because I know I wouldn't have been able to do any of it myself.

The panic still has my body frozen in fear, and it's all I can do to even breathe on my own at this point. *It's done. He's gone. I'm safe.* I repeat those words to myself over and over again, but it doesn't help much.

He steps away from me, leaving the door open and popping the trunk. He's back moments later with towels in his arms, wrapping one around my shoulders and grabbing another to begin wiping the blood away from my legs and hands. I didn't realize I was so covered in blood- I wasn't involved in much tonight, but I guess just being in the same room as the havoc soaked me with it just as much as the rest.

Kain's hands are also bloody, but he makes no move to clean himself first as he wipes hard and fast at my skin. I snatch the towel from him with shaking hands- the last thing I need is the big fucker thinking he has something over me because he helped me.

"I can do it." I bite out, not wanting him to touch me any more than he already has. I know I probably *couldn't* do it on my own, but I don't want to be perceived as weak or unable to fend for myself.

"I know you *can*. I'm going to do it. Don't say another word except to acknowledge what I've just told you."

I don't have it in me to fight him right now, or even to say anything back. All I can do is stare at my lap and nod.

He cleans me up as best as he can with the limited supplies we have. When he's satisfied with his work, he chucks the towel over my head through the gap and into the footwell of the row behind me, gripping my chin and tilting my head towards him.

"You will stay here. I'm going to fetch the others, then we go home. Don't move."

Home. What a joke.

I stare back at him and nod my head twice, watching as the door closes behind him. He takes off running back into the bar, and I start to break down. The tears don't come like I expect- instead, I begin to hyperventilate in my seat, shaking uncontrollably.

My head begins to get fuzzy from the lack of carbon dioxide, and I know it's only a matter of time before I black out. I'm almost glad there's no tears, knowing that they would've raised brows with the guys when they return. Better to leave no evidence, no room for questions. My hands land on my knees and I dig my nails in, desperate for something to ground me and stop the fear.

My mom taught me that when I feel afraid, the only thing that'll help is a bit more pain, then it all goes away. I hope she's right- I hope that the pain I'm feeling right now is just the tiny bit of extra that I need for everything to be okay again, because if it's not, I'm scared that I'm on borrowed time.

My mind can't take much more of what I saw tonight, and at this point I've told these men everything I know. I slump forward, bringing my chest as close to my knees as I can, and silently pray that they'll let me go tonight.

I'm still breathing hard when the edges of my vision start to turn black, and I almost smile at the sweet relief of unconsciousness that is waiting for me.

I fall further over my lap, my eyes rolling backwards into my head and embrace the darkness, knowing that as soon as I wake, the chaos will resume and they'll realize that I'm no longer of use, bringing me closer and closer to my death.

I was lucky tonight that Jax chickened out- I almost wish he hadn't so I didn't have to look at Soren when he inevitably does it himself.

Maybe that's how it's supposed to be. It's for the best. I was never meant to last here, anyway.

Beck

When Kain came back into the bar alone, I was sure he'd tied Georgia up in the trunk of the car and left her there. I was normally eager to get back after a hit like this- sure, I've had my fair share of blood on my hands, but it doesn't mean I like being in the aftermath, surrounded by the smell of blood and gunpowder- especially not when I have a pretty girl waiting for me. However, my focus now was on Jax and making sure he isn't going to fall apart in front of Soren.

He needs to look strong, like putting Emmett Riley down was no big deal. He seems to be taking everything okay, or as okay as you can be after you've taken a life for the first time, I guess.

He doesn't speak, only offering a half smile to Soren and nodding when he's spoken to. Soren is beaming like a proud father- he'd been itching to get Jax made since we took him in, and he's finally done it, and in a huge way. Taking out the second in command of The Iron Brotherhood was a huge win for us, and the fact that Jax was the one to pull the trigger just earned him some major points with the rest of the Vipers- not to mention Soren's admiration.

I roll my eyes as Soren slings an arm over Jax's shoulders, roughing his hair up and laughing-truly laughing- with him. I remember when things were like that with us, before I was the fuck up of our little foursome.

Before Soren's dad died, we were brothers. I guess we still are in a way, but after all the shit that went down, I don't think we'll ever be able to get back to the bond we once had. I'm the first to admit that I messed up a few times, maybe didn't handle things as well as I could have, and probably disappointed him a few times along the way, too. But Soren could've done what I've done tenfold, and I would never have turned my back on him.

I guess it's in the Turner blood. My dad was a kiss-ass to Conner, and I'm no better. I'd forgive Soren over and over again for the shit he pulls- for hitting me, for pulling me away from her. For everything, without question. That was the one flaw I always saw in my father, his willingness to follow and forgive another man blindly.

I told myself growing up that I would be my own man, follow my own path and my own orders- I would never belong to someone the way he belonged to Conner. But now, looking at the way things have played out, I see that I'm no better than he is. Guilt surges through me for faulting my father in the way that I have, and I know I need to call him soon to catch up. *And probably apologize for acting like a dick to him in my head, too.* I shake my head, not allowing myself to wallow in shame any longer, and turn back towards the scene.

"Let's get out of here. The pigs will be pulling up any minute; we weren't quiet about anything." Soren orders, dropping his arm from around Jax's shoulders. "You did good, kid. Let's get you home and into the warm embrace of a woman, huh?"

He walks out of the bar's front doors with Kain trailing close behind him. I roll my eyes. He won't end up in anyone else's bed but mine, not if I have any say in it.

Jax goes to follow them, but I grab his arm and stop him.

"Are you okay?" I half-whisper, tightening my grip on his arm.

"Yeah, I'm good. Let's go-"

I pull him into me and slam my lips against his, effectively silencing him. He hesitates at first, tensing his muscles, but when he realizes I'm not letting him go, he softens into me, kissing me back. I pull away and lean my forehead against his, and out of the corner of my eye I can see his bottom lip quiver slightly. I know he's more fucked up over Riley than he's letting on, and I plan to crack his shell and put him back together before the night is over.

"She means nothing to me, J. I know it hurts, what I said, and I know you didn't like what you saw." The lie tastes sour on my tongue as I spit it out, but at the end of the day, Jax is too important to me to lose over a girl that isn't sticking around much longer anyways, no matter how much I want her to.

"I'm not using you. You're not a plaything to me. I need you, and I can't keep going like this. I *won't*. Just tell me what I have to do, Jax. Tell me what you need from me, what punishment you deem worthy so I can fix this."

He stays silent for a beat, taking in everything I've said. With the way he's acted all day, I assume he'll tell me to fuck off again and walk out, but instead, he collapses into my arms, burying his face in my neck.

"You swear?"

I let out the breath I didn't know I was holding in, leaning my cheek against his head. He's back where he belongs, and I'm not going to fuck that up again.

"I swear, Jaxon. I swear on everything, I won't ever do something like that to you again." I breathe, reveling in his acceptance. "Unless we can fuck her together."

He chuckles and reaches up to punch my arm, but he doesn't say no, and I flash my eyebrows. I file that away to ask him about later. I take the blow because I deserve it- I deserve a lot more from a lot of people, but I guess I'll start with this. I place a few soft kisses to the side of his head and grab his face, guiding him back upright and roughing up his hair.

"Enough with the pussy shit. We've got some celebrating to do, Eight Ball. Someone just earned his place at the big boys' table."

The ride back to the compound is quiet and awkward. I sit in the back with Jax once again, but closer this time, and already sore from the first umpteen hours in the car. My frame contorts at uncomfortable angles with every pothole and bump we hit in the road. Georgia stayed quiet the entire time, staring straight out the window. I notice a slight shake to her hands, placed neatly in her lap, but I chalk it up to the shock of the shit she just witnessed. I can't act like I care too much, not in front of Jax, regardless of how much I want to pull her into my arms and comfort her.

When we arrive back at the compound, a few of the guys are already ready and waiting for us outside to take the car back.

Kain whips into the attached garage, slamming on the brakes hard, and jumps out of the car before it's barely in park, striding over to Georgia's side and opening her door. She gingerly steps out, staring at her shoes, and he wraps a big hand around her bicep, ushering her inside.

I almost feel bad for her- he won't be gentle with her, regardless of what she needs, but I can't bring myself to walk away from Jax right now. It's not like she's anything to me, right? I don't have any obligation to help her. *You can lie to yourself, but that doesn't make it real, dickhead.*

I scrub a hand over my face and lean dramatically against Jax, groaning loudly. He chuckles and opens his own door, crawling through the aisle and sliding out and leaving space for me to clamber out behind him.

I stretch tall as soon as my feet hit the ground- I'm not a small guy by any means, and sitting in the back seats for that long has set an ache into my body that I'm sure isn't going anywhere any time soon. Once the feeling comes back into my limbs, I slide my hand into Jax's and follow Kain and Georgia into the compound, leaving Soren talking with the few Vipers still lingering in the garage.

My heart thrums in my chest, and I'm almost beaming knowing that I've at least begun to rectify things with Jax. It kills me to know that he felt so betrayed, and I know I didn't exactly do anything to make it better until now- add that to my list of fuck ups I need to atone for, I guess. It feels right with him next to me, like things are slowly getting back to how they should be. I'm putting the pieces of my family back together. I know I need to fix shit with Soren, too, but for now, I'm focused on celebrating my boy's victory.

When we get inside the doors, we're met with the deafening cheers of our brothers. Everyone is crowded together in the main room, whistling, cheering, and banging on the tables like a war cry to welcome the new blood. It's a big deal around here when we initiate a new member officially, and I know the party we've got in store is going to be one for the books, considering how long it took Jax to take the plunge to commit to us fully.

I think back to my initiation, and how it was perhaps the first time in my life that I felt I truly belonged to something. I was freshly nineteen when I smoked some drug dealer on one of our corners in broad daylight, and I don't think my dad has ever been that proud of me. He took me back to the compound and every member of our organization was there, telling me how proud they were of me and how lucky I was to have been able to get in so young, but I didn't feel lucky.

Sure, I was thrilled that I got booze and my pick of any girl we had under me for the night, but sometimes I think the price I had to pay to get in wasn't worth it. I panicked at first- freaking out that I was going to get arrested or some shit, not realizing the reach The Vipers had to protect their own.

You never forget the first life you take. Even now, sometimes when I close my eyes at night I see his face, bleeding from his temple all over the pavement. Shit like that stays with you, and I doubt I'll ever stop seeing him.

After it happened, I got so drunk at the initiation ceremony that I holed myself up in the bunk room upstairs and talked to him out loud for three hours, apologizing for what I'd done and begging for his forgiveness.

I looked his family up, found their address, and for a year straight I would send money and groceries to their house to try and make up for it. He had a girlfriend and a son living in some shithole apartment in Oakridge, unbeknownst to me that day, and I tried my best to make sure they were taken care of.

I never wanted to kill anyone, but I grew up in the life. Holding a gun and pulling the trigger was second nature to me. My dad raised me to take no shit, ask no questions, and shoot first- always. It was kill or be killed, and I wasn't going to wait around for the latter- he made sure of that. I made him proud that night, and the way he looked at me after I told him what I'd done was the only thing that stopped me from putting a bullet in my own skull to make it right. I can only hope Jax handles it better than I did, but I'll be there to pick up the pieces if shit goes south with him. He's not going to lose himself to this- I won't allow it.

We're ushered over the bar, and the liquor immediately starts flowing. Jax and I are passed shots right away, and we down those and move onto another round. A bunch of the guys crowd around us, and I tell an animated version of what happened, milking it for laughs.

Jax's shoulder brushes mine, and I glance down, he's beaming- just a quick, private smile before he drops his gaze. Just for us. I want so badly to lean down and kiss him, but I know I can't. We aren't exactly exclusive to the rest of the guys- they don't need to see that. I keep talking, like nothing's out of the ordinary. Like my heart still isn't pounding from the way he looked at me.

My chest starts to heat up, and the ache I previously felt from the uncomfortable car ride is long forgotten as the liquor starts to loosen me up. I almost don't register when Soren takes the spot next to me, and it's not until I feel a hand on my shoulder that I look over at him.

"Can we talk?" He asks in a low voice, only for me to hear.

I nod, and slide out from the bar, heading towards the elevator. Instead of following me, he jerks his head towards the garage, and I cock an eyebrow at him. He gestures that way once more and heads out the door, and I follow behind him. When we walk out to the garage, there are a few Vipers lingering in the space, presumably at their guard posts.

"If you're not my second in command, get the fuck out. Now." Soren barks, and all of them immediately turn and walk right out of the space.

"I'm surprised you'd still call me that, boss. What is this- you bring me out here to take a swing at me again?" I quip.

"We need to air this shit out. Sit" He gestures to a metal chair sitting against the wall, and I immediately plop down.

My leg bounces, nervous energy radiating off me. I don't quite meet his eyes, given that the last time we were alone together, he was trying to knock my teeth from my mouth with his fist.

Something about his energy says that I'm not in any danger tonight, though.

"I'll start. I'm sorry I've been a dick."

"You can say that again." I mutter. He gives me a pointed look.

"I'm on edge with her here, and I can't channel it properly. I don't know how to manage what I'm feeling and it's easier for me to be angry than figure my shit out. I know it makes me look like my dad, okay?" He sighs, rubbing his forehead. "But I love you, brother. This shit between us makes me feel like I've lost my right arm. I don't want to be like this anymore." He rushes out, his voice wavering.

The emotion behind his words softens my heart towards him, at least a little. I know it's hard for Soren to be this raw and vulnerable, and I'm grateful for his efforts.

"But I also can't have you flaunting her around all the time, you know? I can't lie to you and say I don't want her too. I do, bad, but we can't. Once all this shit's over, we're getting rid of her and moving on with our lives, and I don't want any loose ends from any of this. Our family's all that matters in the end, right?"

I almost scoff at him, because there's no way in hell I'll be able to just let her go after all of this, but something about his tone seems... final. My jaw clenches. I try to push away the worry that starts to worm its way into my head. I ache to be close to her-if she's with me, I can protect her. I can convince him that she's not going anywhere. We're in too deep now, and I've never wanted another woman, hell even *looked* at another woman the way I do Georgia. I'll let Soren think what he wants for now, to clear the air, but she's staying.

I'll take another beating later to atone for it.

"I get it. Tension is high right now, and we're in uncharted territory having someone new with us. We can't let our family break over this. I won't let that happen. It's always been us- it'll always *be* us. Water under the bridge, right?" I hold my hands up, a visible sign of surrender in case my words weren't enough. "Just don't give me shiner again, okay? It's embarrassing to explain to the guys."

He laughs as I stand and cross the space between us, pulling him in and resting my forehead against his. The sound of his laugh- the ease of it- lifts a weight from my chest.

For a second, I'm not the man who constantly fucks up. I'm not the one who disobeyed orders.

I'm just his brother again.

I didn't realize how heavy it's been, carrying all this silence and anger between us. But here, with us breathing the same air, it's like it never existed. This is how it should be. How it's *always* been.

We've fought before- brutal, bloody fights that left us both half-dead, but laughing afterwards. This one felt different. This one scared me.

Because for the first time, I wondered if I'd really lost him.

I feel the swell of pride I'm sure our fathers feel- well, felt- for us. I'm sure they shared many moments like this, and they've probably fought ten times worse than we have. It gives me hope.

"Through fire and blood, brother." I murmur, clapping his back a few times and pulling away. "Yeah, yeah." He replies, and I crack a smile. "Let's get back in there, the little one deserves a true celebration. He was a badass today."

I chuckle and start towards the door, shaking my head. When my hand reaches the handle, I'm shoved to the side, hearing Soren laugh as he races to open the door before I do, like he always did when we were kids.

I know that everything is starting to be okay again. We may not have fully repaired the cracks in our family, but the duct tape we managed to put over them tonight might just be enough to get us through. At least, for now.

Georgia

I think I'm in shock. I have to be, right? I just watched the life leave Riley's eyes- the man who tortured me for years.

I always wondered what it would feel like to watch Emmett Riley die. I fantasized about it, every time his hands were on me, every time I was drugged, or hit, or locked in the dark for days on end. I wondered what his blood would look like as it ran out, what he would say in his final moments. But nothing could've prepared me for what it would really be like.

Especially considering the fact that the man who ended it for me was seconds away from ending *me*.

In the end, I was worried for him- because I was conditioned to be. I wanted to jump in to save him. As I heard him die, I wanted to turn around and grab Jax by the shoulders and shake him for what he'd done.

I was mostly so

That's the thing about the Brotherhood; they broke me so badly that I was made to believe I should do anything in my power to save them, if it came down to it. I should risk my life for any one of theirs.

That kind of pain stays with you, and I have half a mind to think it won't ever go away.

I think I must've blacked out the entire way home, because I don't remember anything past Kain trying to clean the blood off me in the back seat of the Escalade after everything was over. When we pulled up again, he made quick work of getting me out of the car and back to the basement.

At first, I thought it was to chain me up again, but as we stand in the en-suite bathroom attached to the room I was sleeping in, I feel I might've misjudged the situation.

My hands start to shake, and I feel like I'm seconds away from collapsing, just being this close to him. I might talk a big game when I need to, but at the root, I'm still very afraid of him. After seeing what he is truly capable of tonight, killing without any emotion in his eyes, I don't want to be in an enclosed space with him.

He stands at the far end of the bathroom, unmoving, staring at me with those dead eyes.

"Strip." He orders, and my blood runs cold. Does he want some sort of favor for cleaning me up? I didn't ask him to do that, and I'm damn sure not doing anything to thank him for that tiny, unwanted act of service.

"It's not like that." He retorts, like he can read my mind. "I need to ensure you aren't going into shock from what you saw. Strip."

He slowly makes his way over to the bathtub connected to the glass shower stall and turns the red tap on full blast, reaching his hand down to plug the drain. I stand still, not moving, and surely not removing any clothing in front of him.

When he notices that I won't comply with his order, he lets out a frustrated breath and grits his teeth.

"I can step out for a moment, if that would make you more comfortable. I can't touch you, anyways, even if I wanted to, so you have no reason to be hesitant."

My cheeks redden at his words, a flush of embarrassment running through me. He read me like a book.

"You really don't have to do this. I'm fine." I manage, but the violent shakes wracking my body quickly prove that I'm lying. He raises his eyebrows once, as if to confirm that he knows I'm lying, and it's clear I don't have much of a choice here. I cut my eyes to the side, trying to find a way out, but I can't.

"Can you at least turn around?" I ask quietly, and he instantly complies, turning to face the wall. I slowly remove the blood-stained clothing and leave them in a heap on the floor. I test the water before climbing in, my pulse loud in my ears.

I don't want to tell him to turn around. I don't want him to see me like this- shaking, exposed. Small. I don't want him to look at me, because if he does, I'm afraid he'll see all of it.

"Are you finished?" Kain asks from his position in the corner

"Erm, yeah. I'm good." I manage, hoping that the red in my cheeks can be chalked up to the heat of the water.

There's no soap in the bath, so I'm fully exposed under the water. Normally I would've never agreed to this, but something about the clinical way he moves assures me that he's not going to try anything. *Nothing I wouldn't want, anyway.*

He turns around and opens the cabinet under the sink, taking out a few washcloths and a bottle of body wash.

I figure he's just planning on handing it to me and walking away, but he dunks a washcloth under the water and begins to scrub my bare shoulder. The touch startles me so completely I forget how to breathe.

It's been a long time since I've had a man's hands on me in this way, and my brain shuts down. It's comforting almost, my mind being completely numb and my body totally pliant, giving full control to someone else, just for a brief moment in time.

There are no ulterior motives, no anxiety about what I'll have to do next- just calm. I've carried so much for so long, and Kain's gentle scrubbing allows me to shut my mind off just enough to bring me slight comfort. I know comfort is not his intention here- he wants to make sure I'm conscious enough to give up more information, but I can't bring myself to care right now.

I catch myself leaning into his touch, and I'm so exhausted I can't stop myself. Kain's breath hitches in his throat, and I can tell he's uncomfortable with the closeness.

As if moving on instinct, I bring my hand up to cover his. He jerks back as if I've burned him, but I grab him before he can fully move his hand away.

"You don't have to do this." I whisper. "I can manage."

"Yes, I do. Stop pushing the issue, Georgia. Follow my instructions."

I nod slowly and close my eyes, relishing in the numbness coursing through my body. The comfort is quickly replaced with panic, though, as I feel his bare hand make contact with my skin. I don't move, I don't even breathe, as his fingers caress my shoulder. His touch is hesitant and slow, and there's a tiny tremor in his hands.

He trails downwards, following the curve of my arm under the water. His breathing is heavy, and I know this is making him uncomfortable- I can't fathom why he's putting himself in this position.

"Stay very still. I don't want to hurt you."

I bristle at his words and try to slowly move my arm away from him, desperate to create some sort of distance between me and this certified psychopath, but he grips it before I can fully move away.

"Listen and obey, little one. Please." Kain's voice is hoarse, but his movements don't stop.

His fingers brush over the length of my arm, down to my wrist, and back up again, moving across my shoulders to the back of my neck. The tremor in his hands grows stronger. I feel like I'm in the bath with a rabid dog, waiting for it to snap and rip my arm from my body.

The image of him pulling the trigger on the men in the bar is forever etched into my brain, and it's almost unbelievable that we're in this position just mere hours after he took those lives. The way he's able to switch it off, the violence and the darkness, makes me believe that there's more to him than he lets on.

The tough-guy exterior, similar to Soren, is just that- his mask that he presents to others, but I'm realizing that these men are much more complex than I initially thought.

He sucks in a breath through his teeth as his hands start to knead small circles at the base of my neck. I let out a small moan- he's talented with his hands, I'll give him that much, and even though I know he's not putting much effort in, I'm melting under his touch. For a moment, I forget that I'm being bathed by a killer and allow myself only to *feel*. The more I think about who he is and what he's done, the worse my stay in this basement will be.

A mangled sound leaves his throat at the sound of my moan, and he grips my neck tighter, drawing a hiss out of me and leans in, his lips nearly touching my ear.

"Don't do that again, Georgia. I won't be responsible for what happens if you do. I'm already hanging on by a thread." He murmurs.

His voice brings immediate heat between my legs. His soul might be covered in blood, but *god,* I can't deny that I want to know how he tastes. Does that make me sick? Probably. But being tended to in this manner, so gently, by a man who could stop hearts with a simple flick of his wrist is turning me on.

He continues his path across my body, his hand now flat against my skin. He finds my other shoulder, squeezing once, then sliding down across my collar bones. I nearly jump out of my skin when his big hand encircles my throat, and his movement stills.

This isn't like before- there's no pressure, no ill-intent behind his grip. He collars me gently, and I tilt my head back and lean against the edge of the tub. I shut my eyes, not daring to look up at him, but just the feeling of his touch quells the fear I've felt when I'm around him, and quiets the horrible thoughts that have ravaged my mind since we left the bar.

"Take a deep breath, little one. Let me feel it." He whispers, and I instantly obey, breathing deeply.

"Good girl, that's it. One more."

I shudder at his words as I follow his instructions, breathing in through my nose and exhaling through my mouth, the air coming out shakily. I hear him growl under his breath, and he squeezes my throat gently.

"I'm terrified of you, little one. No other woman in my life has scared me like you do."

"Why?" I squeeze my closed eyes, waiting for him to shut down. "I'm nobody. If I'm such a problem, why keep me here? Why not let me go?"

"You don't understand." He says under his breath, but I catch it.

I might regret it, but I pry further.

"Make me understand."

"I think you're going to ruin us, and I'm terrified that I might let you." He admits, squeezing my throat harder. "You're not- no one's- *fuck*." He stumbles over his words, trying to find the right ones to say.

I'm not sure there is a *right* thing to say. I reach a hand up again, bringing my fingers to his arm and giving it a small squeeze. His body jolts at my touch as if he's been electrocuted.

"You can tell me."

He exhales loudly through his nose. "We've never let anyone come between us like this. There's never been anything that makes us *act* like this. But you- I want to hurt you, punish you for getting into Beck's head the way you already have, for upsetting Soren so much. And at the same time, I *can't*. I know what it would do to them. To me."

I moan again as his grip on my throat tightens, rubbing my thighs together, desperate for some sort of friction. My core is soaked, and not because of the bath water.

In a flash, his lips are pressed against my ear.

"What did I say? Don't make those noises around me again. Next time you do, I'll put you over my knee, and you won't like it very much."

Holy shit. I will myself not to think about what it would be like to be completely bare in front of him, bent over his lap with his hand on my ass.

I have no idea what's come over him- the cruel facade he wore when I was first brought here has dropped, and today he's throwing himself into… caring for me? I'm not really sure how I'm supposed to react.

My life before was a circle of chaos- see the blood, swallow the feeling, keep moving and pretend like I wasn't terrified. I used to be good at that last part. The pretending. Everything I saw, every scream I heard, I buried it deep down until there was nothing left to feel. I had to. I couldn't focus on the pain, because I always knew there was something so much *worse* to come.

When Isaac died, something cracked. I couldn't push it down that time, and I felt every bit of it, like I was breaking apart from the inside.

But now- God help me- after everything they've done to me, after everything I've seen them do, I feel… safe. Kain's hand steadying me instead of striking me. Beck's need to protect me. Soren's eyes on me, not cold anymore, but searching- human. Even Jax, as much as he hates me, he *killed* for me.

It doesn't make sense, any of it. I should be fighting, keeping my distance. But I can't. I don't want to. Trusting them is starting to feel as easy as breathing- they've proved on many occasions that they aren't going to kill me. In fact, they've protected me- killed *for* me.

Tonight, I've watched another death. But this time, I didn't have to hide from it. Didn't have to hide *in* it. Maybe that's why I can't quite bring myself to hate them. Maybe that's why the fear's starting to feel a lot like something else.

They've shown me a glimpse into a life I didn't know existed before, something more than just waiting tables and eating Thai food alone in a shitty apartment, and there's something to be said for that.

I'm not sure if I should tell the others about what went down between Jax and I, or how ready I was to die at his hand.

I've never considered myself to be suicidal, rather just *tired*. The feeling is like a leaf blowing in the wind, not sure where it'll end up, but unphased all the same if it washes down a storm drain or gets stuck to someone's windshield. I always thought I would be the leaf in the storm drain, forgotten and dying in the dark, but as Kain's hands caress my shoulders, I think I might've ended up stuck to the right windshield.

I might not be free in the wind, but I'm damn sure not rotting underground.

"Do you feel better?"

The sound of Kain's voice jolts me from my thoughts. I nod slowly, sitting up to reach the drain plug, but he grabs my shoulder and pulls me backwards, flattening my back against the side of the tub. We stay like that for what feels like an eternity, the anticipation of his next move electrifying the space between us.

Finally, he leans forward and pulls the plug, hauling me out of the tub and leaving me standing in the middle of the bathroom, dripping wet, freezing, and totally naked in front of him.

The cool air of the bathroom rushes across my skin, my nipples hardening from the change in temperature, and I know he notices. He stares at me, seeming to drink in every inch of my naked body. He doesn't seem repulsed like I thought he would be. The look in his eyes matches that of a wolf about to descend upon a rabbit- hungry, and ready to strike at any minute.

Half of me, the sane half, wants to tuck my tail and run, but the other half, the more primal and unreasonable part of me, wants him to step closer and reach out. As if he can sense it, he moves, taking a half step towards me, locking his gaze onto mine.

"I can't touch you." He repeats, but his hand starts to lift from his side, as if it's being pulled magnetically towards me.

"Why?" I manage to get out. My voice is raspy with need, and if I don't get his hands on me, I feel like I might pass out. Feeling his touch without fear for the first time leaves me undone. I need more, crave it even, and I don't think I'll stop begging until I get it- until I get *him*.

"Soren said. I can't disobey an order, little one." His face is twisted, his brows knitted like something's hurting him.

"A man like you, taking orders from someone else? I didn't peg you for the follow-the-leader type, Kain." I goad him, hoping for the tiniest crack in his unwavering refusal.

"Watch your mouth." He growls.

"Beck's done it. Touched me, I mean. If he can do it, why can't you?" I push him further.

"Beck's an idiot, and you saw how Soren flew off the handle because of what he did. I respect Soren too much to blatantly disregard what he asks of me."

He's not budging, but he doesn't make any move to walk away or avert his eyes from my body.

An idea springs into my mind, and before I can discern whether it's a good one, I act.

"Okay," I start, drawing out the 'O'. "You can't touch. But no one said anything about looking, right?"

He grunts out something that sounds like a 'no', and I lean back against the edge of the bathtub.

Now or never, Georgia.

I part my legs, giving him a full display of my now-soaked pussy, and run my hand down my stomach.

"You may not be able to touch me, but I can show you exactly what I wanted you to do to me, right, Big Guy?" My voice is full of lust as I shamelessly caress my body, my hands trailing across my stomach and down my thighs.

"Be very careful with what you do next, Georgia."

I roll my eyes, but maintain eye contact as my fingers land home, sliding through my slick folds and circling my clit. I keep my eyes on him, focusing on the depths of his eyes. I mentally trace his scar, wanting to reach out and feel it for myself. It adds to his beauty, in a way- cracked China is still fine China.

A breathy moan leaves my mouth as a shockwave of the sought-after pleasure racks my body, and Kain's breath hitches in his throat, his eyes blinking slowly, drinking me in.

"Georgia." He warns, but he doesn't look away. I can see the growing bulge of his cock in his pants.

I keep dragging my fingers over my clit, chasing the feeling of friction as my wet fingers run across my even-wetter pussy. I'm close already, the feeling of Kain's eyes on me as my fingers draw tight circles around my clit turning me on more than I expected it to. My breathing quickens, and I know he can tell I'm on the verge of exploding. I long to slow it down, to show him exactly how I need him, but the sound of his breathing mixed with mine, even when several feet separate us, it is too much and I'm barreling quickly over the edge. My head tilts back, eyes screwing shut as my orgasm takes me and I cry out, only to be met with the sound of the bathroom door slamming shut.

I catch my breath, the euphoria fading as quickly as it came.

Did I go too far? Did I push him too much? A weight settles in my gut, my palms starting to sweat. Do I feel... bad about teasing him like that?

I find a towel draped across the vanity, wrapping myself in it before heading out of the now-empty bathroom.

I find Kain pacing in the bedroom with his hands running across his head, his face red and his cock hard, looking like any girl's bad-boy wet dream. As soon as he senses me enter the room, he stills and looks over to me.

"Don't speak." He growls. "Actually-" He sighs loudly and shakes his head, leaving his sentence open-ended and storms out of the bedroom, slamming the door so hard behind him that I can feel the vibrations in the floor.

Maybe he's a virgin.

Regardless, I know that I have at least a miniscule effect on him, and I've proven the same. The guilt I felt just moments earlier is replaced by something stronger- I hold my head up a little taller, my spine a little straighter. I know things won't be the same between us now, and I can only hope that means he won't be as cruel towards me anymore.

Or maybe they'll finally let me go.

My eyelids begin to droop as the events from the day replay in my mind- Riley's body hitting the floor, the sound of Jax's gun, *Kain.* I drop the towel to the floor and crawl between the sheets, relishing in the way the cotton feels against my exposed skin, and let my eyes fall closed.

I wonder if Kain will tell the others about what happened, what I did.

I almost hope he will. Maybe I *want* them to know.

Let them talk about it, replay it, argue over it. Let them realize I'm not just the terrified girl they dragged here. They don't look at me like that anymore, not really. There's something else behind their eyes now- curiosity, maybe even hunger. Kain's made me realize that.

It's twisted, but the thought makes my pulse quicken. Maybe I scare them, maybe I ruin things just by breathing their air, but they don't want me dead. Not yet.

Maybe they want me, too.

Soren

The party is in full swing, and I feel that for the first time in a week, I can actually enjoy myself.

Clearing the air with Beck was necessary, not only for the sake of our organization, but for my mental's sake, too. Tonight was a huge win for The Vipers, sure- but my eyes are on Jaxon.

He's worn a grin since the moment we walked back into the compound- a genuine smile that reminds me of the scruffy kid we picked up, rather than the shell he's become.

The music is loud, and the liquor is flowing- the epitome of an initiation party. Jax and Beck sit side-by-side at the bar surrounded by our brothers, their shoulders shaking with laughter as Jax no doubt recalls the events of the evening. I notice one rather large hole in the group, though- Kain is missing.

I watched him take the girl back down to the basement, but his absence makes me feel uneasy as I think about what might've happened down there.

I give another glance to Beck and Jax- they're deep in conversation, and the way their bodies are beginning to slouch over lets me know that they're not long for this world. *They won't miss me.*

I slink towards the elevator, grateful that the noise of the party drowns out the *ding* of the call bell.

I board the elevator and mull over each scenario I might find them in on my way down. I can hear my heart beating in my ears. I tap my foot impatiently, mentally cursing the elevator for how slow it's moving. If he's alone with her, if I'm not there... I could be walking into carnage. Him laughing at how pathetic she must seem to him, her crying- *bleeding*. However, when the elevator lands and the doors open, the hallway is quiet.

The door to her holding cell is wide open, the lights off and the room vacant.

My brow furrows- surely, he hasn't already killed and disposed of her this quickly?

I walk quickly towards the kitchen, where I find Kain slumped over the island, holding a cup of coffee in his shaking hand. He looks disheveled, and I can see a wet spot on the front of his shirt. It doesn't look like blood, and he's worked up. *She's not dead, then*.

"Where is she?" I ask him, keeping my voice soft. Kain might respect me, but there's no way I would remain upright if something set him off in this state. *Big asshole*.

"I bathed her. She's in her roo- the spare room. She's not in shock and can continue to provide information." He replies. His tone is that of a good little soldier, reporting his findings, no inflection in his words, no trace of emotion on his face.

He bathed her? I feel like I'm in the twilight zone- Kain can't stomach being touched in hardly any capacity except when he spars, but he willingly put himself alone in the bathroom with her. He's shutting down, so I can only discern that touching her, even in small capacities, was too much for him to handle. I've never seen Kain's hands on a woman unless it was to cause pain- this is out of character. "You didn't need to-"

"Why is everyone telling me what I need to do or shouldn't do? I am perfectly capable of making my own decisions. I might respect you, Soren, but right now is not a good time to treat me like a goddamn child." He bites out. His grip on the mug gets so tight I think it might shatter. *Okay, new approach.*

"I'm sorry, man. You're right." I cross the kitchen and move to stand in front of him. "You're relieved for tonight. Go work this shit off. Tomorrow, we'll regroup and figure out what to do next. We're close, brother."

He grunts out in agreement, standing so fast that his stool clatters to the ground behind him. At this rate, we'll have to have new barstools brought in before the week is over. He moves behind me and throws his mug in the sink, not sparing a second glance at me before storming out of the room. I hear a door slam from somewhere in the apartment, and I hold my breath in anticipation of Georgia's screams. When they don't come, I sigh, scrubbing a hand over my face. He's probably in the gym, and he'll probably be there for the rest of the night.

I should check on her.

I shake my head at the thought- I've developed an unsavory soft spot for her, and I can't stop the feeling of worry that overtakes me when I think about what she had to witness tonight. I knew it was going to get messy, and I knew she would have to see more than she might've wanted to, but I still don't understand how she ended up in the room with Jax alone when he pulled the trigger.

When I'm out on a job, everything always goes according to plan. I know where every person on my team is positioned at every moment- I never leave with questions. I acted on pure emotion at that bar, running off into the next room without a solid plan, leaving her alone with him- something my father always warned against.

He always said that a mind clouded by emotion was a weapon aimed at itself, and I never understood the saying until I had *her* to protect as well. Now, I'm drawing a blank trying to figure out where she was and why she ended up where she did. I should've kept her with me, stuck her between Kain and Beck so I knew she was protected. So she didn't have to look at him. Seeing the way she just shut down after everything happened makes me understand Beck's request even further.

Regret settles in my bones, and it's a deep ache- I should never have put her in that situation. I need to see her myself, even if she doesn't want to see me.

I mindlessly walk out of the kitchen and find myself in front of the door leading to her room. I raise my fist as if to knock, but decide against it, dropping my hand and opening the door, slipping inside.

The scene is reminiscent of my first time inside the room with her. She's bundled in the middle of the bed, the lights off.

"Georgia." I speak softly, unsure as to whether she's awake.

She startles at the sound of my voice, sitting up in bed to meet my eyes. She looks tired, and the sight of her rubbing the sleep from her eyes tugs on my heart strings. She looks so innocent, and guilt washes over me. She's undressed, as she's clutching the sheet to her chest as if her life depends on it.

"Are you okay?" I try, already anticipating her response. I can feel her glare, and even if she didn't physically wear one, the sentiment is the same.

"Sure. Can I go back to sleep?" She retorts, but my part in this conversation is far from over. Fixing my shit with Beck inspired me, I guess, and I'm not leaving this room until I've cleared the air with her, too.

I'm tired of treating her as a hostage here. I never expected this situation to take a turn like it has, but I'm determined to prove that I'm *not* my father, and showing her kindness is the beginning of that. At least, that's what I tell myself to distract myself from the fact that I'm aching to sink my cock into her and never let her go.

"No. We need to talk."

"I don't want to talk, Soren. I'm tired of talking, and feeling, and having to make decisions. I just want to sleep. I'll help you in the morning, but I don't have it in me tonight." She murmurs, and *god damn it,* there's the guilt again. "I'm sorry." She whispers, and I know it's still out of fear.

I step over to her bed and settle on the edge, getting as close as I possibly can without letting the fragile thread of my restraint break.

"You have nothing to apologize for." I whisper.

My hand drifts out and lands on her calf, rubbing small circles through the sheets. She stills, but I don't stop. Something about her reduces me to my most primal form. With her, I'm not the man I make myself out to be to the rest of the world. I want to sink to my knees in front of her and let myself be completely at her mercy. Coming to grips with this, I realize I can't fault Beck for his interest in her. She's a siren, and we're the helpless sailors drawn to her song. She's even begun to worm her way into Kain, which is a feat not even I have been able to achieve. I move closer to her, sliding my hand further up her leg until it rests on her knee.

"You have no idea what you do to us, pretty girl." I murmur, continuing to circle her leg, wishing I could feel her skin instead of these damned sheets. "When Beck brought you here, I hated you. I hated what you represented, who I thought you were with. Part of me still does. But now… We're fighting over you like animals, baby, and I don't think I'm going to be able to let you go."

She lets out a shaky breath, and I can feel her leg twitch under my touch.

"I'm sorry for all the shit we've put you through. I thought it was the only way, and until now it *was* the only way. For me. But I feel so fucking guilty, and I hate that you make me feel this way, but you do. I feel guilty for keeping you in that cell, guilty for hurting you, guilty for making you watch that man die. I'm running on overdrive trying to figure all my shit out while all I can think about is *you*. How much I hate you. How sorry I am for what I've done. How much I want you." I admit.

Laying my thoughts out like this is strange- I'm not one to speak my mind this freely, especially in front of someone I don't fully trust.

Yet with her, it's different.

There's something disarming about her, something that makes me feel like the human parts of me that I've spent years hiding don't need to be hidden anymore. For the first time in a long while, I want someone to see me, to fully understand what I'm thinking.

When she doesn't respond, I still my hand on her leg, but don't remove it.

"You still don't feel like talking?" Again, no reply. I shake my head, pulling my hand away from her leg in preparation to stand and walk out of there, leaving everything I just said for her to chew on. But then, something snaps, and I forget the one rule I've imposed on everyone.

Fuck it.

I rush forward and grab her shoulders, crashing my lips to hers. She resists me at first and fights to pull away, but there's no way in hell I'm stopping now. After a beat, she kisses me back, feverish and hungry.

Maybe I'm not thinking straight- call it riding out the adrenaline rush from tonight, but I plan to claim every inch of her. I take her bottom lip between my teeth and bite down hard enough to elicit a moan from her. The sound goes straight to my cock, my pants suddenly becoming too tight. *Music to my fucking ears.*

I pull her closer, the covers falling away from her body. Before I can fully look at her, she breaks the kiss, gasping for breath, her hands frantically searching for the sheet to pull back around her. I grab both her wrists in one hand, pushing her back against the bed until her back hits the mattress, pinning her arms above her head.

"Not a fucking chance, pretty girl. Let me see you. All of you."

I rip the sheets away from her lower half, exposing her completely, and I swear I start to drool at the sight. I can't make out much given how dark the room is, but my eyes have adjusted enough to make out the curve of her tits, her hips, and how her legs have already begun to part for me. My free hand begins to explore her body freely, running across her chest and cupping her breast, brushing across her nipples. They're already hard under my touch, and the pad of my thumb chases the pebbled skin.

My mouth moves to her neck, leaving a trail of sloppy kisses as I lick and suck at her skin. I make sure to leave my mark there, and I'm sure the morning light will reveal a masterpiece of purple and red across her throat. I find my way back to her lips, kissing her hard enough to bruise. Georgia tastes like heaven, so goddamn sweet that I fear I'm already addicted.

I pull my hand lower, circling her navel, then lower, to where I've been dying to be since I first laid eyes on her. She's *soaked*, and my mouth is watering for her. She's wet enough that I can sink two fingers into her with ease, and I waste no time pushing them in and pulling them out, relishing in the tiny moans she gives me. I start to move faster, curling my fingers as I push them inside, and she gets louder.

"That's it, pretty girl. Let this whole fucking building know how I'm making you feel."

I fuck her faster with my fingers like a crazed man, desperate to hear what she sounds like when she comes. I angle my hand so that my palm makes contact with her clit, brushing against the swollen bundle of nerves with every thrust of my fingers, and it sends her over the edge. She clenches around my fingers as she cries out, throwing her head back as she comes, and her release soaks my hand. I nearly blow my own load as I bear witness to the goddess writhing beneath me.

My goddess.

I take my fingers into my mouth, savoring her sweet taste, and release her hands. Again, she searches for the sheet- realizing it's long gone, discarded somewhere on the floor, she crosses her arms in front of her chest to cover herself. I wrench them away, pinning them at her sides.

"What did I say? Not a fucking chance. I'm not done with you."

I rip my shirt over my head and fumble with my belt. Her small hands reach up and carefully stroke the sides of my body, mirroring my previous movements on her leg. I melt under her touch, shoving my pants down my legs and kicking them off. I hope she's on birth control of some kind, because I have no time to search for a condom in this godforsaken labyrinth of a basement. I need to be inside her *now*.

My cock is painfully hard and leaking as I grab the base, slapping it against her clit a few times before lining it up with her entrance.

"I'm never letting you go, pretty girl. You're mine."

She gasps as I shove inside, burying myself inside her without warning. I let out a string of curses as her pussy grips me like a vice.

Her arms wrap around my neck, her legs around my waist, and *fuck,* I'm a goner. I fuck her furiously, giving her everything I confessed before. I give her all of my hate and anger towards her, but all of it is replaced by the most intense lust I've ever felt with every thrust into her. Her legs start to shake around my waist, and I know she's close.

"Say it, Georgia." I grunt, hearing her cry out in response. "Say it. Who do you belong to, huh?" I slow my pace, giving her a chance to answer me.

I want to hear her say it. I *need* to hear her say that she's mine- at least for tonight. At least for right now.

"You." She breathes. "Only you."

Good fucking girl.

I pick up the pace again, determined to give her another before I explode, my hips snapping against hers.

"Come for me, pretty girl. I'm not going to last much longer." I get out through clenched teeth, desperate to feel her come around my cock before I finish.

I slide my hand between us to find her clit, pinching it hard and thrumming it with my thumb.

"F-fuck, Soren, I'm so close. Please don't stop." She whimpers.

"I'm not gonna stop, baby. Not until you give me one more."

Her legs are shaking violently now, and with one final thrust, she's coming violently pulling me in deeper. I'm close behind, spilling into her until I feel like I'm going to seize. I've never come this hard before, not with anyone.

I press my forehead against hers as we catch our breath.

I know I shouldn't have allowed myself to get this close to her, and I damn sure shouldn't have taken her and claimed her like this.

But it's too little too late, because I don't think there's a force of nature that could get me to give her up.

I slide out of her, running my fingers across her swollen pussy once more, not ready to get my hands off of her quite yet.

She quivers and whimpers beneath me, her hips writhing against my hand as if she can't decide if she wants more or not. I lean in to kiss her once more, before quickly locating my clothes and pulling them back on. I find the comforter and sheet and drape them back around her, resting my hand on her head in place of words. I tuck her hair behind her ear, lean in and kiss her forehead, and start for the door, unable to form words.

Don't be a dick, Soren. I pause right before the door; almost sure I can hear the even breathing of sleep taking her again.

"I meant everything I said, Georgia. Good night."

With that, I slip back outside, as quietly as I entered, and rush for my bedroom. When I'm safely inside, I throw myself onto my bed, the ghost of a smile on my lips.

This was a mistake. A damn good one, maybe one I want to repeat again. And again. And again.

I smell like her, and it consumes me. For the first time in a long time, sleep finds me easily- call it pleasantly sated and thoroughly fucked, but truthfully, I know it's because I finally gave into the one thing I've been avoiding like the plague. She's mine, fuck the intel, and I'm going to do whatever it takes to ensure she never leaves my sight again.

Georgia

I sleep easy for once, a dreamless, calm rest that I've craved for almost a week. When I wake, I'm *deliciously* sore, and scenes from last night dance through my head, clouding my flashbacks of Emmett Riley's lifeless eyes. I can't rid myself of the smile that dances on my lips, and I don't want to.

I'm still a bit in shock at Soren's words- he's never letting me go. I don't let myself get too attached, though. I've been with enough men to know that the things they tell you when your legs are spread are *never* true, and I'd be stupid to believe him. Still... hearing it did something to me. No one's ever said anything like that before- not in a way that didn't make me feel dirty or afraid. For once, it didn't.

I sit up, the sheets slipping from my shoulders as a run my hands through my hair. I can't help but think about Beck. I shouldn't feel guilty- what we did wasn't anything *real-* it was heat and chaos and too much adrenaline, not a promise. But even still, the thought of him finding out about what Soren and I did... it makes my stomach twist in a way that *really* feels like guilt. Maybe because he was the first man in a long time to touch me without taking something from me. Maybe because for a second, I felt like his, in the same way I feel like Soren's now, too.

And now… now I've gone and let someone else have me. Someone who scares me just as much as he fascinates me. It's not real feelings- I know better than that- but it's something, and that something feels dangerously close to betrayal.

I groan as I roll out of bed and stretch, stepping into the bathroom. After a shower and a quick brush of my teeth, I dress and carefully make the bed, crisp corners and all. This isn't *my* space, and I always leave it the way I found it, just in case. I don't want to make them angry- Sykes always made me make the bed before I left our- *his* bedroom.

When I step out of the room, I smell something cooking, and I follow my nose into the kitchen. Beck and Jax are there, hunched over the bar, engrossed in something playing loudly on Beck's phone.

Kain stands at the stove, shirtless and wearing- an *apron*? My jaw goes slack. He's got his back to me, but I can tell the apron is made for a woman, teal with red flowers. It looks like something you'd see your grandmother in as she cooks Thanksgiving dinner- not something a nearly seven-foot-tall thug would typically be caught dead in.

They hear my footsteps, and Jax throws a look over his shoulder, scoffing and rolling his eyes at me before turning his back again. Beck doesn't look back, and I try not to let it sting- I guess what happened between us meant nothing to him. I'm not sure why I dwell on it- it means nothing to me, too. *Right?*

When Kain turns around though, he frowns, surely taking in my shocked expression.

"What, Georgia?" He remarks, glaring at me.

"Nothing. Nothing at all." I manage, choking back laughter.

He looks down at himself, and back up at me, his face unamused.

"It's for the oil. I don't like it when it pops, it hurts. Have something to say?" He challenges, raising an eyebrow. I say nothing.

"Nah," Beck starts. "He wears it because he feels pretty in it. Don't let him lie to you, I've seen him wear it while making a salad."
Jax chuckles, and I breathe a laugh.

"Yeah, he wears it out sometimes, with nothing underneath. Sometimes he wears it with fishnets." Jax continues, pulling a full belly laugh out of Beck.

"That's enough from the peanut gallery." Kain growls, shaking his head and turning back to the stove.

He reaches up to one of the cabinets, and while the apron looks silly, his back muscles do *not* as they stretch.

He grabs a stack of plates and begins dishing up whatever he's made. I lean over to see past Beck- egg whites, tomatoes, spinach, and a grey-colored toast are arranged neatly on each plate. He slides a finished plate in front of Beck, and a second one to Jax, his without tomatoes.

"Give me Jax's tomatoes, Kainy-baby." Beck calls out, and though he glares at Beck, he obliges, spooning a few extra tomatoes onto Beck's plate.

"Jax hates tomatoes, Georgia. Can you believe that? They're like the best fruit. He's insane." He says to me through a mouthful of food.

"First, quit telling her shit about me. Second, they're vegetables. Third, don't call people names for not liking the same things as you, it's rude." Jax retorts, reaching over and taking a bite out of Beck's toast. He gasps dramatically, and leans over, stealing Jax's clean off his plate.

I chuckle. It's strange to see them so… normal, after seeing them in action.

"Actually, they are fruits." I say under my breath, and the guys stop eating, turning towards me. "And they're great. Very high in antioxidants."

"Ha!" Beck calls out. "I'm going to make you eat one someday. Maybe while you're sleeping."

"I'll make *you* eat something while you're sleeping, but it won't be a tomato." Jax mutters, turning back to his breakfast.

He looks up, like he's going to ask a question, and Kain's there- a bottle of hot sauce in his hand, pulled from the fridge. Jax takes it, puckers his lips, and blows Kain a few noisy kisses. Kain grumbles- per usual.

"Thanks." Jax mumbles, opening the bottle and *drenching* his eggs in hot sauce.

"Jesus." I murmur, and he holds up his middle finger, not turning to look at me.

"Here." Kain gruffs, placing a plate on the edge of the island, in front of the empty barstool next to Beck.

"Oh, uhm, I'm not hungry. Thank you though." I lie. My stomach is growling so loud, I'm surprised they can't hear it.

"Shut up." He drawls, clearly seeing through my lie. "Eat. Don't make me tell you again."

That earns a chorus of 'oooohs' out of Beck and Jax, like a child hearing his friend get called to the principal's office.

"Enough from you two. I mean it. What is this, a fucking kindergarten?" Kain snaps, and they stop. After a beat, Jax's shoulders begin to shake with quiet laughter, which sets Beck off, and they start up again.

"Jesus fuck." Kain whispers and turns back towards the stove.

I walk over to the barstool, slowly sinking into it, keeping my limbs as close to my body as I can to avoid touching them. I'm uncomfortable and feel out of place- I feel foreign being thrown into the dynamic that is so clearly established. I tuck into my food, trying to eat as fast as possible so I can get away from them quicker.

I hear the creak of the door, and I jerk my head backwards, feeling a bit of relief as a zombie-like Soren rolls in, looking as disheveled as I've ever seen him. He's dressed in an oversized hoodie and sweats, his hair a wreck, his skin still creased from the sheets.

We lock eyes, and I turn back around. I'm not sure that he wants the others to know about last night, and I'm sure not going to be the one to spill the beans. My heart nearly drops out of my chest when he steps closer and places a kiss to my cheek, lingering for a moment.

It's barely a brush, but the heat of it brands me, a quiet claim that everyone in the room feels. He lingers long enough for the air to tighten around us before pulling back, his gaze flicking to Kain- still in his apron, still watching.

The low sound that rumbles from Kain's throat makes the hairs on my arms rise. Soren's brows jump once, a faint smirk ghosting over his mouth before he turns away, leaving the silence to choke the rest of us.

I glance at the others- their faces in varying degrees of disgust, anger, and confusion. The room is wound tight as a wire, and for a second, I swear even the air forgets to move. I drop my head, my cheeks burning with embarrassment.

I can feel Beck's eyes on me before I even look. The weight of his stare burns through my skin, and guilt settles heavy in my chest. I don't even know why- he's got no claim on me, not really- but the thought of him seeing Soren touch me like that makes something in my heart crack.

Jax scoffs, muttering something about PDA and eating, and Kain's eyes are still hard, set on Soren, but he doesn't seem to notice. He heads to the fridge, brushing my back with his hand on his way past, and grabs a can from the middle shelf.

"So, are we just not going to talk about tha-" Jax starts, but Beck cuts him off with an elbow to the ribs, and Jax hisses. "Ow, fucker. They're still not healed."

Soren chuckles, but doesn't acknowledge Jax's unfinished question, at least not out loud. Instead, he comes to stand behind me, leaning over and resting his chin on top of my head, answering the question all of them probably have- loud and clear. I don't move, and stare back into my lap. Beck jumps up, grabbing his unfinished plate and throwing it into the sink. He turns to me, his eyes sad, his brow creasing. It makes my stomach hurt. I say nothing.

When he turns to Soren, it's all anger, his glare vicious, his eyes hard.

"Hypocrite." He spits, before turning on his heel and stalking out of the room. Jax follows closely behind him, leaving his plate on the island.

Kain scoffs, reaching over and scraping it into the trash before placing it gently into the sink. He doesn't stop staring at Soren, though, his gaze hard and unwavering.

"Animals, both of them." He mumbles.

"What did he mean, Soren? Why was he so pissed?" I question, sliding out from the barstool to turn and face them.

"It's because of you." Kain mutters under his breath.

"Kain." Soren hisses, but he doesn't deny it.

"No, don't yell at him. What does he mean? Why is Beck angry?"

I can guess why Beck's angry. I just want to hear Soren say it, to make it real.

Soren stutters, unable- or unwilling- to give me a clear answer. I look towards Kain, a brow raised. I don't want to push my luck too hard with him- I know he'd make good on his threats to take me over his knee, and I've already muddied the waters enough.

"If you won't tell her, I will." Kain says, matter-of-factly.

"Kain." Soren repeats, his tone sharp. He doesn't elaborate.

"Someone better start fucking talking." I grit, earning me a look from both of them.

Kain's brows raise, eyes sharp with a challenge.

"You know better than that. Watch your mouth. What did I tell you?"

"What the fuck? *You* watch your mouth with her. What did you tell her?" Soren grills.

"That's between her and I. You won't answer her questions, I won't answer yours." He quips back.

I have to hide my smirk.

"Fucking fine." Soren says, exasperated. "I told them to keep their hands off you- no touching, no *anything*. Frankly, I am a bit of a hypocrite, because it's clear that I *have*."

Oh.

"That's why you hit Beck, right? That night after we saw Jax fight? You hit him because he touched me." I state, already knowing the answer, and hating myself for it.

"Yes, Georgia. That's why I hit him." He replies.

I look over at Kain, a knowing look in my eyes. His eyebrows jump, a silent 'told you so'. He told me last night he wasn't allowed to touch me, no matter how badly I wanted him to. He didn't want to face Soren afterwards.

"You're a dick." I glare at Soren, and he holds his hands up.
"Listen, I didn't expect it to happen, Georgia. I didn't do it to spite my brothers, if that's what you're thinking. If you regret it, just say that." He challenges, and he's got me there. *Shit.*

"I don't *regret* anything, Soren. But you can't treat me like I'm a fucking object! I don't belong to anyone but myself." I tell him.
"That's where you're wrong, baby. You're mine now."

With that, he picks me up, throwing me over his shoulder and starting for the door. I pound on his back, but he ignores me, laughing. I spare one final look at Kain, and he mouths one word- *ours.*

What? My eyes widen, and he smirks at me, sending heat to my core. *I'm so fucked.*

Kain

It's been two weeks since my private encounter with Georgia. Two weeks since she bewitched me so badly that I haven't thought of anything but her. Two weeks of her presence in our lives, and it doesn't seem like the others have any plans to send her away any time soon.

She consumes my every waking thought. I have visions of her, standing naked in front of me, her own hands giving her the pleasure that I so desperately wanted to reach out and give her myself.

I fucking *hate* her, maybe more so now than I did before. She's turned from this fragile, delicate thing to something fiery. She's gotten too comfortable with us, and she makes us all too aware of it. But I was right- she is going to ruin my family, and I left that door wide open for her.

I know now that Soren's claimed her for himself- several times, and quite loudly, at that- and he practically pisses on her every time she's around. He hasn't asked her for any more intel and has given her free reign of the compound, on the condition that she doesn't leave.

It infuriates me, seeing her standing in *our* kitchen, over *my* coffee pot, wearing *his* clothing. I haven't felt anger like this since the fire, and I vowed

that I would never let anything make me this angry
again.

I can't escape her- her smell has ingrained
itself into the basement, and every time I come home
I'm reminded of that night.

I don't know whether to be ashamed of my
cowardice- of needing Soren's unspoken order not to
touch her to mask my fear and justify doing nothing
but staring at her- or proud that I did what he wanted
and left her untouched, albeit nearly under duress. All
I know is that I need her *gone*, and for my life to go
back to how it was- for our family to be restored to
what it was.

I find her one morning alone in the kitchen,
wearing one of Soren's shirts and a pair of cut-off
shorts. Georgia wakes unusually early for someone
with nothing but time on her hands. She's typically up
before Soren is, around five or so.

Today, she's completely lost in her own
world, humming something quietly and darting
around the kitchen like she owns it. I can't quite make
out what she's doing as she flits around, but I know it
can't be anything good. I stand and observe her, as I
often do these days, trying to compel her with my
mind to vacate the space. She never does, much to
my dismay.

When she finally looks up from the island and meets my gaze, she startles, eyes wide, her hand flying to her chest and a dramatic gasp leaving her mouth.

"Holy *shit*, Kain, you nearly made me pee my pants. You've got to warn a girl when you're in here."

"Apologies. I didn't realize I had to announce myself in my own kitchen." I grunt, moving towards the coffee pot. It's then that I see it- what she's been up to. I turn to her slowly, catching the sheepish look written all over her face.

"What the fuck is this?" I question, not making any attempts to hide my frustration with her.

There are *stickers*. All. Over. The. Kitchen. At least twenty, all brightly colored and absolutely nauseating to look at. The fridge, the cabinets, and worst of all- *my motherfucking coffee machine*. Right in the center of the lid, a big, red sticker. I can barely make out what it says, but I can read the word 'spite', and I'm seething. It can't say anything useful.

"Where did you get these, and why the *fuck* did you ruin the kitchen with them?" My voice is deadly calm- I don't want to explode on her, but I'm very close.

"Erm, Beck got them for me. I figured this place needed some, I don't know, lightheartedness?" She replies, a blush creeping up her neck and onto her cheeks. *Goddamn it Beck.* "Come on, you can't deny that this one is *so* fitting, right? It's you to a tee!" She giggles, but this is nothing to giggle about.

I want to ask her what they say, and the twinge of embarrassment I feel about not understanding only fuels my rage further.

I scowl at her, silencing her laughter, and begin to peel at the edges of the sticker. It peels back unevenly, the adhesive stronger than I anticipated, and I nearly launch the thing off the counter in frustration.

Since the night I bathed her, she's done everything possible to get under my skin. She's constantly commenting on my demeanor, my clothing, my habits, and anything else she can find to pick at. I can usually ignore it- I can usually ignore *her*, but this is a step above her previous annoyances. This is vandalism at its finest, and I won't stand for it.

Acting out of pure frustration and instinct, I rear back and deliver a sharp smack to her ass, giving her just a taste of what I want to do to punish her for this. Realizing what I've done, I jerk my hand back as if it's been burned, while her face pales as though she's seen a ghost.

I want to apologize for my lapse in control, but my anger surges, dominating my thoughts.

"Remember when I told you I'd take you over my knee, little one? That promise still stands. You will remove all of this mess from my kitchen immediately, and you will not do anything to tarnish the space going forward." I growl, my glare sharp enough to ignite a flame.

Instead of cowering and obeying like I expect, she raises her chin, a look of defiance in her eyes.

"No." She replies simply, the one word making me see red.

"Excuse me?"

"I said *no*."

I stare at her for a beat, then approach her slowly. When we're nearly touching, I stoop down, getting eye-level with her.

"You will not tell me *no*, Georgia. Do what you're told or take your punishment. Your choice." I manage.

Being this close to her is clouding my judgment, and I know if I don't step away soon, I'll do something I may not be able to take back.

She cocks a smug eyebrow at me, and my hand reaches out, encircling her wrist where it's planted on her hip. I squeeze hard, almost missing the flash of lust that crosses her face.

"Is this really the hill you want to die on, little one?" I murmur, tightening my grip on her wrist. As if by divine intervention, the door bursts open and Jax strides in, rolling his eyes at the sight of Georgia.

"Saved by the bell." I murmur, releasing her and stepping back before Jax noticed our close proximity.

He's been steering clear of her at all costs since his initiation, even going as far as delegating his work here to others, and I'm jealous of him for that.

He's been fighting nearly every night since he was initiated, keeping him mostly away from the compound. He sleeps at the warehouse, only coming home when he needs a change of clothes or a decent meal. I have half a mind to go with him most nights, to stay away from this place as well, but I know I'm needed here. I've taken more jobs, keeping our corners clean and our men in check, throwing myself into my work. Unfortunately, that usually ends with me having to come back to the compound, back into the lion's- or lioness's- den.

Jax walks over to the fridge, his hand pausing on the handle as he takes in the new additions. That bastard actually *chuckles* at it, like it's not a heinous crime.

"Who did this?" He asks, hiding his laughter under his breath when I groan out of frustration. He turns to look at Georgia, raising an eyebrow at her. When she shrugs and turns away, he laughs again, out loud this time.

"You must have a death wish, fucking around in here like this. Shit's funny though, I'll give you that." He snorts, pulling out an energy drink, which coincidentally has also been marked with one of her stickers. I can't read his either. Heat flashes across my face- my embarrassment slightly begins to overtake my anger. I'll make it a point to practice more this week.

"That one wasn't meant for you, but if the shoe fits, I guess." She murmurs, clearly anticipating a rash reaction out of the smaller man. He picks up the can, eyes narrowing as he reads the sticker. A smirk tugs at the corner of his mouth, but he quickly wipes it away, masking his amusement. "This is rude." he mutters, before cracking it open and taking a long sip, acting like it doesn't faze him at all. He looks at the can again, and his eye roll is all I need to see to confirm that whatever's written on that sticker would've pissed me off. *Maybe I'm glad I can't read.*

"Clean this shit up before Kain has a heart attack. Soren might put up with it, but the rest of us live here too." He snaps, taking his can and stalking out of the kitchen.

"Barely." She mutters under her breath. When I shoot her a glare, her cheeks flush and she drops her eyes.

"You will respect my brothers in my presence, Georgia. That is non-negotiable." I growl.

Her fire returns, any embarrassment she might've felt at my scolding gone as she returns my glare with one of her own. My dick twitches, and I have to will myself not to bend her over the counter.

That's it. Keep pushing me. Strike one.

"You don't get to tell me what to do. And neither does he, for that matter." She squares her shoulders, planting her feet and crossing her arms over her chest.

Just like that, little one. That's strike two.

She's riding a fine line, and if she doesn't back down, I'm not going to be able to keep my hands off of her for much longer.

"Georgia." I warn, a low growl leaving my throat.

"What, are you going to hit me?" She turns and drapes herself across the island, sticking her ass out dramatically. "*Oh,* Kain, please don't spank me! I've been a good girl, I swea-" She croons, but I cut her off with my hand around her throat.

Strike three.

I move at lightning speed, boxing her in with my hips pressed against her ass. I have no idea what I'm doing, but I know that I want to hurt her. Badly. And the worst part about what I want is that I know deep down, in the darkest and most masochistic parts of her, she wants it too.

"Is this what you want? Soren's not enough for you? You need me to put you in your place too?"

"Kain-"

"That's not an answer. Is that what you need?"

"I- I don't-"

I tighten my grip on her throat, stopping her sentence. The fingers on my free hand act on their own accord, tracing a light line down her spine, stopping at the top of her ass. I lean down, my lips touching the shell of her ear and her scent invading my nose. She smells like the cherry blossom soap Soren brought in for her, and it drives me *crazy*.

"A good rule of thumb, little one- don't talk back, and don't ever assume that I'm not a man of my word. If I really wanted to, I could spank your ass raw over this counter, and you'd enjoy it, though I plan to make that as difficult as possible for you. I bet if I reached down right now, your panties would already be soaked with the thought of that, right?" She mewls in response, unable to form proper words with how hard I'm pressing against her throat. "Soren might've had you first but believe me when I say that means *nothing* here. You're a tool for us to use, and when we're done, you're gone, and if you keep this up, I may have to start using you for more than just intel and claim that ass before he does." With that, I release her, shoving her forward into the counter and stalking out of the kitchen, not wanting to wait around for her to push me further. She's a spitfire, I'll give her that, and as much as I want to hate her for it, it turns me on so much I don't know what to do with myself.

As I enter the hallway, I'm nearly knocked over by a very winded, very frazzled looking Nate. I'm stunned into silence- the others never venture down to the basement, especially not our resident hacker who tends to keep to himself in the cave he's established upstairs. He's got every piece of equipment readily available, and even stuff that you can't find- military grade shit.

His normally neat brown hair is slick with sweat, clinging to his forehead and shoulders, and he reeks like an ashtray. His glasses are hanging halfway off his nose, probably from running into me. Nate's a small guy, maybe 5'11", and skinny as a rail- smacking into me at full speed probably felt like he was hitting a brick wall.

"What the fuck, Nate?" I growl, steadying myself after I'd gotten a good look at him.

Something must be very wrong, or he wouldn't be standing in front of me.

"I'm sorry, I didn't want to come down here, but I couldn't wait, and no one would answer the damn phone." He gasps, bracing his hands on his knees to catch his breath. "I ran all the way here. I'm so fucking out of shape, man."

I give him a pass this time, because I have no idea where I left my phone. I hate the thing, but Soren makes me carry it around, something about always being connected. It's a distraction at best- the amount of time Beck spends on it should be considered criminal, and I refuse to have it on me unless I'm on a job.

"Spit it out, Nate. I'm not getting any younger."

"I found it." He manages.

I cock an eyebrow at him, waiting for further explanation. As far as I knew, Nate wasn't assigned to find anything other than the places The Iron Brotherhood frequents and given that it'd been two weeks since we'd heard anything from him, I was sure that his leads all ended up dead.

"Elaborate. I'm not a goddamn mind reader."

"The clubhouse, Kain. I fucking found it."

"You'd better be absolutely sure that what you *think* you found is real before you bring this to anyone else."

"I'm sure, man. I've never been surer of anything else. I have the street address, and I've tapped into the security feed. There's too much leather walking in and out of there for it to be anything else."

"Soren!" I shout, loud enough to hopefully rouse him from sleep and get him moving. "Soren, now!"

Within seconds, he's scrambling out of his bedroom, hopping towards us as he tugs his boots on, his shirt halfway on and his gun peeking out of his waistband.

"What? What happened?" He barks, righting himself, his hand reaching for his gun. He spots Nate and his face drops, his eyebrows knitting together.

"Who's dead? What happened? Why are you down here?" He questions at rapid fire.

"Tell him what you told me." I whisper, gesturing towards Soren.

"I found the clubhouse, boss. I've got an address and security feeds."

Soren's hand flies out, grabbing Nate's collar and shoves him into the wall.

"If you're fucking around, you're dead. I don't care how much I need you." He growls, pressing the smaller man harder into the wall.

"I'm not joking, man, this is the real deal. Come see for yourself if you don't believe me." Nate rasps.

I lock eyes with Soren, giving him a small nod.

If Nate found what he thinks he found, this could change everything. Jax will avenge his parents, the Vipers will finally get back on top, and I'll finally be rid of the blonde-haired blue-eyed devil that's wormed her way into our lives.

Beck

"How did you even find this?" I ask Nate, who sits in front of his wall of monitors, preening like a peacock.

"Honestly? I didn't even try. I've never seen these cameras before, and they were wide open- no encryption, no firewall, nothing. Either someone's sloppy, or someone's baiting me, but I cover my tracks. This is legit."

We've been sitting around Nate's computer for what seems like hours, watching men come and go from the abandoned-looking house on the monitors. My jaw is slack in disbelief.

We've been searching for this spot non-stop since the murder of Jax's parents, and it almost doesn't seem real staring at it now.

"Play that again." Soren commands, and Nate rewinds the footage for the tenth time in a row.

It's unassuming, an old house on the outskirts of Shadeview Heights that we must've passed over dozens of times. Soren's meticulous and slow to start, which I- of course- complain about. If it were up to me, we'd go in guns blazing and handle it- none of this boring strategic shit. To punish me, he's making us watch old security footage as some kind of planning exercise- why, I have no idea. I'll give Soren this- with the number of men in that house, we have to go in ready and with a solid plan- our anger alone is not strong enough to take it down.

I glance over at Jax, who stares into his lap. He refuses to look at the screen, partially because his nerves are shot, but mostly because he's reliving all that shit over again. The last time we went into something like this, it was a trap, and he didn't come out whole. I reach out, squeezing his knee twice and offering a small smile. I won't let anything happen to him again.

"Let's go." I whisper, just loud enough to where he can hear me. "We've seen enough. We're not doing anything tonight."

He nods and stands, trudging out of the room. The others shoot me puzzled glances, and I shrug as if I didn't just tell him to leave.

"I'll handle it. We'll be back."

"Hurry. We need to finish strat-" Soren starts but I cut him off before he can bore me to death.

"Yeah, yeah, yeah. Plans, strategy, don't go in blind. I think I got it. I'm going to get him; we'll be back when we're back."

I slam the door behind me quickly to shut Soren up as he protests- something about being fast. *Yeah right.*

I might come right when he calls me, but one thing for certain- I don't come quickly any other time.

I catch Jax in the hallway outside Nate's office, slumped against the wall waiting for me. It's loud in the main part of the warehouse, filled with bass-heavy music and the chatter of the men and women who occupy the space. I gesture towards the stairs, and he starts for them, his head hanging. I've had enough of this mopey bullshit, I've decided, and I run to catch up with him. He needs a pick-me-up, and I want to get him alone, away from the prying eyes of the others.

I dart in front of him, grabbing his wrist and pulling him towards the garage.

"Beck, I don't want to go anywhere. Please, just let me go to bed." He murmurs, but I'm not having any of that.

I push him out into the garage, where we find our bikes parked- two black Aprilia RS 660s. I texted a few of my guys to bring them around, as to not make Jax wait any longer than he needed to.

We stole these a few months back from some rich idiot just outside of Oakridge. It took us a few hours to coordinate getting them back here without getting caught, but we did it and spent hours in the garage fully customizing them- and scratching the VINs off. They're not cheap bikes by any means, so we haven't really been able to take them out and open them up yet since we figured they'd still be too hot to ride, but I think tonight is the perfect time. The helmets I ordered are hanging from the handlebars, equipped with Bluetooth mics in each so we could talk to each other during rides.

I glance over at him, and his face lights up like he's just seen his favorite toy. I arch an eyebrow and nod toward the bikes, and he practically skips over to them, grabbing a helmet and looking it over. Already, there's a bit of a spark back in his eyes- a tiny sparkle in those deep blues. The tension in his shoulders begins to fall away. It's not much, but anything's better than the look on his face back in that office.

"Are you sure? I really don't want to go to jail tonight." He asks warily, his eyebrows raised as his fingers ghost over the handlebars, like he's too afraid to touch them.

"I'm sure, Eight Ball. Pick one and let's go before the others realize we've left them."

He wastes no time climbing onto one of the bikes and throwing his helmet on. I jump onto the other, turning the key to start the ignition and relishing at the purr of the engine beneath me. I close my eyes and lean my head back, a wave of nostalgia washing over me.

This is how it used to be, before everything got complicated and Jax fell apart. Before our focus became only about revenge.

When we were happy.

I don't have much time to reminisce, though, as I feel a gust of wind and hear the squeal of tires. Before I can even blink, Jax is already out of the garage and halfway down the block. I shake my head, quickly throwing my own helmet on and pulling out after him.

When the Bluetooth finally connects and I've caught up to him, I can hear him singing- okay, more like screaming- something, an angry sounding song that I don't recognize. I'm right behind him, and I know he knows I'm there, but he weaves in and out of traffic without a care in the world.

This is what I wanted, for him to forget everything for just a moment and just *be*. I chuckle at his singing, and he quiets, seemingly having forgotten about the connection between our helmets.

"I liked it, keep going." I tease, a smile dancing on my lips. "At this rate, you'll be able to leave the life behind and do whatever *that* was full time."

His laugh comes through, and warmth floods my chest. It's always been the one thing that can truly ground me, and I don't hear nearly enough of it these days.

"Whatever man, you're just jealous that you don't have these pipes."

I roll my eyes under my helmet. "Slow down speed racer, you're riding that thing like you stole it. I can barely catch up."

"We *did* steal them, Beck."

He's got me there.

"I'll race you. Bet you can't outrun the cops faster than I can." He calls out, and his bike takes off like a rocket, leaving me in a cloud of dust. He's got something loud and violent playing through the Bluetooth on his phone, blaring inside my helmet. I know it's only a matter of time before the blue lights flash behind us, so I kick my bike into fourth and tear off after him.

We weave between traffic, cackling at angry honks of horns that follow us, flipping off the drivers as we blur by them. If there's one thing Jax and I are good at, it's this- organized chaos in places it doesn't belong. He splits the lanes, causing other drivers to swerve to avoid him, and I can only laugh and shake my head at him.

He rides like he's the only one on the road- with the type of expertise that only comes after years of trial and error, and more road rash and wrecked bikes than we'd care to admit.

After a while of causing minor traffic infractions, I see the signs for exit thirty-nine, and the memories flood in. When he pulls off on the all-too-familiar exit, I grin. He's heading to the spot, *our* spot.

It used to be a hiking trail, way back in the day, but when some old dude got robbed at gunpoint, the public seemed to avoid the area, making it a perfect spot for Jax and I to come and be left alone when things got too much. It's overgrown and kind of a dump, but it's ours.

After following the dirt path right off the exit, we reach the edge of the woods and he kills his bike, parking it far enough under the tree line that it's out of sight. I follow suit, and pull my helmet off, leaving it on the seat of the bike. My hair is damp with sweat and sticking to my forehead, and as I lean against Jax, I can feel that his is too. We stay like that for a moment, foreheads resting against one another, relishing in the quiet that seems to be a stranger to us these days.

Before, when Jax first came to us and his parents were still alive, we would find any excuse we could to come out here and just *be*. We'd smoked countless joints up here, camped here- this was our sacred spot- albeit just a forgotten trail on the outskirts of Oakridge.

After everything happened, I brought him out here to pick up his pieces without the distractions of whatever was going on back home, holding him through near-overdoses and wiping his tears. Now, I'm hoping the good memories will bring him out of the funk he's been in tonight and help him zero in on what we have to do.

I take his hand and lead him further down the trail to the clearing, taking in the view like it was the first time I'd ever seen it. The clearing looks over a rocky cliff, giving you unpolluted access to look at the moon. The cicadas are singing tonight, and it feels like something out of a fairytale- or as close as people like us can get.

I plop down in the dirt at the edge of the cliff and pull Jax down with me. He goes down easy and leans into me, his head nestling into my neck, and I wrap an arm around him, running my fingers idly through his wild hair.

"I missed this." He murmurs, snuggling deeper into my side.

I can only sigh in response- I know he's talking about the spot, but I missed having him close to me more than I missed this dumpy trail.

"Are you keeping your nose clean?" I ask him, tangling my fingers further into his hair. He's silent, and that answers my question more than his words could. I noticed his pupils before we left, and they're near blown- I know he's been using at some point today. "You need to get that shit in check, Jax. I mean it."

"Yeah, I know." He goes to push me off, but I catch his jaw and tilt his face towards mine.

"Seriously. You need to be focused. We're so close to putting an end to everything, and I'd hate for shit to get messed up because you can't stay clean for more than twenty minutes." I come off harsher than I intend to, but everything I'm saying to him is the truth. He shoves me away, turning his back to me.

"If you brought me out for another half-assed intervention, it's not going to work. I'm fine, and I don't need help."

My words immediately set him on edge. He begins to absentmindedly pick at his nails, looking anywhere but at me. I roll my eyes and fist his hair, yanking him backwards until his head's in my lap, his big blue eyes staring right up at me.

"I worry about you, you must know that, right? This shit eats at me until it's all I can think about. I don't want to plan your funeral, Jax."

My voice breaks- I can't let my tears slip out yet. Not in front of him. I can tell he's surprised by my honesty- like Soren, I don't tend to wear my heart on my sleeve like this, but I need him to hear it. He stills, refusing to meet my eyes. I'm almost glad he doesn't, because I swear if he looks at me, I'll start to

sob- I don't want him to see that right now. *Or maybe
I do*, I think. *Maybe he'll believe me if he sees it for himself.*

"I know." He murmurs after a while, and I
exhale loudly.

"I don't think you do. But I'm going to tell
you over and over again until you finally fix it."

When he doesn't respond, I let the silence
envelop us like a blanket. Sometimes the things we
leave unspoken resonate the most, and in this
moment Jax's shame is louder than anything he
could've said.

He rolls over, his cheek against my thigh, and
my hand finds its place back in his hair, letting the
soft strands ground me and ease my fear.

"Do you remember when we stayed up here
for so long that the guys thought we were dead?" I
chuckle, hoping the nostalgia will break the
awkwardness. He breathes a laugh, and I feel his
shoulders shake. *That's a start.*
"Soren was so mad at us. I've never seen his face that
red before."

I laugh- a real laugh- as I recount the memory.
We were new, still exploring what *this* was, and we
packed enough supplies to last us weeks up here. We
spent days in a tent with our phones off, tangled up in
each other, forgetting any responsibilities that we had
back with The Vipers. After the third day, I finally

turned my phone back on and it almost crashed with the number of incoming notifications from Soren and Kain.

When we finally made our way back to the compound, Soren yelled at us so badly that I'd thought the vein in his forehead was going to burst open, but it was all worth it. Having Jax to myself was- and still is- a rarity, and I'll deal with Soren's rage, even if it's just for a few minutes alone with him.

"His face wasn't the only thing that we left red, was it?" I quip, bouncing my thigh and making his body shake. I can't see his face, but I know him well enough to know he's blushing like a madman.

"I think you left bruises inside my throat that week." He laughs, sitting up to avoid being shaken any further. "I couldn't swallow right for days after we got back." *Damn straight.*

When his eyes lock onto mine, I can see the lust in them. His cheeks are red and flushed, and I reach out and trace his bottom lip with my finger.

"Do you need me to take care of you like that?" I ask him, watching his eyes widen at my question.

I've never given that to him; it's always been the other way around. I don't know if I've been hesitant or greedy, or maybe a bit of both, but he's always been the one on his knees- not me. But after

everything that's been working against us- the shit
with Georgia, the drugs, the death and the loss, I need
to show him what he means to me; how much I care
for him, how much I want him.

"I don't- Beck, I've never done that. I'm not-"

I shush him, effectively cutting off his word
vomit, and move to undo his belt.
"Trust me on this. Let me show you how I feel about
you."

He sighs, and I can feel the anxiety radiating
off him. "Jaxon. Relax. I've got you. I've always got
you."

I can feel how hard he is already, just from my
words, and I ache to touch him again, to feel his soft
skin. I work his jeans and boxers down his legs,
letting his cock spring free, salivating at the way it
smacks his stomach. I pause, feeling slightly
intimidated- I've never done this before, and I'm sure
I won't be any good at it. What if he doesn't like it?
But when my hand finally wraps around him, the
groan he lets out is loud enough to startle the birds
from the trees and leaves me feeling like a pro. All I
have to do is take care of my boy- I can do that. I've
always done that.

I push his shirt up a bit, exposing the
lower part of his stomach, and press soft kisses to his
navel. I can feel his ribs poking through his stomach-

he's always been small, but I have to fight to suppress the worry I feel at how skinny he is now. I move slowly, losing myself in his smell. He smells like he always does, like amber and gunpowder; the kind of smell that makes most people feel uneasy, but his kind of danger is the kind I want to get closer to. *Focus, Beck.*

When my lips finally wrap around the head of his cock, he cries out, a strangled sound that makes me hesitate. But when his fingers wrench themselves in my hair, pushing me further down, I smile, my mouth full of him.

"F-fuck, Beck, please don't stop." He whimpers, and I happily oblige. My hand never leaves his shaft as my lips slide down to meet my fist, carefully working him over. His whines grow more desperate, his hands pulling my hair so tightly that I'd be surprised if he didn't yank some out. I swirl my tongue around him and hollow my cheeks, taking him so deep that I gag- my knees buckle when he does the same to me- and he gasps.

"Oh, shit, Beck. I'm so close. Don't stop, fuck, please don't stop."

I'm aching to taste his release, so I oblige- I keep going, and his hips begin to snap upwards to meet my mouth. I release him with a pop, my hand continuing to work him over.

"Are you going to be my good boy and come for me?" I murmur, pausing to spit on my hand to reduce the friction.

"Yes, but please use your mouth. Please Beck, please let me come." He whines, pushing my head back towards where he needs me. I chuckle under my breath and give him full access to my throat. He fucks it hard, and I'm gagging, which only makes his thrusts come faster. He cups my face with both hands and drives in one final time, stilling when my nose meets his stomach, and his release pours down my throat. It's salty, but it tastes like him, and I greedily swallow every drop, lapping at the head of his cock when he moves to pull out of my mouth. He leans back on his hands, his breathing ragged, and I get to my knees and pull him into my arms.

"Thank you." He breathes into my ear, making me grin so hard my cheeks hurt.

"Anytime. That was fun." I can hear his breathy laugh, and the load in my chest feels almost nonexistent.

"I love you, Beck." I almost don't hear him, but we rarely say these words to each other- I could make them out in my sleep, and I don't think I could ever grow tired of hearing him say it.

"I love you too, Jax. Always will."
And it's true- I will always love him. He holds a piece

of my soul that I can never get back, and I don't think I'd ever want it back, anyways.

I stand, pulling him to his feet, giving him a second to redress, before pulling him back towards the bikes. I grab his helmet from its perch on the handlebars and press a quick kiss to his lips before sliding it over his head and fastening the buckle under his chin. I pat the top of his helmet twice, before turning and grabbing my own.

"I'll race you back. Whoever wins gets to top tonight."

He cackles, his laugh echoing through the speakers in my helmet, and I'm elated. My plan worked- this is the Jax, *my* Jax, that we need right now. He tears out of the drive, and I follow close behind him, hoping I get to keep him this way for more than just the twenty minute ride back home.

Jax

The ride back home has my legs feeling like concrete. I don't want to go back- the thought of planning to face my parents' killers again makes me want to puke. Spending those few moments with Beck almost makes up for what's waiting for me, but I know they won't be enough to stave away the anxiety that's bound to catch up to me.

I feel terrible for disappointing him in the way I have, what with my inability to keep sober for more than twenty minutes at a time. I know I need to get clean, I just don't know how. Things'll be better once I feel at peace again- once this shit is done and the girl is gone for good. Once I have my life back, and I'm not full of pain and rage and- everything else.

I don't even want to look at Soren right now, not until I've processed the shit that went down at the bar. I feel like a coward and a hero all at once- I got the job done, the one we were supposed to, right? I feel nothing for the man I shot. I thought it would feel worse, like maybe I'd be upset or cry or something, but I feel nothing.

What I don't understand is why I couldn't kill her, too. I hate her and what she stands for, what she reminds me of. But I see a little of myself in her, too. That just might be the root of my cowardice. She's broken, just like me. Her eyes reflect the same pain as mine do, and the look she wore when she thought she was going to die was eerily calm- I'm sure if I could've looked in a mirror on that night, I would've looked the same.

Sometimes I wish they would've done me the kindness of killing me, too. Living without my parents after watching them suffer, isn't worth it, and I'm too much of a pussy to handle it on my own. They were the best people. We never had much, but they always looked after me.

My dad was a Viper once, that's how the guys ended up picking me up. He left the life when I was born, something about not wanting me to grow up looking over my shoulder and seeing things that I shouldn't. He stayed around as a mechanic, picking up the jobs Soren's dad would throw to us, but it was never enough money to provide, not really.

Pregnancy was hard on my mom, and she wanted to be around, so she stayed home. She taught me how to read, how to ride a bike, how to cook and clean and take care of myself. She was a light in the dark world- just a ball of yellow and warm and softness. I miss her more than anything.

When I turned seventeen, I caught wind of how my family was really living. As a child, you never really understand- you might see that other kids have better toys and nicer houses, sure, but that's that. You don't think about money, or rent, or a nest egg. But when I got older, I couldn't turn a blind eye to it anymore.

Beck's voice crackles into my ears through the speakers in my helmet, a welcome distraction from my thoughts.

"Why are you so quiet? I gave it to you so good that it made you speechless, right?"

I can only laugh.

"You don't have to tell me, I already know. I've got mad skills." I can hear his quiet chuckle. Warmth floods my chest.

"Seriously though, get out of your head. I just got you back- give me a little more time before you shut me out again." I can't miss the sadness in his voice, and it makes my stomach hurt all over again.

Pulling back into the compound, we park the bikes right where we found them, making sure to shut the doors quickly in case we were followed.

Looking around the garage, nostalgia hits me like a truck.

I remember running off one night, after my parents went to sleep, and finding Beck on a street corner. I begged him for work; he was barely older than me and didn't really know what to do. When I mentioned who my dad was, he brought me right to his father, and I never left.

The compound became home after that. I sent money where I could, but I was needed here. Being close meant I got first pick of the jobs and learned the ins and outs fast.

Beck and I got close- closer than anyone could understand. I've been at his side since day one. He protected me, showed me the ropes of how a syndicate operates. Without him, I don't think I would've made it.

I find a few of my guys hanging around the garage, smoking and talking amongst themselves. When they see me walk by, they almost bow their heads. It makes me laugh.

"Where are we at with the stuff for Afterglow? It's nearly the weekend. Do they have what they need?" I ask the group.

Karim, the only one I trust to run our numbers, is the first one to respond. "Joey dropped off a few cases of E earlier this week. He put it in the back, and the rest is coming in tomorrow night. We'll be straight, Eight Ball, I promise. Another weekend in paradise- either that or they'll all be so high they won't care where they are." He laughs, his silver lip ring glinting in the fluorescent garage lighting as it moves.

"That's what I like to hear. Y'all have a good night, I'm getting a drink." I nod to dismiss them, and head inside, straight for the bar. I don't bother waiting for someone, instead hopping the bar and grabbing the first bottle my hand touches. I walk around to our normal spot in the back, with a perfect view of everything that happens on the floor.

When I sit, I can see Beck walk in, his eyes scanning the room. When they fall on me, his eyebrows knit together, a look of concern on his face. *You good?* He mouths giving me a thumbs up. I nod, waiving him off. I need to be alone right now anyways.

He flashes me his signature smile and heads for the elevator, making me consider following him down to continue what we started earlier. I'm still in shock that I had him that way- we've fooled around for years now, and he's *never* done that for me, no one has. Now that I've had it once, I know I'll be begging for his mouth forever.

I'm pulled out of my daydreams of watching Beck on his knees by an unwelcome flash of blonde hair. Ever since Soren climbed into Georgia's bed, he's let her roam free, with the request that we keep the keys to any vehicles under lock and key, hidden away from her. She may feel a bit freer, but she's

every bit the captive that she was locked in that cell-
she's either just too stupid or cock drunk to realize it.

I take a big swallow from my bottle as I watch
her nervously walk around the room- I'm tucked away
in the corner, behind the lights, and virtually hidden,
so I know she can't see me. She flits around, not quite
sure where she fits in. No one makes a move to talk
to her or even spares her a second glance.

The corners of my mouth lift- I take pleasure
in how uncomfortable she looks. If I wasn't terrified
of Soren, I'd toss her the keys to any car she wanted
just to get her away from me.

My smile drops immediately when her eyes
meet mine. Her eyes widen, and she begins to walk
over to me.

Fuck.

I take another drink- I don't want to be sober
if I have to talk to her, especially not alone. I ache for
something stronger, something to *really* take the edge
off, but Beck's words are still fresh in my mind, and I
don't want to disappoint him. *At least not yet.*

Anxiety constricts me, but the closer she gets,
the more it starts to feel like anger. Georgia stops
about two feet away from the table- she's close
enough where I can see a slight shake in her hands,
but not close enough to where I could grab her if I
wanted. The distance is comfortable for both of us- I

don't think I could stomach being any closer to her without one of my brothers as a buffer.

She murmurs something, but it's loud in here and I can't hear what she's saying.

"What?" I snap. "If you have something to say, get over here and say it."

She edges closer and tries again, but I still can't make it out. Rolling my eyes, I decide I've had enough of the dramatics. I stand and reach out, grabbing her wrist and yanking her towards me, shoving her into the seat across from mine. Her eyes narrow, landing on the spot where our skin touches, but her cheeks slightly flush. *Hm.*

I let her go and sit back down, grabbing the bottle and sliding it to my side of the table.

"What the fuck's the problem, trouble? I'm not going to bite you." I snarl. "You'd like that too much, right?"

She's so close to me that I can smell her, and as much as I hate to admit it, she smells *divine*, like something I can corrupt so easily. I shake those thoughts off quickly- I have Beck, and I'd never dare get my hands that dirty.

Her eyes are wide as she speaks again- I clearly scared her. *Good.*

"I'msorrytobotheryoubut-" The words tumble out too fast, and I raise a hand to stop her word vomit.

"Take a breath. Speak like a person. It can't be this hard." I grunt.

Her eyes narrow at me again, her lips pressing together. *That fucking attitude of hers.* She takes a breath, and I have to look away to stop from staring at her chest as it rises and falls. *What the fuck is wrong with me?*

"Soren sent me to find you." She says, her voice even now, calm but clipped.

What?

"Why? Why didn't Beck come up to get me?" I ask, taking another drink. My chest feels warmer, my limbs looser- her presence less grating than it was before.

She crosses her arms, glaring at me. "I don't know Jax, I didn't stop to ask for a reason. I just did what Soren said. Come downstairs or don't- it's not really my problem." She huffs, standing to leave, but I'm faster than she is.

I grab her arm, yanking her back down. I don't know why I want her to stay, but as I begin to lean into the liquor that's coursing through me, I do.

"You know, you should really start thinking for yourself if you're going to make it around here, Georgia. Doing what Soren says is great and all, if you want to be another one of his stupid sluts he keeps around. But he's got a thousand of those, right? Does he *really* need another one?" My speech is starting to slur now, and I can feel her bristle across from me with every word. "No, he doesn't." I chuckle.

"Fuck you. I don't need advice from *you*." Georgia bites back, pushing out of the chair and climbing to her feet. The bitterness in her voice is rich, venom dripping from her words. I almost laugh- she really means it. Cute.

"Don't you?" I goad. "I really don't give a fuck what happens to you, and frankly, I'm the only one not trying to get my hands down your pants. If I were you, I'd at least listen to what I have to say."

Luckily, she takes the bait.

"Fine." She sighs, but doesn't sit back down. "I'm only listening to you because I want to be useful. I want to see someone put Sykes down like the animal he is. I don't want to be left behind like I know I would be, and I'm damn sure not a *stupid slut*."

I can tell I really struck a nerve with that comment. Good.

"So, tell me- what do I have to do to make sure Soren doesn't lock me up again when he goes to do it?" She asks me.

The earlier bitterness is still there- she's still full of

attitude, but there's a touch of something earnest under the surface, too.

I grin at her, and her eyes go wide for a moment, but long enough for me to notice.

She wants to play? Let's play.

Before I can stop myself, I've got her hand in mine, dragging her back out to the garage. She struggles to keep up, partially because she doesn't know where she's going, but also because she doesn't trust me to lead her. *Smart.*

My guys are still standing around where I left them, and I bark at them, to no one in particular, to get my bike.

"You sure that's a good idea, Jax? You look pretty messed up." It's Karim that raises the question, and I'm on him in an instant, my forearm against his throat, and his back against the concrete wall of the garage.

He hits it hard, letting out a grunt when his body makes contact. No one tells me when I can and cannot leave, and no one who works for me gets to tell me what to do.

"Who puts food on your plate, huh? Who makes sure you morons have work? When I say jump, you say 'how high?', right? If I ask for my fucking bike, you'd do well to go and get it, Karim." I growl, our foreheads nearly touching.

"Fine, but you reek of booze. Don't call me when you need bail later. I saved your ass on the last one, I'm not doing it again." He fires back.

I shove off him, returning to my place in front of Georgia, and train my eyes onto him, following him all the way out of the garage and around the corner.

I can hear Georgia's breathing- it's shallow, and I can nearly smell the fear on her.

"Where the hell are you going, Jax? You know it's not safe for you to ride like this, and Soren'll be-" She starts, but I cut her off.

"Where are *we* going, trouble? I haven't decided yet. Soren can choke on a fat one, for all I care. He'll thank me for this later, I'm sure. You wanted to prove a point, right?"

When I hear the rumble of the Aprilia come into the garage, I push Georgia forward.

Karim skids the bike to a noisy stop just inches in front of her, kills it, throws the helmet at me, and storms out of the garage, shaking his head. I laugh, throwing up both middle fingers in his direction, before shoving the helmet down onto Georgia's head.

"You won't be able to hear me. I don't have Beck's helmet, so you'll be deaf. I'll be behind you."

She tries to protest, digging her heels in as I guide her over to the bike. She weighs nothing, so I pick her up by her hips and sit her down, nearly on the tank, and throw my own leg over, sliding on behind her. She's cramped, but she's small, so she fits- somewhat- between me and the handlebars, and I can still comfortably ride.

I don't want to admit it, but she feels *good* between my legs. The feeling pisses me off- I'm more drunk than I thought, I must be to even consider her like that. I shake the thoughts away as I start the bike back up. On instinct, she grabs me- first my thighs, then my arms, trying to find a secure position. She's wound tight and clearly doesn't trust me. She's a bundle of nerves, her muscles taught, her fingers digging into me- but I'm don't think fear's the only thing twisting her up.

"Hands over mine." I bark, the words ragged in my throat. "You're driving it- I don't feel like going to jail for another DUI, but I'm not letting you wreck it, either. This bike's worth more than you are." I manage, barely audible over the engine's roar.

She does it, hesitating, her fingers barely brushing mine. Her touch jolts through me like a punch- hot, electric, infuriating. I fucking *hate* it. I hate her.

God help me, I don't.

Georgia

Fear doesn't even begin to describe what I'm feeling. I'm at the mercy of a drunk man who *hates* me, in front of him on a motorcycle, going 100 down a dark street. If anyone were to want me dead, it would be Jax- why would I put my life in his hands like this?

Deep down though, it's exhilarating- the speed, the recklessness, and the longer I'm on this bike, the more fun I begin to have. Even though I know he could kill me in an instant, and he probably wants to, I feel... safe?

I'm scared out of my mind, but it's a good fear. I feel it in every synapse, every inch of my skin tingling with anticipation as our hands make the winding curves of the road we travel, the bike dipping so low with each one that I'm sure he'll lay it down. I know he's being careful with his bike, but in a distant part of my brain, I feel like he wants to keep me safe, too- at least to save his own skin when it comes to the others.

I already know Soren's going to pissed when he finds out I've left- I knew that from the moment I stepped foot into the garage. I'm sure they've already noticed our absence and are tearing the compound apart looking for us. But this'll prove that I'm worthwhile- that I can stick around and pull my weight, not cower when shit gets scary.

The way I reacted at the bar embarrassed me- I don't know what Jax is doing or where he's bringing me, but I can only hope it'll help toughen me up so I don't freeze again.

Jax's words echo in my head- *another one of Soren's stupid sluts.* That's all I was with the Brothers, a whore at everyone's disposal, the perfect submissive. I would've never been allowed to help, or plan, or execute, or experience *anything* like this. But here, I don't want to be that. I won't be that girl anymore. I want to be an equal, at least for right now, because one thing that these men and I have in common is the desire to see the blood of The Brothers run through the streets of Shadeview Heights.

I want revenge, just like them- and if I can stomach being alone with Jax, putting myself in a situation this dangerous, maybe they'll realize I can hold my own- that I might just be useful, too.

The longer I'm here, the harder the thought of leaving is. That's the plan, right? When all this is over, when Sykes is dead and we have our grand finale, I'm back on my own. I won't have Kain to put me in my place, no Beck to make me laugh and push my buttons, and Soren- I can't even begin to describe what our dynamic has shifted into, but I can't imagine being without anymore. He's given me a taste of what it feels like to be wanted- desired, even. He sleeps in my bed nightly now- he's gentle with me, tends to me. I might still be stuck there, but he's kind now.

I feel a twinge of guilt- Beck hasn't said much since Soren made it clear what had happened between us, but I know he's still there. Still watching me. There's still a flame, regardless of the way things were left.

As much as that complicates things, it makes me realize how much has changed, and how differently I see all of them now. They make me feel truly free- the same feeling I get being on this bike.

It's terrifying, yet amazing- I want to tell Jax to take me back, put me back in my bubble of security, but another part of me, one that's growing louder and louder with each day, wants to tell him to speed up. For the first time, maybe in my life, I feel like *me*.

The night air whips around us, pulling me out of my longing and back into the present. It's a perfect night for riding- the air is crisp, but not too cold, and feels good against my bare arms. The only light on the road is coming from the headlights, and even though Jax is drunk, he's mostly in control as his hands guide the bike from their place underneath mine. I might feel like I'm driving it, but he's the one keeping us upright- only wobbling a bit.

I know this is stupid, and I should've never gotten on this bike with him. But even still, I slowly let his hands go, my knuckles aching with the release from how hard I was squeezing them. At first, I drop my arms to my sides, and I feel Jax tense behind me, nudging me with his thighs, probably trying to get me to put my hands back. But after a moment, I raise my arms to my sides, letting the wind surround me and leaning my head back, resting my helmet against Jax's shoulder.

This is dangerous territory, and before I can right myself and apologize, I feel a deep laugh in his chest. He lets out a howl, like a wolf, and it's so loud that I can hear it over the bike and through the helmet. I smile- he can't see it, but it's a real one, one of the few genuine smiles I've had since I've been here. I follow suit, letting out a battle cry of my own.

We continue like this down the dark street, my arms outstretched and my head against his shoulder. Losing myself in the moment, I reach back and wrap my arms around his neck, pulling him closer- I might as well flirt with death all the way, and as far as I'm concerned, he's sitting right behind me.

To my surprise, he leans into it, instead of pushing me away like I expected him to, the heat from his body enveloping me like a warm blanket. I feel him groan, and though I can't hear it, the rumble in his chest is all I need- he *likes* it. My stomach flutters, and heat rushes to my core. It feels like kissing a loaded gun- deliciously dangerous, deadly yet exciting.

This night could never end, just Jax and I on this bike forever- the wind, the night, the darkness- I'd be content. This feels as close to normal as I've felt in the weeks I've been here. I'd be *happy*. This is a side of him I didn't expect- softer, carefree. I want more- more of this, more of him. I don't doubt I'll be chasing this high for a long time.

The excitement dies down, however, when the signature blue and red lights begin to flash behind us. He shoves me forward with his hips, and my hands shakily grab for him again. What we're doing is extremely illegal, not only my position on the bike, but also the fact that Jax has had one too many to be driving, and we were definitely speeding.

I brace myself for him to run- it seems like the likely option for him, but instead, he slows the bike and pulls slowly over to the shoulder. It's dark, really dark, and the headlights from the police cruiser cast an eerie glow on the road in front of us. He tears the helmet from my head, letting it fall to the pavement, and pulls me against him, his lips grazing my ear.

"Do not say a fucking word." He growls, squeezing me tightly, driving his point home.

"I won't, I swea-"

"I mean it, Georgia. Not a sound. Stop talking. Now." He cuts me off, releasing his hold on me.

We wait for what seems like an eternity for the cop to approach the bike, though in reality it's probably only a few minutes. I'm trembling, and Jax notices. He brings a hand up to the side of my thigh, his thumb rubbing small circles against it. Memories flash through my mind of the night in the bar when he shot Emmett Riley, and how he managed to calm me, even slightly, with just one touch. Is this how he feels comfort? Does he want to be touched, too? *Fuck it,* I decide, and reach down, grasping his forearm and mirroring his movements, tracing small circles against his skin. He inhales sharply, his entire body tensing under my touch, but doesn't stop.

Finally, the officer approaches the bike. I can barely see, but I recognize him from somewhere- I just can't place it.

"Evening. Officer Crowley with the Oakridge Police Department. Any idea why I stopped you two tonight?"

Jax laughs, and I wish he hadn't- he reeks of liquor, and the cop is so close I'm sure he can smell it, too.

"No idea, officer. Enlighten us." He chuckles, and I want to kick him.

Lay low, I'm screaming at him in my head, but I don't dare say it out loud. I'm shaking so badly that my teeth are chattering, and Jax squeezes my thigh hard to get me to stop. It doesn't work.

"Well, big shot- there's a few infractions I can spot right off the bat. Your speed, your passenger, and your breath. Which one should we start with?" He retorts.

"Fuck you, man. Just get it over with, you taking me or not?" Jax spits. I squeeze my eyes shut, panic sinking in like a stone in my stomach. *Please don't let them take us.*

"Get off the bike, son. Don't make this harder than it has to be." Officer Crowley snaps, his hand moving behind his back. I've seen this move before- but aren't cops supposed to wear sidearms? He's dressed like a cop and pulled behind us in a marked cruiser.

No.

Jax dismounts, standing in front of me, blocking me from the cop. He's shaking too, but only slightly.

"Her too. Two birds with one stone."
Crowley laughs, his hand still resting behind his back.
Realization hits me like a truck. I know where I
recognize him from. *They found me.*

"Gun." I choke out.

All hell breaks loose.

Crowley swings, catching an off guard Jax in
the jaw and knocking him to the ground. Jax is
smaller and faster, so he recovers quickly- by the time
Crowley gets to him, he's righted himself, his own
gun drawn. They struggle, and Jax is thrown to the
ground again, the gun skittering across the pavement,
out of reach. He's on his stomach, the bigger man
straddling him with a knee in his back, Jax's cheek
pressed painfully into the pavement.

"Leave her alone." he grunts out. "Do what
you want with me, you fucks. Leave her here."

"That's not how this works, son." Crowley
drawls, gripping Jax's hair and wrenching his head
upwards. "The boss has been looking for you both,
and it just so happens that you're here together.
Makes my job so much easier." With that, he slams
Jax's head into the pavement, hard. His eyes go wide
for a moment, and then his body relaxes. He's out
cold, surely a serious concussion forming with each
passing second.

I cry out, jumping off the bike and making a break down the road, trying to put as much distance between them and I as possible, but in several strides, my hair is pulled, and I fall flat on my back.

"Not so fast, *princess.*" Crowley sneers. "You're the big door prize. I can't have you getting away from me."

My blood runs cold. *That name.*

I fight, thrashing like a rabid animal to get away from him, but it's no use. I'm not trained, and he's too strong. He throws me into the back of a van parked in the tree line, just behind the cruiser. Before he closes the door, he jabs something into my neck- a needle, and I feel the moment whatever was inside of it enters my body as he pushes the plunger. I close my eyes, unable to fight back as my teeth chatter wildly, and I'm unable to stay fully still as my body is wracked with shakes.

I know what's about to happen- I've lived it before, and I know who's waiting.

Numbness creeps in as the drugs take hold. The door opens, and a masked man throws Jax's limp body into the footwell beside me. He looks so small like this, folded in on himself.

My hands are free, and before the darkness wins, I reach out, threading my fingers through his hair. It's soft, damp with the blood pouring from his temple and a cut at the base of his neck. *I didn't see that happen.* My fingers trace the wound, and I shiver-something about it feels... off, though I can't name why.

"I'm sorry, Jax," I breathe, my hand still buried in his hair as the darkness edges closer.

I can't lose him. I won't. *I'm sorry.*

Soren

I can't recall a time I've felt this angry with my team before. When Georgia didn't return after I sent her to collect Jax, a test in and of itself to see how she'd react being sent into the compound alone, alarm bells started ringing in the back of my mind. Thinking they were just coming to blows and needed a chaperone to step in, I headed upstairs, only to find our usual table empty, and no sign of either of them.

I storm out into the garage, finding a few of Jax's guys huddled in a corner, talking amongst themselves, heads down and nervous looks on their faces. They stop when they notice me, their eyes meeting mine, but no words are said.

"Speak. You know why I'm here." I bark, and their spines straighten.

That's right, motherfuckers.

They might report to Jax, but that's only because I *allow* them to. It's high time to remind the crackhead sector of my syndicate who's really in charge. Still, even after my order, no one speaks. They're loyal, I'll give them that. I roll my eyes and pull my gun from my waistband, firing a round at the concrete near their feet, scattering them like roaches as they dodge the shell's ricochet.

"Speak!" I bellow. "I've lost something of mine, and you have five seconds to tell me where they are, or my next bullet ends up in someone's kneecap."

"He's gone, okay? He was drunk. He took the girl and left on his bike. I don't know where he went." One of them blurts out, his hands in his hair. "He's going to fucking kill me."

I growl, wrenching my phone out of my pocket and dialing Kain, my gun still trained on the group in front of me.

"Get up here. Now. Bring Nate and pull his fucking location. He's gone." I spit, jamming my thumb against the screen to end the call.

"Get the fuck out of here." I retort, not even sparing them a glance, and they waste no time vacating the garage.

I close my eyes and run my hands through my hair as I hear the scramble of boots and the slam of doors. I feel a twinge of worry, and my brow furrows. Why would Jax have taken Georgia? *Where* would he have taken her? He's been so vocal about his hatred for her, and how much he disagreed with my decision to keep her here. He's had every opportunity to hurt her, to get rid of her. Why now? I find myself feeling panic for Georgia- a foreign feeling that causes my hands to slightly shake. He has my girl. *Mine.*

I told her I was never letting her go, and I meant it. No one has ever made me feel the way she does. I've never *slept* beside another person before, ever. The sex is great, sure- her body was simply made for mine, but that's not it. As of now, it's pure emotion. Primal urges, to protect her, to cherish her- to *worship* her. She's so much different than anything I've ever experienced before, and I hate myself for keeping these feelings from her.

She's mine, my girl, and if he did something to hurt her, or if he's *touched* her- I'll skin him alive without a second glance and hang him in the middle of the warehouse to serve as a warning for every other bastard in there- do not touch what belongs to me.

Bishops don't share easily.

The door slams open, quelling my murderous thoughts only slightly, and Kain appears with a breathless Nate and a furious-looking Beck in tow. I nearly laugh at Nate's current state. His glasses are fogged with condensation as he steps into the night air. He lets off a string of curses, leaning against a workbench to catch his breath, before righting himself after a nasty glare from Kain.

"I pulled Jax's tracker, I have a pin. Devin and Axel are pulling the Escalade around and we're leaving. Now." Kain reports, no emotion in his voice.

His face is impassive, his eyes hard and set. He's a good soldier, and in times like these, he's numb- fully analytical, tactical. No time for feelings. The anger will come later.

As if they heard us, Kain's Escalade comes screeching into the garage, Devin and Axel in the front seats.

I'm pleased to see my men. They may be the only two that I can trust outside of my brothers. They leave the engine running as they jump out, ripping the back doors open and climbing in.

"No way we're leaving you high and dry, boss. We want to see this." Devin calls from inside, and my chest warms with the thought of my men at my back.

Before I can get into the car, Beck grabs my arm, and I stop.
"Don't panic. He always makes it back. You know Jax- he wouldn't have hurt her- he wouldn't do that to you, Sor. I know him best- it isn't like him."

I know he's trying to calm me down, but he's tense, his shoulders taught and his jaw clenched.

I'm nearing the point of no return and am in no mood for a pep talk, or words of encouragement.

"We'll see. I hope you're right, Beck. You'd better be, for his sake. Because I promise you, if he's done anything to her, I'll-"

"Save it, boss. I'll beat you to it if he proves me wrong." He says grimly, holding up his hand to silence me.

I let it slide, just this once, doing my best to suppress the possessiveness that I feel, and nod, jerking my chin at the open back door, gesturing for him to get in the car and ending the conversation. It won't go anywhere good, at least not right now.

I get into the passenger seat, Kain sliding in next to me, his phone already connected to the infotainment system with the directions pulled up and ready to go. I stare at the map, hard. They aren't far from the compound, maybe fifteen minutes away. Maybe Beck's right. *He really fucking better be.*

The car ride is silent- save for Nate's constant heavy breathing- and I prefer it that way. I draw three different conclusions in the twelve minutes it takes us to reach the pin of Jax's tracker.

One, he took her out here to kill her. Point blank, period. We'll arrive at her dead body on the side of the road, and he'll probably have split, for good, more than likely, knowing what would be waiting for him if he dared to return home.

Two, Beck was right, and he pulled over to dry up. This is the most unlikely scenario I've drawn up- Jaxon has four DUIs, and his license has been suspended for roughly three years. He has *never* 'pulled over to sober up'- why now? If this is the case, chances are we'll find them in one piece, Jax passed out and Georgia pissed, but whole. This still does not explain why they left together with no notice.

Three, he wrecked the bike, and we'll find him in a ditch somewhere, one or both of their bodies mangled and riddled with road rash and broken bones. This is an unsavory thought- I can't picture Georgia in this way without getting sick to my stomach.

Another foreign feeling. I shut my eyes tight as we approach the blue dot, savoring the last few minutes of mental clarity I have before I inevitably step out of the car and lose my shit. I hear the car doors open, close, and then- *silence.*

When I open my eyes, I'm no longer myself, not really. I am Soren Bishop, son of Conner Bishop, leader of The Vipers. At this moment, I am my father's son, wholly.

"Soren!" Someone screams, but I can't tell who.

I exit the car calmly, walking around the hood. No scenario I could've drawn up, no warning, nothing could've prepared me for what lay in front of me.

They were *gone.*

Like they vanished into thin air, right off the back of the motorcycle. There was nearly nothing to go off of- blood on the pavement, the black Aprilia, kickstand still up, parked on the shoulder of the road, a helmet on the ground. There was a lot of blood, and with no bodies, it's impossible to tell who it belonged to. I hoped it was Jaxon's.

I see red.

"Where the fuck did that goddamn thing take us, Kain?" I scream, my eyes wild, scanning the group for his face. I land on Nate, and I swing before he can take another breath. My fist lands in his stomach, and he doubles over in pain, groaning loudly.

"I thought you said the trackers were accurate, you fucking keyboard warrior." I snarl. "If they're so accurate, where the *fuck* is our brother, huh? Where's my girl?"

He coughs, unable to answer me, and I raise my fist to hit him again.

"Wait! Goddamn it, Soren, wait." He sputters, clutching his stomach. "Fuck man, I think you broke a rib."

"You better start talking, or you're going to swallow your teeth." I bite back. I still want to hit him- hard.

"That tech is never wrong. He must be around here somewhere. He's still here, or the tracker itself is, but either way- it's accurate."

A cold weight settles in my gut. I hadn't thought of that. Surely, Jax could've held his own, right? He wouldn't have let someone remove his tracker- he'd want us to find him if he was in trouble. *Did he cut it out himself?*

"Motherfucker!" Beck screams, and turns the flashlight on his phone on, searching the ground.

The team follows suit, and the only thing I can hear is my blood beating in my ears and Beck's curses, coming out in strings as he struggles to find the tiny piece of plastic.

"It's lost," I start, but my words falter as my own flashlight catches on something shiny a few feet away from the motorcycle. I pick it up, and my heart sinks. *Shit.*

A tiny, plastic device, the size of a grain of rice- covered in blood.

"Here!" I shout, getting the attention of my men. "He's gone."

"No." Kain mutters.

Beck screams, swearing and shoving the motorcycle to the ground. He targets the mirrors, the windshield- anything that'll shatter underneath his boot.

I don't know what to think. There is no way Jax would've cut this out on his own- outside of his loyalty to our family, he doesn't have the balls to do it himself, he's too green, too scared of inflicting that much pain upon himself. The trackers are implanted deep, and it would've taken an even deeper cut to get it out in one piece like this. We've never told Georgia about the trackers either, so unless he told her about them himself- unlikely- that rules her out. There's only one other option- they've been taken.

I've failed.

I promised her I'd protect her, that if she helped, gave us information, I'd make sure nothing happened to her. I failed her. I failed my brother.

I take a breath. We've been at war, that I can deal with- as hard as it is to lose family, to lose our own, nothing compares to this. I didn't feel pain when my father died, when my mother left me, when Beck's mom passed. I felt nothing, at least not compared to what I feel now.

This is pain, real and raw, and unlike anything I've experienced. The feeling winds itself through my body, constricting my nerves like a snake, until I'm gasping for breath. Every nerve in my body feels as though it's on fire. My stomach twists, bile rising in my throat. My chest feels tight, like it's being squeezed from all sides. Even the air tastes sharp in metallic in my mouth as I suck in a breath.

I don't make a sound- I don't scream, I don't swear, I don't dare cry. I compose myself, standing straight and steeling my spine. *I am my father's son. I am a Bishop.*

"Nate. Find them. As fast as you can." I command, my voice like ice.

"On it, boss." He gets back in the car, and I'm grateful for his immediate compliance. Nothing and no one will stand in the way of my finding them and continue to breathe.

"Get in the car. Contact every available resource, cash in all your favors. If I don't have them back by the time the sun is up…" I don't finish my sentence. I don't have to.

My team moves, and I stand in the headlights, composing myself and suppressing any lingering anger and fear.

I might've failed her once, but I will not fail her again.

I am my father's son.

Georgia

I open my eyes, and pain is all I feel. My vision is blurry, like the room is shifting with every blink. My eyes feel like someone's thrown sand into them, my throat screaming for water, but I can't remember the last time I drank. *Where... where am I?*
My head pounds with every tiny sound- the hum of lights, the soft scrape of something across the floor- and nothing makes sense. I try to move, but my limbs feel heavy.

For a moment, I forget- I forget where I am, what happened, *who* happened.

But then, I remember. And when the realization hits me, I start to scream.

Loud, uncontrollable screams, turn into sobs that wrack my body and consume me completely.

I remember then that I wasn't alone, and I start to scream for Jax. I scream his name until my throat is raw, only stopping when I hear a faint grunt from somewhere close by.

"Georgia?" He groans, and my body sags with relief. He's here. He's alive. He's breathing.

"Jax? Jax, is that you?" I cry out, willing myself to stop crying for long enough to find him. When my eyes lock onto his, I almost wished I hadn't looked.

He's *covered* in blood. Streaks of it across his face, matted into his hair, and most noticeably, a blooming crimson stain on the front of his shirt. He's sitting upright, at least, but hunched over against the wall, his arms wrapped around his midsection. The ground where he sits is dingy and stained, the concrete yellow. The stones he rests on look uncomfortable, but as I look around, there's nothing around that I can use to make him more comfortable. In fact, there's nothing at all- no cots, no chains, no buckets; *nothing*.

Jax's eyes are black and bruised, one of the whites turned blood red with busted vessels, making the blue even more brilliant. I haven't been cuffed, at least not yet, and am free to move around, so I run to him, as fast as I can in the haze I still feel. Any danger or apprehension I had towards him is gone as my hands roam every part of him- his face, his neck, the back of his head. I check him everywhere, to make sure he's real, that I'm not dreaming- that I'm not alone again.

"I'm fine, Georgia." He gruffs. "It's not all mine."

"What's this? What happened?" I start for his stomach, and the large, red, wet stain on his shirt, but he stops me.

"Don't. Please, don't touch it." He breathes.

"What happened?" I ask again, and he looks away from me, wincing at the small movement.

"They stuck me on the way in. It's not a big deal." He murmurs.

"Not a big deal? You're bleeding, Jax, it's re-"

"Stop it. Please, just stop. We need to find a way out. Worry about the rest later, yeah?" He cuts me off, reaching a shaky hand up and cupping my face, leaving wet streaks of blood on my cheek. "We need to get out. They cut my tracker out, Georgia. No one's coming. It's just us. I'm bleeding bad, and I- I don't know how long I can stay awake. You need to *think*, okay? You gotta keep it together."

He's shaking like a leaf, teeth chattering, pupils blown and unfocused. He had a tracker? Where? It must've been implanted if they had to cut it out. My stomach turns over, trying to block out visuals of a knife entering his skin.

He's freezing to the touch, but sweating profusely, the blood caked onto his skin running like wet paint. He's really fucking pale, and- *damn it, focus.* Think. I need to think. I can't help him if I panic.

I look around, taking in our surroundings further, and my heart sinks when I realize I don't recognize anything. This is a basement, or at least it has to be with the lack of windows. A garage, maybe? The room is derelict, to say the least, with deteriorating stone walls and creaky, old wooden floors. The ceiling has open rafters, but there's no skylight or opening. There's a small staircase leading to a door, and I stand, leaving him slumped, and rush over to it, twisting and jerking the handle as hard as I can. *Locked. Of course.*

I try the handle again, my hands shaking in desperation as I realize it won't give. I throw myself into the door, but I'm not strong enough to even shake it right now. Instead, I pound on it as hard as I can, screaming for help, for someone, anyone to come. It's useless. I'm met with silence.

I don't give up- I can't. Someone has to hear me. I scream for what feels like hours but is probably more like fifteen minutes before my throat is so raw that I'm scared I might cough up blood.

I sink down against the door, bringing my knees into my chest, fresh tears falling down my cheeks.

"We're going to have to wait for someone to come." I call out. "There's not another way. We're going to have to wait, just a little longer." I manage.

"Fuck." He whines, throwing his head back against the wall.

I stand shakily and approach him cautiously, like one would a nervous dog- not sure if he'll bite or cower and show his belly. To my surprise, he cowers as I sit next to him.

He inches closer to me and reaches out, groaning in pain, and wraps a shaky arm around me. I tense, unsure of his intentions. My gut tells me he needs me, so I lean in, pressing my cheek into his shoulder, as carefully as I can, and he doesn't push me away.

I melt into him, pulling my knees up into my chest, trying to get as close to him as I can- he's weak, but he's *here*. He can protect me. They won't hurt me if he's here. *Right?*

He slumps even further, and I look up at him- his eyes are starting to close, and I reach over, patting his face to get him to come to.

"Jax. Hey, Jax? You need to stay awake. Open your eyes, please." I whisper, but he falls further forward. I catch his shoulder, sitting him back up as best I can. "Jax!" I shout, and his eyes snap open, wide and wild, darting around the room. "That's it. Look at me, please. Keep your eyes open." I plead.

"Fuck." he whimpers. "Don't let me fall asleep, please, Georgia. Don't let me-" He nods off again, his head slumping forward.

I pat him again, harder this time, but it's no use. I shake him, not caring how badly it'll hurt.

Maybe the pain will keep him conscious- at least, it always did for me.

His head snaps back up, and he cries out, his breathing shallow, whimpers coming out with each exhale.

"It's not just the stick. I'm crashing hard, okay?" He's panicked, the words tumbling out so fast I can hardly understand him. "I need you to check my pockets. I can't- fuck- I can't do it myself, but check them, okay? I need anything that's in there." He begs.

I do- reaching into his front pockets, feeling for something- I'm not sure what I'm looking for, but there's nothing there. My fingers feel blindly against his leg, my heart racing. Only a small sheet of fabric separates my skin from his, and much as I want to deny it, it feels nearly electric being this close to him. It feels *right.* When he realizes I'm coming up empty, he lets off a string of curses.

"I'm sorry. Maybe I can help-"

"You can't, Georgia!" He cries out, whimpering again at the exertion. "Unless you have a half ball of blow on you, you have nothing that can help me." He snaps, leaning his head back against the wall.

I say nothing. I always knew there was something different about him, something... off. I didn't know he was this bad.

"It's going to be okay." I try, taking his face in my hands.

"No, it's not." He murmurs, trying to shrug me off, but he can't- he's weak from the blood loss, and exhausted. "I'm going to die in here, Georgia."

"No, you're not. I'm not going to let you." I tell him, holding back tears.

I try to think of anything to tell him, anything to talk about to take his mind away from where it is.

"It's my fault we're here, you know that? He came for me. You were just collateral." I start, and he exhales hard through his nose.

"I think they wanted us both. You don't know the full story. I never told you." He mumbles.

"Shhhh. Let me talk. When we're out of here, you can tell me your side, okay? Just keep your eyes open." I try, and he nods.

"I was a rebellious teenager. My parents hated it, but they were so busy with work that they didn't really care all that much what I did. I met Isaac about five years ago, at a bar. He was in his cut, and the leather really did something to me. Embarrassing, I know. So, I let him take me home- well, back to the clubhouse. I was so drunk that I couldn't remember where I was, and when I woke up the next morning, he told me he loved me, and that was that. I was his."

Jax snorts. "If I'd have known you were into leather, we would've worn it weeks ago, trouble."

My brow furrows. *What?* He's exhausted and strung out. He doesn't mean it. He hates me. *Right?*

"Shush, I mean it." I pat his forehead, and he rolls his eyes, but there's nothing behind them. "I never went home again, except for one time to get all my stuff. I called home a few times a week, told my mom who I was with, but she already knew who he was and knew who he ran with. They disapproved, and I can't fault them for that. When I told Isaac I wanted to go back, he blindfolded me and put me on his bike. It was fun, at the time- I was young, and didn't understand why he did it, but now I really wish I could've seen where we were. Things may have ended differently for me if I knew." Tears well in my eyes, but I need to tell him. I need to finish the story, at least once, out loud. This is the first time I've told anyone the full truth.

"My parents tossed my shit on the lawn and changed the locks. I was nineteen, and he convinced me that they didn't love me, and I'd be better off with someone who did. So, I moved in. Moved into the clubhouse, into his life- into their ways. It was fun, until it wasn't." I pause, looking up at him to make sure he's conscious. His eyes bore into me, analyzing every word I'm saying, drinking it all in.

"He was killed on a job, a job Sykes put him up to. It was supposed to be simple, but then… it wasn't. He went fast, one between the eyes, and that was it. They brought him home, and the service was quick, rushed, almost. I had no time to grieve before Sykes was on me like I was a shiny new toy." The words get stuck in my throat, but I force them out anyway. *Keep talking. Keep him awake.*

"From then on, I was expected to be a perfect housewife for him. I cooked the meals, did the cleaning, and was an open pair of legs whenever he wanted. I was tricked, you know? He told me he could take care of me, that he'd provide, make sure I didn't want for anything. He wouldn't let me leave, to go anywhere outside of the clubhouse property, and I was barely allowed outside.

I tried it once, just to step into the parking lot for some air without permission. He chained me up in the basement for seventeen days in the dark because of it. He said he wanted to 'teach me to be grateful for what I had, not want what I didn't'. It all got worse after that."

Jax inhales sharply, and his fingers brush my arm, his little circles starting against my skin. I close my eyes, focusing on his touch, letting it ground me.

"He would do things to me, things I didn't want. His men would do things to me. By the time I finally escaped, I had broken almost every bone in my body, and I wasn't anywhere close to a virgin." I mutter, breathing a laugh, but there's no humor behind it.

He pulls me in, and I don't fight it. With my ear against his chest, I can hear his heartbeat- it beats wildly, like a butterfly stuck in a jar, trying to escape. His breathing is so shallow, and I know he needs to rest, but I can't let him close his eyes.

Someone has to have noticed we're gone. They'll be coming soon. He can rest when we're safe.

"It's okay. You don't have to say anything else. I've got you. I'm so sor-" His gentle whispers are cut off by the sound of the door banging open, and a thunderous voice booming through the room- a voice that has always ripped me into a ball on the floor and now is no different. I cower, tears flowing down my cheeks freely, and I shake, almost worse than Jax does.

"That's not exactly how the story goes, is it *princess?*"

Kain

I haven't slept in thirty-four hours. My eyes burn from staring at the computer screen for hours before we left, and even more so now that I'm blinking back tears. We regrouped at the compound after leaving the bike, which is how I found myself standing in Nate's office.

I don't know why I'm crying- I don't think I've ever cried before, at least not a time I can remember. My eyebrows thread together- I can't decide if I feel this strongly for Georgia, or if it's because Jax is missing, but my stoic mask is beginning to crack, just a bit- but enough. They have my brother. If I'm correct, which I usually am, he's been taken by the very people who want him dead more than anything.

As for Georgia, I decided quite some time ago that she is *mine*. Soren can delude himself, and Beck can dream- she isn't theirs. She was made for me, whether by divine right or dragged up from the depths of hell itself- it doesn't matter. She was put on this earth for *me*. I blink hard, forcing the tears back inside.

Soren bursts in, with Beck in tow. He has a file in his hands, and I grit my teeth. Without missing a beat, Soren sweeps an arm across the desk against the wall- luckily, not holding any of Nate's computer shit-, sending a stockpile of tech to the floor.

My eyebrows jump, and I refrain from sounding off the sarcastic remark that enters my head at his childlike actions. He begins to unpack the file, unloading pages of coordinates, instructions, and instruction manuals for security systems. I feel uneasy- no maps, no pictures. I can't help like this. I shift a little, and the guys notice.

"What?" Soren snaps.

I cast my gaze downwards, trying to hide the shame. I know my face must be flush. I pick at my fingers, trying to find something, *anything* else to focus on.

He must've forgotten, what with all the stress.

"What's the issue now, Kain?" He grumbles. "Am I not doing something right? Do you have a better idea?"

"I can't read these." I murmur, feeling my face heat up. I've never admitted this nasty little factoid about myself to Beck, and it makes me want to run.

"What?" Soren asks, his tone annoyed and dismissive. I snap.

"I said I can't fucking read this shit, Soren!" I yell, throwing the papers from the table. I really can't judge him too harshly for his previous display- that really was very therapeutic.

Beck raises an eyebrow, a confused look on his face. "Is it the print size, or-"

"I can't fucking read, Beck! Is that what everyone wanted to hear?" I'm screaming at them now, my fists balling, aching to throw a punch. I don't.

"I can't fucking read the words on the page. I've *never* been able to read the words on any page. Ever." I breathe. I'm embarrassed, willing the redness in my face to recede and looking for an escape route. I feel ashamed because I've failed at my job, because I'm failing my brothers. I'm failing *her*.

As angry as I am, it's not their fault- it's mine. It's my mother's. It's my father's. But it is *not* my brothers'.

Soren bows his head, bracing himself against the table.

"Shit, Kain, I'm sorry. I forgot, okay? I was trying to move quickly, and I just-"

"It's fine. I'll go make myself useful somewhere else." I murmur, not wanting to stick around to hear their teases that are surely coming.

"No." Beck calls out, moments before I reach the door. "We're a team. Get your big ass back over here, I'll read it to you." He offers, without missing a beat.

His voice is empty of judgment. No hint of mocking. I stop, pausing by the door, my back still turned to them. This is not the reaction I was expecting, nor one I know how to process. It would be so much easier if he'd called me an idiot and told me to get lost- that I can handle. But offering help? I don't accept help from anyone. No one's ever offered me help like this. Sure, Soren prints photos, but it was unspoken.

My eyes burn once again, and this time I don't blink the tears away. One falls, sliding from my eye and down the length of my scar, and it burns on the way down, too. It's time, and it's been time- I've blocked them out for so many years, and I can't anymore. I need to let them in, fully, and it starts with this.

I turn to face them, not bothering to wipe the lone tear, and their eyes go wide, Beck's eyebrows nearly melting into his hairline with the look of shock he wears.

"Fine. You want to help me? Then do it. But after tonight, we will not speak a word of this to anyone, and I will continue to learn. On my own." I bark, looking back and forth between them.

Beck gives a halfhearted salute, and I walk back over to the table.

"So, it is like big words only, or just nothing at all-" Beck starts, but Soren and I cut him off with a yell at the same time. We make eye contact, and Soren gives me an exasperated look, shaking his head.

"Sorry, sorry. Let's get back to work." He rushes out, holding his hands up.

And we do. I spend the next three hours listening, as Beck and Soren read to me, every word written on the paper, never missing one. They ask me questions, making sure I understand what they're saying. I want to tell them that I'm illiterate, not deaf, but the warmth in my chest shuts me up.

Before, I was terrified that Georgia would ruin my family. I thought she'd split us into four and leave us stranded, broken, or worse. But now, listening to my brothers, watching them jump to my rescue, it feels like it should. It feels better than it did before, and as much as they can blame this newfound camaraderie on saving Jax, I know it has every bit to do with getting her back too.

By the time we call it, I know way too much about security systems and blueprints, and way too little about where they are. *That's where Nate comes in,* Soren keeps telling me. *He has the location; he'll get us there. Be patient.*

It makes my stomach twist- that little hacker isn't good for anything that's not in front of a screen, and this is the one time we can't fuck up. I don't want to be patient. I want to kill them.

I leave the office, needing a break and a stiff drink. The others follow me out, and we end up at our usual table in the corner of the room. Soren grabbed a bottle of something clear- I normally only drink beer or brown liquor, but right now I'll take anything that'll quiet my mind. He tips the bottle in my direction, and I grab it, taking a big swallow, thankful for the burn in my chest to distract me.

I pass it to Beck, and he does the same, hissing through his teeth as it goes down. Soren takes two, slamming the bottle down on the table.

"I don't understand this, Soren." Beck murmurs quietly. "We know where to look. Why are we still here?"

"We *don't* know, Beck. We don't even know if this is them, or someone else. What if they ran, huh?"

I knit my brows. They wouldn't run.

"That's a non-issue, boss. He wouldn't leave with her."

"Fine. I'll buy it- for now. Regardless, we need to be prepared before we gun anyone down. We need to know how many people are in that house, what shifts they work, the layout- we're not ready."

"If it were up to me-" Beck starts, but Soren quickly interrupts him.

"It's not up to you, Beck. You either get in line, or by all means, go in blind and kill yourself. You're just as useful to them dead as ill-informed."

Soren has a point. As much as it's killing me to sit here knowing they're gone, we can't show up knocking at the doors of The Iron Brotherhood without cause- they would sign our death certificates. Besides, from the camera footage we have seen of their clubhouse, there's more than forty men in there, all armed. We won't do any good without strategy.

"I can't fucking do this." Beck hisses, shoving back from the table, his chair clattering to the ground. He picks up the bottle and throws it against the wall, glass and liquor flying everywhere.

"They've got them. I know they've got them. I'm not going to step on your toes, Soren, but you better know what the hell you're talking about. If he winds up dead- if *either* of them ends up dead because you're fucking sitting on your hands, I'm done."

The table goes silent, and my jaw goes slack. Soren's face is impossible to read- he's nearly expressionless, save for a slight tilt of his head and a slight furrow of his brow.

"You don't mean that." I try, my voice soft- or at least, as soft as it can be given Beck's anger.

I can handle a lot, but this? This is different. Beck's threat feels like someone's pulled the rug out from underneath me. My teeth grit, my fists clenched. I can't- I *won't* let it happen.

"Try me. We bring them back, whole, or I'm out. I mean it. You have until the morning to make a move or I'm going in alone." With that, he storms off, towards the elevators.

"He's not fucking going anywhere." Soren grits, his hands gripping the edge of the table. His mask cracks- anger seeps through. "If he thinks he can walk away, just like that- he must not know me as well as I thought."

His face falls as he runs a hand through his hair. "We're going to find them. I just… need to be ready. I can't lose more than we already have because I make a move too risky, or don't fully understand-"

"I get your position," I cut him off, holding my hand up to silence him. "But you're never going to feel ready, boss. There will always be more to learn. Don't let them suffer because you don't want to fail."

He stands with a huff, his eyes not meeting mine. He's being torn apart, and I wish I could help him. But now, the only thing that will ease any of us is the safe return of our brother. *And our girl.*

"I'm going to check in with Nate, see if he's been able to get anything. I locked his door from the outside; he won't come out until we have answers."

I watch Soren walk away, his shoulders slumping forward. I trust him. He's a good leader- smart, strong. I'd trust him with my life any day. But Beck has a point- he needs to trust his gut.

We all know where they are, even though we don't have proof, and gunning down a few members of The Iron Brotherhood wouldn't be the worst thing, even if we were wrong. But nothing else makes sense. Jax and Georgia are the only two who have history with them, the only ones they'd ever want. We don't need proof- we need them back. I trust Soren with my life, forever.

Do I trust him with *theirs?*

Beck

It's been ten hours since I last saw Jax. Ten hours with no news, no information- no idea whether or not they were alive or dead. Ten hours spent with a piece of my soul missing.

My first instinct was to get angry- I was pissed at him for leaving and not telling me where he went. Angry that he wasn't being safe with Georgia.

But when I saw his tracker, cut from his body and covered in blood, my brain shut down.

I felt *nothing*, which was strange, at least at first. My brain is constantly going, thinking of the next funny thing to say, the next bad thing that could happen, the next job- my head is always loud. But when I saw that tracker, one thought was all that would come.

Find them.

A switch flips.

Everything in me sharpens- my head clears, my pulse evens out, my thoughts line up like weapons on a rack. The noise, the racing thoughts- they fade away into nothing. I don't care how much blood I'll have to spill, how many buildings I'll have to burn down- the sun won't rise without Jax back where he belongs, without my boy back to me. Without Georgia back home.

I find myself in Jax's bedroom, still with no news about where he is. I hate Soren- I don't, not really, but I don't agree, and sometimes that feels stronger than hate could. I just want them back- I can't understand why he won't go look. We don't have to be sure- I need them back so badly that I would knock on the biggest and baddest doors in this city just for a clue as to where they are. I don't care what happens to me- I just need them to be okay.

I know where he is. My gut knows where he is, and we need to *go*- I just can't convince Soren of that.

I didn't mean what I said, either- something else I have to apologize for, I guess. I wouldn't leave him, even if we never found them. I wouldn't know what to do on my own.

I clutch Jax's sheets to my face- they smell like him, and if I close my eyes, it's like he's here. Tears fall quickly, and I let them- no one's here to see. I can cry, just for a second. I talk to him, out loud- tell him how sorry I am for losing him, and I can hear his response in my head, asking me how in the hell *I* lost *him*. I almost laugh.

I pray. I haven't in a while, not since my mother forced me to as a child, before… before she was gone, but I do now. I pray to find him, for some kind of divine intervention to make him magically appear in the doorway. Nothing happens. I weep harder.

My eyes fight to stay open- I'm exhausted, but I don't want to sleep, not before I know the plan. I reach out, fumbling blindly on the nightstand for my phone. When my hand closes around it, I open it and fire off a text to Soren, asking for updates.

No reply.

"Fuck." I mumble, throwing the phone down on the empty side of the bed- Jax's side. I can't be this tired and expect to help. I can close my eyes, just for a second. Sleep comes easy, but so do the nightmares. I never did sleep well if he wasn't next to me.

I wake to shouts in the hall. Several voices, some I don't immediately recognize, fill the basement. My body still heavy with sleep, I reach over, blindly searching for Jax next to me. When I only find cool sheets, I jolt up, a bitter reminder about last night's events. I grab my phone- it's nearly six. Why are they yelling?

I dress quickly, pulling on my clothes from last night, and pop my head out into the hall. My gun's in my hand, slightly behind the door.

"You better be really fucking sure, Nate!" Soren's screaming.

Walking a bit further out into the hallway, I see a wild-eyed Nate against the wall, his feet dangling.

Kain's got him pressed, his forearm against Nate's neck, and Soren- damn it, Soren's got his gun drawn, nearly pointing it at Nate.

"What the hell is going on?" I call out, jogging down the hallway to meet them. They don't let up or even acknowledge my questions.

"I'm sure!" Nate wheezes. "I know what I saw."

"Tell me again. From the beginning." Kain grunts, shoving him harder against the wall.

"Fucking ease up, will you King Kong? I can't talk with your tree trunk of an arm pressed against my trachea."

Kain hesitates, shoving him one more time before dropping his arm and stepping back.

"I'm going to need some goddamn workman's compensation for the shit you all put me through, Jesus." Nate groans, rubbing his neck. Soren cocks an eyebrow. Nate swallows hard. *Pussy.*

"Like I said, I was able to tap into a camera I couldn't see before. Camera's pointed straight at the front of the house- clean shot, no blind spots. Way better than the crap angles I had before. Last night at about eleven-thirty, a cop rolls in with four guys built like hired muscle, and they're bringing in two bodies wrapped in some kind of sheet. I couldn't see the faces, couldn't tell who they were, but c'mon, man-two bodies, showing up the same night Jax and Georgia go missing? It's them. It has to be them."

"I told you." I grit my teeth, boring my eyes into Soren. "I fucking told you!"

I shove him hard, but before I can take a swing, Kain's on me, holding my hands behind my back.

He's silent, for a moment, regaining his footing. Soren stares at me, and there's something *more* behind his eyes this time. If I didn't know better, I'd call it remorse.

"I should've listened. I'm sorry, Beck."

My chest warms, but it's a strange feeling-usually I'm the one apologizing to him. He turns to the others.

"No more waiting. Get strapped and let's go."

I get to the armory in half the time it normally takes, impatiently tapping the screen of the security system as it takes its time verifying my identity. Once inside, we arm ourselves, taking just about everything that will fit in a pocket, waistband, or boot, and strap our Kevlar to our chests. Soren gives us a once over, nodding his head.

"The rest is in the car. The kids are bringing the car around now." He stares at me, our eyes locking. "You good?"

I feel my eyes glaze over. In truth, I'm anything but *good*. We've lost so much time, and they could be hurt, or worse, because Soren refused to listen. But I push that aside- that's a fight for later. What matters now is getting in and getting out- with both of them *alive*.

A switch flips, once again.

"Let's get it done."

Nate, Devin, and Axel are waiting for us, Kain's Escalade already pulled around and idling. Devin's grinning from ear to ear, rubbing his hands together and Axel's jumping in place, like a boxer preparing for the first round. *Fucking psychos, both of them*. They've all got Kevlar on, as do we, but Nate's appearance nearly makes me double over.

He looks like a war journalist, with a vest that is two sizes too big- nearly bumping his glasses from his nose with how high up it sits, his bulky laptop clutched in his arms, and *a helmet*- a fucking half helmet for riding a bike. I take one look at him and nearly fall to the floor with laughter, wiping my eyes. Even Soren barks out a laugh, and Kain hides a smirk with my thumb.

"What?" Nate asks innocently, looking around. "We're fucking *going in*, right?"

"Dude," Axel starts, but I hold up a hand, still shaking with laughter.

"Don't. Let him. When we find Jax, he's gonna piss himself." A fit of laughter takes hold of me again, and tears are rolling down my face by the time I catch my breath.

It's been a while since we've heard real laughter out here, and god knows we need an ounce of relief right now.

"Why are we laughing? What did I miss?" Nate asks- I can't fathom how he misses the fact that he's the butt of the joke, but somehow, he does.

Soren shakes his head, muttering something about Nate being a moron, and motions for us to get in. I take my usual spot behind the driver's seat, with Soren in the passenger's seat. Kain drives, with Axel and Devin cramped in the back. Nate connects his laptop, the GPS loading instantly and displaying a map.

"It's nearly an hour away, Kain. When we get there, park two blocks from the house. There's a tree line that'll give us enough coverage but still leave the car open if we need to run." He says, perching his laptop on the center console between Soren and Kain. As he backs out of the garage and into the night, Kain murmurs something- it's barely audible, but his words might as well be a battle cry.

"There's no running. We're not coming home without them."

Jax

I can't move. The man stands over her, dragging her to the center of the room. I'm too weak. *I can't get to her.* She screams, and my head lulls backwards, hitting the wall.

"Rowan please, you're hurting me. I won't fight, please just let go of my hair." She cries. He doesn't listen. He doesn't let her go. I want to reach out, to hit him, shoot him, snap his fucking neck- but I can't.

Rowan Sykes. The man who took everything from me. The one who killed my parents.

He looks nothing like the whispers swirling the underground. He's not the all-powerful villain Georgia made him up to be. Greasy hair hangs over a sallow complexion, with skin stretched too tight over sharp cheekbones. A three-day beard coats his jaw, and when he grins, showing yellowed, uneven gums, it makes me want to run.

A gut pokes out of his sweat-stained button up, the buttons straining, and his neck has a slight green hue left behind by the cheap jewelry hanging from it. No, this man doesn't radiate power at all- he radiates *rot.*

I groan, trying to tell her to fight back, to do *something,* but no words come- just a sound. He stops, his hold on her hair loosening.

"I didn't realize you were still alive, boy. You've got some fight in you, that's for sure." He drops her, her small frame hitting the floor with a loud *thud*.

I shuffle, trying to get away as he walks towards me. I can only get so far before he's standing right in front of me. He smells like death- like an omen. Exactly how I remember.

"You look just like your daddy did the night he died; did you know that?" He drawls, grabbing my face in his hand and squeezing hard. "I wonder if you'll bleed like him too."

"Get the fuck away from him!" Georgia screams.

"Shut up, bitch!" Sykes fires back. Georgia cowers.

Good. I don't want her to get hurt for trying to defend me.

"How's your head?" He sneers. "Yeah, I recognize dope sick from a mile away. Have the cravings really started yet?"

I lean forward, and spit at his feet. I miss his boots completely. I think I get my point across anyway.

"F-fuck you." I manage through clenched teeth. He backhands me, my ears ringing, face aching from the blow.

"If you were polite, I'd offer you something to take that nasty edge off." He grunts, reaching into his pocket.

No.

He pulls out a small, dirty plastic bag. I stare at it. The white powdery substance calls my name, like a beacon.

"I'll give this to you, if you promise to keep quiet and turn your head. She and I have a lot of making up to do, and I wouldn't want you to get in the way. Can you do that, boy?" His voice is sickly sweet.

My exhaustion is telling me to trust him, to take what he's offering. Everything hurts- my body twitching, muscles spasming in ways I can't control. Sweat pours down my face, cold and hot at once, and my teeth are chattering so hard it hurts. My heart races, then skips, and nausea twists in my gut.

I can't think straight. My thoughts ricochet between panic and despair. If I just took it... Just a bump. Just a tiny bit of what he's offering would make a world of difference.

But the rational part of my brain, the part that's growing weaker by the minute, is telling me to kill him with my bare hands and not think twice about whatever's in the bag.

If I'm honest, I don't know what's in it. He could've laced it with something, hell, it could be rat poison for all I know, and I'm not stupid enough to think this guy would give me anything clean. But even still...

I need it. Just *something* would ease the pain enough to get us out. If I just had a little bit, I could take him- I wouldn't even think about the wound from the screwdriver those assholes stabbed me with earlier, and I could fight. I could stand. I could grab Georgia and get us out of here- get us back alive.

"Come on, Jaxon. I don't have all day. It's not gonna hurt you- well, no more than the shit you do at home." Sykes taunts. *He's right.*

My hand drifts out, slowly reaching towards his- towards salvation.

"Jax, don't take it." Georgia whimpers. "Don't. He could kill you with that!"

I almost don't hear her over the blood rushing in my ears, but then I remember something.

She and I have a lot of making up to do. My hand falls. If I take this, it'll hurt her. I can't do that to her. I won't. If I'm not awake, I can't do *anything* to stop what he's going to do to her.

"No." I whisper. It's all I can manage.

My eyes start to close again. I can barely make them stay open.

"I figured you'd say that." He growls, reaching back into his pocket and pulling out a syringe. It's full of something amber in color, and it fills me with fear.

"I don't know if you've ever tried this one. It's fun while it lasts, but the comedown's a bitch. You'll see. Can't be any worse than you're feeling now."

I jerk, willing my limbs to listen to my brain, to get away from him, but I can only thrash in place. *I can't get away.*

Sykes grips my hair, sending a knee into my nose. Blood gushes down my face, and I taste it. My head falls backwards, and I'm too tired to pick it up.

Too tired to fight. Too tired to breathe.

He grabs my arm. I don't pull away. I can't.

The needle hits before I even understand what's happening. Sharp sting. Then burning.

Somewhere far away, I hear Georgia screaming at him to stop. He doesn't.

The plunger pushes down. I feel it- every inch of it- liquid fire racing through my veins. My chest catches heat first, then my arms, my neck.

My eyes go wide- the rest of me, stone. My skin's too tight- too hot. Like it's shrinking, trying to crawl off my bones.

He laughs. It's low and ugly. My stomach flips. I taste blood.

"You took it like a champ, kid. I'm impressed."

The needle clatters to the floor. I stare at it, dumb and useless, heart pounding somewhere deep inside. What did he just do? What the fuck did he put in me?

Then- silence. Everything in me goes quiet. Like a cord's been cut.

Numbness seeps in slow, syrup thick. My thoughts stop firing. I can't even panic.

My breathing's shallow. My chest barely moves. My head tips forward, eyes hooded. Mouth slack. There's something wet on my chin- drool, blood, I can't tell. Doesn't matter. For one second- one awful second- I don't *care*. About the pain. About the wound. About her.

I just float. Like I've been unhooked from everything that makes me human.

And that's worse than anything else he could've done to me.

"Jax!"

A voice breaks through, soft, warm- sounds like home. Like my mother, before she stopped saying my name.

It calls my name again. Soft, far- like through a wall. I can't lift my head. Don't know if I can't, or don't want to.

Someone's crying. It's loud. Then another voice- sharp, angry.

My head tips sideways, too heavy to hold. The floor tilts with me.

Georgia. She's there. Right there. I want her closer. I want...

I can't speak. Can't move my mouth. My tongue feels nailed down.

He's on top of her. Knees caging her in.

Too close. Too much. She doesn't like that. I can see it in her eyes.

Get off her. Get off her. GET OFF HER.

The words don't leave my throat.

He's tearing at her clothes. She looks cold. She's shaking. I wish I could give her my shirt.

He's yelling at her. She's apologizing. Why's she sorry? She could never do anything wrong. That's what made me hate her. That's why I don't anymore.

I want to help her. Or look away.

He hurts her. I watch- can't help. My stomach flips. She lays still. I think she's passed out until her head turns- slow, broken. She looks at me.

A tear falls.

"Shhhh," It's barely a whisper. "I-it'll be alright." It's won't. She knows it. She cries harder.

He doesn't stop. Doesn't even slow down.

I want to stand up and push him away. I can't move.

"Get o-off of h-her." My voice is wrong. Warped. He laughs at me.

"It's real big of you to try and protect her, Jaxon. I commend you; I do. But we've got unfinished business, right princess?" His hands slide around her throat. She gasps, face going red. "My lady and I have got an awful lot of catching up to do, and I just don't think I can wait to get her upstairs. You don't mind, do you boy?"

My vision pulses. Black at the edges.

"She's n-not yours." I choke. "She's *ours.*"

His face twists- the movement fast. A flash of his fist.

Contact. Silence. The lights go out.

When I wake, I think I'm dying. Or maybe I already did. Everything hurts- my limbs, my head, my stomach. It's all sharp and distant at the same time. My mouth floods and I think I'm going to throw up, but nothing comes.

There's something tied around my stomach- fabric, I think. It's dark, hard to see. I blink until my eyes sting, trying to focus. The bleeding's slowed, maybe. I didn't... I didn't tie that, did I? My brain lags, skipping. Someone else.

Georgia.

I jerk my head- too fast- and the whole world shifts sideways. She's there. Curled up next to me, knees to her chest. She's shaking. Part of her shirt's missing, torn, I think. I look back down to my stomach. Something shifts inside me, even through the haze.

My tongue sticks to the roof of my mouth. It takes me a few tries before any sound comes out.

"Georgia?"

It's barely a whisper, but she hears.

She moves too fast, crashing forward, her hands on me, her breath hitching. Her face finds my neck, hot and wet.

"Oh my god." She says. Again. Again. Like it's the only thing she remembers how to say.

"I-I'm," The word catches, and I force another. "I'm okay, I promise, trouble. It's g-gonna be okay." My teeth won't stop chattering, so I press my face into her hair. It smells like blood and sweat. Real.

I try to move. My fingers work, slow and stupid- but they work. My arm lifts next, heavy as concrete, but mobile. I grab her and don't let go.

"What happened? What did he do?"

She moves away, but I yank her back as best I can, our fingers tangling together. I need to know she's real. Need the proof of her skin under my palm.

"Nothing." She breathes. "Nothing he hasn't done before. I'll be okay. We need to get out of here. Can you stand?"

Can I stand? I want to laugh. Of course I can't stand, but the room's spinning and she's right. We have to move. We have to get out.

Where are we? The others- Jesus, the others will be burning Oakridge to the ground trying to find us, but I don't even know where we are or how we got here. We could be hours away from the guys. They took my tracker- they'd have no way of finding us quickly.

"If you help, I can stand. Don't let me fall."

"Never."

She hauls me up and pain explodes- stomach flaring, the pain white hot. My knees buckle. I hate that I'm weak. She holds me anyways.

Solid. Warm. Real.

"Try the door." I rasp, stupidly alert. I need something- any damn thing to protect us. Nails glint in the doorway, and they're rusted- *perfect*. I curl my fingers around them, slip them between my fingers like claws. It feels obscene and right.

She tries the door. It doesn't budge. Of course it doesn't.

Teeth chatter. My handles tremble so bad I can barely form the grip. But I lock my jaw, steady my voice- focus on what I can feel.

"Call them back, Georgia." My voice is thin, but it holds. She nods.

Let's do this.

Beck

We're ten minutes out from The Iron Brotherhood's clubhouse, and the car is silent. No one speaks. There's no planning, no pep talk- nothing. We all know what we have to do, what's waiting for us. Each of us are running countless scenarios through our mind, trying to prepare ourselves for what we'll find when we get there. I don't think anything will prepare us enough.

The silence is pierced by a ringtone, a loud trilling coming from Soren's phone. He growls, grabbing it from the dashboard and clicking the green button on the screen to answer it.

"What?" He answers, and after a beat, his face falls. He wrenches the phone away from his face, fingers fumbling against the screen before finally clicking the speakerphone button.

"It's a pleasure to make your acquaintance, Mr. Bishop." A gravelly voice drawls; one I don't recognize.

"Who is-" I begin to ask, but Soren's hand flies up, silencing me. I listen.

"My name is Rowan Sykes. We haven't met officially yet, but I think we're going to, very soon."

He's got an accent, one from somewhere much further south, but it's the tone of his voice that shake me to my core. It's honey sweet and razor sharp, all at once.

My blood runs cold.

"What the fuck do you want?" Soren grits, his teeth clenching so hard I'm shocked they don't shatter in his mouth.

"Well, it seems I may have picked up one of your strays, and you may have picked up one of mine, come to think of it."

"How did you get this number?" Soren's seething, his whole body beginning to shake. He's not scared, though- no, he's much worse than scared. "That doesn't matter now, does it, son? What's important is that we can talk freely, now, understand? I've had my eye on you for quite some time. You've been very successful with your little band of thugs, right? I'm almost impressed- it's a good start." Sykes replies.

"I'm not your fucking son."

I turn to Nate- *trace the call*, I mouth, and he rips his laptop from the center console, typing furiously.

"What do you want?" Soren questions.

"Nothing really, honest. I have my princess back where she belongs, that's all I ever wanted. I just want to make sure we get this young man back to you in one piece. It'd really be a shame if something were to happen to him. He's looking awfully pale, and he's bleeding pretty bad. You boys better hurry up."

"Don't fucking touch him!" I scream. Axel reaches forward, wrapping a big hand around my mouth and pulling me back against the headrest.

"Shut the fuck up. Your mouth won't help them." He hisses into my ear. He doesn't let me go. *Smart.*

"You will return both of them back to me. Where are you, you motherfucker?" Soren commands, his tone even.

The boss of The Vipers, son of Conner Bishop, taker of lives and king amongst men is here, and he's *lethal.*

"Well, judging by my sights, you're nearly there. You boys are smart, I'll give you that- I'm surprised you found me so quick. You've built a great team, Mr. Bishop- it's time to put them to the test. You just keep pulling that nice black car around- don't miss the turn, now. I'll leave the light on for you. I'll see you soon." With that, the line goes dead.

"Fuck!" Soren bellows, throwing his floor in the footwell. Kain veers a sharp left, taking the Escalade into the tree line on the side of the road. Once we're completely covered by the canopy, he kills it, the lights turning off. It's completely black, the dark of the night giving us cover.

"I can't find any cameras," Nate sputters. "I don't know how he can see us. Scouts, maybe?"

It doesn't matter. He knows we're coming, and we're fucked. It's a suicide mission.

"Nate, comms?" Soren asks, and the other man produces them, slipping an earpiece into each of our hands.

"We're going in through the front. He's already expecting us, so might as well make it easy. Take out as many as you can from the car, then we go in. I'll find Georgia. Beck, you get Jax, but if someone else gets to them first, you grab them and get back to the car. No questions. Sound off if you find them, but otherwise, you all focus on covering us. Understood?"

There he is. Our fearless leader.

"Yeah, boss. I hear you."

"And Georgia stays. Once I have her back, she will not leave us again. I want no push back, no argument. She is *mine*. I'm bringing her home."

I nod my head. I wouldn't have fought him anyways, not on this. That girl's got me in a chokehold, and she has from the moment I found her in that goddamn diner. She belongs to all of us- she's changed all of us, more than any of us expected her to in the weeks we've had her. Even if he hadn't said it, I wouldn't have let her go. Ever. It's our fault she's back here, and I'll spend the rest of my life telling her how sorry I am for it if I have to.

"She's *ours*, Soren." Kain corrects, and my jaw goes slack. I didn't even know he could feel anything outside of anger and annoyance, but… it looks like she's gotten to him too, and he must have it *bad* for him to go toe to toe with Soren.

"You might've had her first, but when we get her back- she belongs to all of us. She's got the three of us tied in knots, and you know it. You're not the only one who feels something *more* with her. You don't get to keep her for yourself. We're past that."

"Agreed. Either she chooses and we live with it, or we make it work. End of story." I chime in. "And to set the record straight, I had her first."

Soren growls, and the corners of my mouth lift, just a bit.

"If you three are done, we need to move. We're sitting ducks out here, and the longer you three argue over your toys, the longer they're in there with *him*." Axel calls out from the back row. He's right.

"Kain, get us there."

Kain starts the engine and pulls out of the tree line, turning the headlights off.

"Pull right into the driveway." Soren commands. "We leave *with* Jax and Georgia, or we

don't leave at all. Watch your backs. Make it out alive-
I'm not burying anyone today."

I lean back in my seat, my face stoic, my head
calm. We say nothing else. We don't need to.

When we arrive, it's eerily quiet. No men
waiting for us, no gunshots- just *silence*. We're deep in
the woods, but the light from the house casts a glow
to the front yard.

That motherfucker. He left the light on for us,
just like he said.

"Don't get out. Something's not right." Soren
directs.

We keep our heads low, but I can't stop my
eyes from wandering and peeking out at the windows
at the house. Some part of me expects to see them
somewhere, their faces behind a pane of glass. It's
pathetic, really- thinking it would be so easy. *I hoped it
would be.* My heart sags.

"Soren…" I start, but he holds up a hand.
"We're wide open. We need to move." I push further.

"Something's not right." He says again.
"Where are they?"

Before anyone can answer, shots drop. They
surround us, nicking the body of the Escalade and
cracking against the windshields.

"Get down!" Soren barks, all of slumping into the footwells of the car. Nate grabs his laptop and crams himself nearly under his seat, typing furiously.

"I can't get the feed, Soren. We're blind."

"No, we're not." He bites back. "Right window, second floor. Someone get a clear shot and start picking them off, now!"

Axel leans forward, reaching up to crack the window slightly and wedging the barrel of his Glock 19 out. He squeezes the trigger once, his bullet shattering the window in question.

"Hit 'em again." I urge, my voice low.

"Are you sure? I don't want to waste-"

"Fuck it." I retort. I grab my own weapon from its position in my ankle holster and pop my door, sliding out of the car and onto the gravel drive. "Beck, what the hell are you-"

Whoever that was, I cut them off, slamming the car door shut and shimmying underneath the car, moving up to just underneath the hood. The gunfire continues, and I'm breathing heavy, trying to focus- easier said than done while you're being shot at from like fifteen different angles. I'm on my stomach, arms out in front- I have a clear shot and a shelter overhead.

They don't call me Trigger for nothing.

I aim for every window, shattering them on impact. As my bullets hit the glass, the shots surrounding us start to stop. I must've hit a few of them, at least. The car doors open and boots hit the ground heavy on all sides. I scoot forward, slowly moving to stand, still crouched and at the ready.

"Fucking idiot." Soren hisses, jogging past me. "Move, now!" He orders.

We head straight for the front door, wasting no time to check the locks. Kain plants himself in front of the door, shoulders squared, his massive frame blocking our view. He shifts his weight and drives his boot forward, right beside the lock. The first kick makes the entire door shudder in its frame, the wood splintering with a sharp *crack*. He doesn't hesitate, letting out a grunt as the second blow lands like a sledgehammer slamming into the wall. The strike plate tears loose, and screws fly as the screech out of the frame, and the door explodes inward. Kain lowers his foot, his chest heaving, but his face impassively calm- like it was nothing more than kicking open a stubborn cabinet.

"Jesus, fuck." Devin whispers.

The interior of the house is quiet, and there isn't anyone waiting for us in the entryway. We don't speak as Soren looks to Axel and Devin, gesturing with two fingers towards a wooden staircase on the left. He directs Kain forward, into the house, and he goes without a word. He looks back at us, once, then twice, realizing Nate is in tow, too. He gives me an exasperated look and jerks his head violently towards Kain. Nate scurries off, following his new babysitter into imminent danger.

Soren locks eyes with me, his face grim. We hear shots coming from upstairs, and every part of me wants to run to the aid of my brothers, to help, to fight, to do *something*. But when Soren jerks his head towards a descending set of stairs, I realize that I can't. They're close. I feel my heart tugging. I know they're here. Just through the door. We start edging slowly towards the staircase, my grip unsteady, my gun trembling in my hands.

"Quit shaking. You'll shoot yourself before we get to them." Soren bites out, moving past me to take the lead, echoing the voices of our fathers and their instructions throughout the years of training we went through together.

It's all I need to hear, and I tighten up, steeling my face and forcing my hands to stop shaking.

As we step closer to the door, Soren's boot comes down on a board that gives off a sharp *click*- a noise that old, wooden floors don't normally make.

Shit.

"It's rigged." Soren breathes.

One small step, one mistake and we could kill everyone in this house- including ourselves, our brothers, Jax and Georgia.

"Don't move." I urge him, and he doesn't, his boot planted in the same spot.

"What do we do, Beck?"

I shake my head, unable to find the words.

We're so fucked.

Georgia

Before I can raise my hand to pound on the door, gunfire erupts. I look at Jax, my eyes wild, but his face is calm, a smirk playing on the corners of his mouth- he almost looks like himself again.

"I'd know the sound of that gun anywhere." He whispers. I don't understand, and my face must give it away. He breathes a laugh- a weak, guttural sound. "Our boys are here."

His mind must be gone. He said it himself, no one's coming for us. His smile never falters, a gleam of hope in his eye.

"Jax," I whisper, grabbing his arm to usher him away from the door. "They're not. Come on, come sit back down, okay?" He lets me lead him away, and I sit him back down on the floor. "It's too dangerous right now. We don't have any weapons. We have to keep waiting."

"No, Georgia. They're coming. I know they're here. *Beck's* here. He c-came for me."

"Just relax." I whisper.

I pull him into me, tucking his head against my chest. He's pliant and goes willingly. I smooth my hand over his hair, trying to calm him. I don't even know how to help him- there's too much wrong. He's weak and starting to hallucinate.

Every time I look at him, I start to cry. In this moment, he's so... *broken*. The same man who killed for me, who holds his own in a fight- is unrecognizable.

The smell of his blood, the raw agony etched across his face, the twitching limbs- it's worse than anything I could've imagined. Every nerve in me is screaming that he could die, right here, and I couldn't do anything to stop it. I want to scream, to tell him it'll be okay, but the words freeze in my throat.

The gunfire grows louder, and I tense, pulling Jax closer. I'm not sure how much longer he can stay awake before he passes out again. I just hope Rowan is caught up in whatever's going on out there and stays away from us.

It was awful, finally being in the same room with him after all this time. He hadn't changed.

He is still every bit as horrible as I remember. His smell, the stains on his shirt, his breath- all of it sent me back, and maybe I am *back*. Back in hell, but this time, I drug someone down with me. I'm just glad he didn't witness what happened. *He didn't see me undressed. He didn't watch.*

I dressed quickly after Rowan was finished with me, and besides- Jax is so out of it, I'm not sure he would've recognized what happened even if he was awake to see it. I can hold onto at least a shred of my dignity.

I'm still not sure what he gave Jax- I just know whatever it was made him *so much worse.* I need to find a way out of here, and fast.

I hear a shout from right outside the door, and then another. The voices are familiar, but I can't place them with the sound barrier muffling them. Jax picks his head up, swinging it towards the door. He must've heard them, too.

"Beck?" He whispers.

"No. He's not here. Look at me." I force his face to mine, leaning our foreheads together. I don't have time to break. I can't let the emotions take over. I cannot shut down. He needs me.

"Beck isn't here. It's just us. Only the two of us." I tell him, nodding my head against his as I talk. "Say it. I need to know that you understand."

"No." He whimpers. "He found me. H-he came for us."

"No he didn't, Jax!"

"I got so m-mad at him, you know? So mad..." He trails off, his eyes starting to close. I sit him back against the wall, patting his cheeks.

"Why? Tell me why you were so mad. Keep your eyes open, let me see them." I look down, and he's bleeding again. *Badly.* He must've bumped the wound when he stood up.

"He likes you. Maybe more than he likes me, s-sometimes."

My brow furrows. He's delusional.

"I don't like to share. He was mine first. B-but..." His eyes roll back, and he's gone. Out cold.

Panic slams into me. I rip what's left of my shirt over my head and press it hard against his stomach. I'd hoped the pain of the pressure on his gut would wake him, but it didn't. I reach up with one hand, feeling the side of his neck for a pulse- I find one, but it's *faint*, so faint that I'm worried he'll... I can't think like that.

I keep calling his name, screaming it until my throat's raw. I don't care who hears. I press hard on his stomach with one hand and slap his face with the other. Nothing. Not even a twitch.

When the pounding starts against the door, I scream louder. He can't protect me if he's not awake, and *I* can't protect *him* against Rowan. I sob uncontrollably as I try to wake him, but then- a *boom* shakes the entire room, and the vibrations force us to the ground. I scream, clinging to Jax. He remains still- eyes closed, unmoving.

I smell smoke. It's faint, but it's there.

Fire.

My eyes widen, as I right myself and sit back on my heels. I take in our surroundings, and realization hits me like a punch in the face. We're trapped in this room, no way out, no one to help us, and something somewhere just exploded. If this building goes up in flames, or something down here blows- we're going with it.

The first wisps of smoke slither under the door, and dread consumes me- I realize that it doesn't matter if Jax dies in this room. *We're already dead.*

Soren

I can't move. Beck barks out orders to the others, fully immersed in his role as my second, but I can't hear anything over the blood rushing in my ears. I don't even blink. That *click* will haunt me for the rest of my life. If I move, I'll kill them. I'll kill them all.

"Soren!" Someone calls. I don't look. "Soren!" Beck's in front of me, his hands on my shoulders, shaking me. "We gotta move, bro. Take a small step. Just a small one. See if you can feel anything."

"I-I can't. What if-"

"You *have* to. No choice. Small step, right to me." Beck presses. He's right- I might be able to feel a shift of a plate, hear another click, *something*, if I just move my foot slightly...

"I wouldn't do that if I were you, Mr. Bishop."

I whip my head around. It's that voice- that gravely drawl, laced with poison. It's *him*.

"I worked real hard on that. It's some of my best work, really."

"What the fuck did you do?" Beck grits out.

"Just a little home security, that's all. You never know what kinds of snakes you'll find crawling around your home." He sneers, his eyes boring into mine. He's an idiot- doesn't he know that if I move, I'll take him out with us?

I don't look away from him- I won't give him that satisfaction. If I could move my fucking foot, I'd be chest-to-chest with him.

"Where are they?" I ask him, my tone even and calm. The firefight upstairs gets louder, Devin and Axel's shouts getting closer.

"If you move, they'll be scattered around the property. It'll be a nasty cleanup- I doubt you'll be able to separate their parts from your guys here."

"What do you want, huh? We're here. What's the plan?"

"I've got what I wanted all along. I don't want anything more than for you and your little operation to keep your nose out of my business." He retorts. "Don't think I haven't noticed your constant prying into my affairs. Who do you think gave your hacker access to the cameras? I've just been waiting for you to be man enough to show up here yourself. Shame it took you so long."

What? He knew we were trying to find him? That can't be right. We've been careful, crawling through everything, piecing it together in silence. I glare at him, my nostrils flaring. How would he know?

"But we both know you'll never stop, don't we? You're angry, and I get it- if someone took out a few of my own like we did, I'd be angry too. But anger like that won't quit, and the only way I'll be rid of you is to put a bullet between your eyes." With that, he reaches into his waistband and pulls his gun, aiming it right where he said he would. Right between my eyes.

Beck tenses. "He's bluffing." He breathes. "He's bluffing about the plate. Trust me."

"If you asked me nicely, boys, I would've already turned over your little friend. I have no use for him, but man, was he fun to play with." He grins, eyes glinting with sick amusement. "You might be too late- I doubt he's still alive, but you're welcome to confirm that. Just step off that plate, Mr. Bishop, and you'll know for sure."

Beck swings before any more words are said. He charges Sykes, tackling him to the ground and landing blow after blow upon the other man's face. Sykes tries his best to protect his face from the raining punches, but Beck thrashes him like a storm unbound- no tact, no skills. Just pure, unbridled *rage*. I almost smile.

"Do it, Soren!" He screams, his voice rasping. "Fucking move!"

I think back to when we were young. *Beck will be yours one day, like Mr. Turner is mine. You'll have to learn to trust him,* my father would tell me. Back then, I was just excited to have a friend- someone to do everything with. But he was right- I had to learn to trust him. After all these years, he's become a part of me, our minds thinking in tandem, our bodies moving through the same motions.

I trust him.

I take a small step forward, bracing myself for something- I'm not quite sure what, but my hands fly up to cover the back of my neck as I crouch forward. When I stand, puzzled, Sykes starts to laugh. Beck only hits him harder. Nothing happened. They're okay-

A white light fills the room, followed by the loudest noise I've ever heard. I'm thrown backwards with the force of the explosion, my head smacking the floor. I give myself thirty seconds to lean into the pain- my body is screaming, and I'm sure I've broken something, but thirty seconds is all I allow. My brothers are here, hurt or worse. My *girl* is here.

I sit up as best I can, taking stock of the carnage. It's not good. The stairwell that I sent Devin and Axel up is now completely crumbled, impassable. Beck's laying on his back, his eyes open. *I need to get to him.*

I stand, clutching my ribs and fumbling through the dust for my gun. I sag with relief when my fingers close around the pistol grip- I can still protect us.

I stumble over to him, leaning forward. One of his pupils is blown, the other tiny- he's got a nasty concussion.

"Beck!" I slap him a few times, his cheeks, his shoulders- anything I can reach. He's breathing heavily, probably in shock, but I need him. I can't afford to lose him right now.

"Come on, we'll get you checked out. You need to get up now. We have to find the others."

Like they read my mind, I hear Kain calling for me from further into the house. I exhale- if he's that far away, they weren't near the blast. Two sets of footsteps thunder down the hallway. We're almost whole. *Almost.*

"In here!" I shout. "Beck's real bad, man."

"I'm fucking fine, Soren. Help me up." He groans from the floor.

I do, slowly. He grabs my forearms, hoisting himself up, mostly on his own.

"Where the fuck is he?" Beck growls, and it's then that I realize Sykes managed to slip away in the explosion. He could've gotten to them- he knows this place better than we do.

"We need to move, Beck. Can you walk?"

"Yeah, I can fucking walk. I can do a little dance if you want me to. Stop fussing and let's go." He spits.

I tap the comms earpiece twice, hoping for some sort of signal. "Kain!" I call for him. Seconds later, he bursts into the room, a wide-eyed Nate in tow, and rushes towards me. He scans us, methodically checking us for any injuries or blood. He looks at Beck's eyes, and his expression goes murderous. I put my hand to my ear again, calling out for Axel and Devin.

"Check in. Tell me you're okay." I demand.

"We're fine, boss." Devin answers, but he's coughing. "No fucking clue how we're getting down, but there's no one else up here- we took care of them before the blast. What the fuck happened?"

I don't stop to answer any questions.

"One more room left to clear. We couldn't get in there before shit hit the fan. I'm going in." I start for the door, but Beck falls in line next to me, grabbing my arm and stopping me in my tracks. "If they're in there, I will be too. You're not going in alone."

I give him a once over, checking him once more for myself. I nod once, jerking my chin towards the door.

"Cover us." I direct to Kain. "Sykes is still here somewhere. Do not let him through that door."

I muster every ounce of strength I have, kicking open the wooden door. When it splinters on impact, I charge through, finding a dingy set of stairs. I hold my gun in front of me, creeping slowly down the stairs, heart hammering, breath sharp and ragged. Beck's behind me, gripping the banister like his life depends on it.

We're met with a dust-filled basement, the smoke and dust from the explosion having already infiltrated the space. I scan the room, gun drawn, looking for anything or anyone that might attack first, but my breath hitches in my throat as my eyes lock onto a heap of bodies in the corner of the room.

I see Jaxon first- he's pale, face streaked with blood and bruised so badly he's almost unrecognizable. He's still- too still. My heart sinks.

No.

Beck sees him too, and he freezes for a fraction of a second- then, he's on him, crouched over his body and screaming his name, shaking him so hard that I think his head might fall from his shoulders.

Then I see *her*.

Georgia.

She's shirtless, left in a sports bra with her eyes wide and her chest heaving, the smoke from the open door curling around her like a living thing. Relief crashes through me, sharp and overwhelming.

I rush towards her and drop to my knees beside her, grabbing face, her neck, feeling every exposed part of her skin. She's hysterical, uncontrollable sobs wracking her body. She grabs my forearms, squeezing hard- trying to ground herself.

"I'm here. I found you. I'm so sorry, baby." I manage to get out. *Do not cry. Protect them. Get them out.*

"It's really bad. Get him out. Please, get him out of here. He won't make it much longer." She weeps.

I look towards Beck- he's still shaking Jax, swearing under his breath, his hands trembling over Jax's body. He feels for a pulse, and my chest tightens.

His eyes widen, and he nods. "I've got him. We need to move, now!"

"Get him out of here, please!" Georgia screams again.

Beck lifts him like he's made of glass, turning and starting for the stairs. He turns, right before he reaches them, and looks back at Georgia. His brow furrows, his eyes full of sorrow and a million unspoken apologies.

"Go!" I bark at him. We don't have time for making up. I need them *out,* safe- then, we can begin to repair what I know has been broken.

I stand, grabbing Georgia's hand and pulling her to her feet. "We have to go, baby. I'm so sorry, you're going to have to run. Can you do that?" I ask her.

She nods furiously, and I don't wait- I start for the stairs, pulling her behind me.

We've got them. For a second- just a second, I let myself breathe. He's alive. *She's* alive. We're going to be okay.

My feet hit the stairs, pounding the treads as we make our way back to the main level of the house. As I reach the top, I lose my grip on Georgia's hand. I turn around, looking back to find her, and…

She's gone.

Another deafening *boom* rattles the walls, sending a wave of heat and debris down the stairwell, the dust and smoke burning my eyes and lungs. Pieces of wood and plaster rain down, and I hear her scream somewhere beneath it- it's muffled, but unmistakable.

"No!" I roar, lunging forward, taking a false step down the stairs, my leg sinking into the debris. I stumble, coughing, choking, searching through the gray haze for something, *anything* to pull myself out, and then I feel it.

A faint, but real, scrape against my ankle.

One, two, three.

Three scratches in succession.

One, two, three.

Kain's at the top of the stairs, yelling for me to grab onto him, that he'll get me out. I don't listen.

"Hold on, baby, stay with me." I yell, hoping she can hear me. Her fingers scratch again, weak but steady- a desperate signal that she's alive.

One, two, three. Relief punches through me, sharp and sudden, and I feel the tiniest spark of hope.

"Keep doing that, Georgia. I'm coming." I urge her, pulling debris aside.

My hands bleed as I rip wood and plaster away from the stairwell, fighting like an animal to get to her.

Another scratch- she's still fighting, still here. I press forward harder, breath ragged.

"Kain, help me! Get this shit out of the way, now!"

He's beside me in an instant, as is Nate- the little cockroach- moving the rubble away from the stairs.

"Georgia?" I call out to her. No response. No scratch.

"No." I whisper. "Don't you dare! Georgia, please!"

I'm screaming now- all control I had is lost. All I can think, all I can do is to try and get to her. My stomach twists as fear seizes me. She's buried under all of this, invisible in the smoke and rubble. Every second she doesn't signal, my mind races through worst-case scenarios.

I tear at the debris, hands raw, nails breaking, pulling splinters and chunks of wood as if sheer force can reach her faster. Every motion is desperate, frantic, but I can't stop, no matter how much it hurts me. Not until I feel her scratch again, until I know she's still here. I promised I'd protect her. I tried- I can't fail. I refuse to fail.

But as the smoke thickens, Kain's big arms pull me away. I fight him, kicking and screaming like a child as he pulls me out of the stairwell.

"You can't do anything if you die from smoke inhalation. She's safe underneath it- she has time, she'll have air pockets. We need to get out of here. We can search again. Let's move."

I start to disagree, my heart clawing out of my chest to get back to her, but he leaves no room for negotiation. He pulls me outside where the rest of the team waits, Devin already behind the wheel of the Escalade still parked in the driveway.

"We gotta go, boss. Eight Ball's fading fast- we need to get him to a hospital." Devin calls out.

Kain stares at me, trying to calculate my next move. He shakes his head, turning back towards the car.

"Go, send someone for us. He's not leaving without her. Do not let my brother die."

They don't say another word as Devin tears out of the driveway, the wheels screeching, gravel flying.

I look over at Kain. He's watching the taillights disappear down the road. His jaw's tight, hands shaking slightly.

"What's the plan?" I ask. My voice sounds far too calm for how bad this is, but I can't fall apart. Not yet.

"We take a breath, then we go back in. We're not leaving her here." He murmurs, laying a hand on my shoulder.

I wish I could take her place. I'd trade every breath in my lungs if it meant she was safe. I promised I'd protect her- swore it, like it meant something- and I know in this instant- I couldn't.

The guilt burns, but it's hollow, too. I want to cry, but there's nothing left in me but rage and the echo of her name. I'll find her. Make no mistake- I *will* get her back.

Even if I end up dead trying.

Acknowledgments

I have so much I want to say about this story, about my experience, about everything- it's hard to find just the right words to express how incredible this entire process has been.

Firstly, thank you to everyone who has contributed, read (and reread), and listened to me complain, stress, and freak out. Without all of you, this story would've forever remained in my mind, untold.

To Lindsey, you have no idea how much I appreciate you. You took this from something I was excited about to something that I am truly in love with. Your guidance, expertise, and overall commitment to this book have not gone unnoticed or unappreciated, and I don't think I can put into words how grateful I am for your efforts. Here's to many more.

To K- I love you, I love you, I love you. You're the best friend I could've ever asked for. Thank you for loving this story from its inception to its final form- for loving me. Thank you for getting excited with me. I couldn't have done this without your encouragement.

To all readers- I am so glad you're here. My whole life, I've just wanted to tell stories. This one is the most powerful one I've ever written, and I'm so glad you stuck around (or at least, hopefully you did, if you're reading this). I am beyond excited for you to see where this story will go, because believe me when I say that it is far from finished.

To Retribution, thank you for giving me purpose. Thank you for this journey, however hard it was. I'm so proud of you.

Connect With Me

You can find me on all socials, under the handle **@shinygreyauthor**. Follow me there for updates, exclusive content, and everything else!

If you have questions, want to tell me what you thought, or anything else, drop me an email at shinygreyauthor@gmail.com. I want to hear from you!